Nicola Cornick's novels have received acclaim the world over

'Her books are fabulous.'
—*New York Times* bestselling author Julia Quinn

'Cornick is first-class, queen of her game.'
—*Romance Junkies*

'A rising star of the Regency arena'
—*Publishers Weekly*

Praise for the SCANDALOUS WOMEN OF THE TON series

'A riveting read'
—*New York Times* bestselling author Mary Jo Putney on *Whisper of Scandal*

'One of the finest voices in historical romance'
—*Single Titles.com*

'Ethan Ryder (is) a bad boy to die for! A memorable story of intense emotions, scandals, trust, betrayal and all-encompassing love. A fresh and engrossing tale.'
—*Romantic Times* on *One Wicked Sin*

'Historical romance at its very best is written by Nicola Cornick.'
—Mary Gramlich, *The Reading Reviewer*

Acclaim for Nicola's previous books

'Witty banter, lively action and sizzling passion'
—*Library Journal* on *Undoing of a Lady*

'RITA® Award-nominated Cornick deftly steeps her latest intriguingly complex Regency historical in a

Nicola Cornick

One Night with the Laird

HARLEQUIN®MIRA®

Harlequin MIRA is a registered trademark of Harlequin Enterprises Limited, used under licence.

Published in Great Britain 2014
by Harlequin MIRA, an imprint of Harlequin (UK) Limited,
Eton House, 18-24 Paradise Road,
Richmond, Surrey, TW9 1SR

© 2013 Nicola Cornick

ISBN 978 1 848 45302 9

59-0414

Harlequin (UK) Limited's policy is to use papers that are natural, renewable and recyclable products and made from wood grown in sustainable forests. The logging and manufacturing processes conform to the legal environmental regulations of the country of origin.

Printed and bound by
CPI Group (UK) Ltd, Croydon, CR0 4YY

For Alison Lindsay. Thank you!

Pleasure's a sin and sometimes sin's a pleasure.

—Lord Byron

CHAPTER ONE

Edinburgh, Scotland, April 1815

IT TOOK TEN minutes to cross from Edinburgh New Town to Edinburgh Old Town in a carriage, and for all of those ten minutes Jack had an almost uncontrollable erection the like of which he had never experienced before in his life. He had learned over the previous ten years that anticipation was one of the greatest aphrodisiacs of all; the anticipation he felt tonight was acute and almost impossible to bear.

Opposite him sat the woman who was the cause of his discomfort. He could not see her clearly in the drifting lamplight, but his awareness of her was sharp. Jack could smell the jasmine perfume that lingered on her hair and on her skin. He could see the shadow of a smile that curved her lips beneath the mask and he could still taste her from the kiss he had snatched a few minutes earlier. She had pushed him away then, but playfully, in a way that promised more, much more.

He had a rake's reputation, but it was a long time since he had bedded a woman. He wondered if that accounted for this reckless urge to throw caution to the wind and take this woman he had met a mere four hours before. Jack did not know her name. He had not seen her face. He knew only that his sexual awareness of her was so keen that if he did not have her, and soon, he would be in danger of exploding with the frustration.

She knew it too. He could tell that she could feel the tension in the carriage, the expectation wound as tight as a spring. He wanted to wipe that satisfied little smile from her face with a kiss. He wanted to take her here in the carriage with each lurch of the wheels over the cobbles driving him harder into her body. He had no notion why she affected him so and he did not like it because it pushed him close to losing control; he only knew that from the moment he had first seen her he had wanted her.

The coach drew up with a sudden jerk. A groom, black-clad and inscrutable, opened the carriage door and let down the steps. Jack sat back to allow his companion to descend first. She gathered up the filmy silver skirts of her gown in one hand and stepped lightly down. Jack followed, glancing about him curiously. The carriage had stopped on Edinburgh's Royal Mile. He could see the dark bulk of St. Giles's Cathedral. The streetlamps glimmered in the soft falling rain.

She took his hand and drew him along one of the narrow alleyways that plunged downhill away from the main thoroughfare. The darkness was absolute here. He could hear the tap of her slippers on the cobbles and feel the rain cold against his face, soaking his hair and his jacket. The walls of the tenement buildings pressed close on each side.

He was rushing headlong into danger; in these deep alleys he could be robbed and murdered and no one would come to help him. A knife in the ribs would be rich reward for his reckless pursuit of passion. He paused, good sense overriding lust for a moment, but then she turned to him, pressing her body against his, reaching up to kiss him. The cold tenement wall was at his back, but she was all heat and sweet fragrance. Her kiss was fierce and urgent, sweeping away any polite preliminaries, demanding a response. She put one hand on the nape of his neck and held his mouth on hers, tangling her fingers in his hair. He felt the hot slide of her tongue against his and groaned into her mouth.

He slipped his hands beneath her cloak and felt the slippery silk of her gown slide beneath his palms. He caught her about the waist and drew her closer. Her breasts were pressed against his chest and she rubbed her hips against his. It was galling to be so at the mercy of his senses when he was a man of experience and not a schoolboy, but Jack seemed powerless to resist the molten lust that was coursing through his veins.

The faintest thread of light glimmered in her eyes as she smiled at him. She broke away, but only to turn the handle of a door set back in the corner of the wall, deep in shadow. She took his hand again and pulled him inside.

The house was not as he had expected. Here, in this poor neighborhood of peeling walls and dirt-strewn cobbles, it was like a miniature palace. Everything was polished and rich and gleaming, wood, silver, gold. He saw it all only in a brief flash as she pulled him up the stone stairs: the jewel-bright colors in the long curtains that shut out the night, the scatter of cushions on the settle. When she stopped at the turn of the stair to kiss him again, she slipped a hand inside his pantaloons and stroked his shaft and he almost came there and then. He was panting with anticipation and lust, his mouth was dry, his heart pounded.

The room she took him into was all in darkness. Only the embers of a fire burned low in the grate. There was no candle. She shut the door with the quietest of clicks and stood for a moment with her palms resting against it. He could feel her looking at him. The dark sharpened his senses; he could hear her breathing, hear the little hitch in her breath that told him she was neither as calm nor as in control as she seemed. The knowledge gave him a savage satisfaction. He would have hated to be the only one to be so close to the borders of control.

There was a soft hush of velvet as she untied the ribbon of her cloak and allowed it to fall. The gossamer silk of her gown glinted again as she moved, coming over to him, placing one hand against his chest. Her fingers were sure on the buttons of his jacket; she slid it from his shoulders and then burrowed beneath his shirt to find the heat of his skin. He heard her sharp intake of breath as her hands slid over his bare chest. Despite the raging need inside him, he kept quite still and let her have her way. It felt like a small victory to resist her.

She reached up to kiss him. She was tall but he was taller still. He caught a curl of her hair in his fingers, satin-soft. He had no idea of its color as she had been wearing a hooded domino. His questing fingers found some pins holding more curls in place. He tugged. They fell with a tinkle onto the wooden floorboards, and her hair cascaded over his hands.

She nibbled his lower lip, then slid her tongue into his mouth, and his mind spun away into a dark realm of sensation. He drove a hand into her hair to hold her head still for his kisses, seeking the heat and demand of her mouth, meeting it and demanding more in return.

Wherever he led she followed eagerly. She tangled her tongue impatiently with his. She nipped at his lips and tasted him deep.

Sometimes she ran ahead with needs of her own; it was she who pressed the cold handle of a dirk into his hand and then spun around in mute order that he cut her laces. It was madness in the dark but he managed somehow, sliding the blade beneath, hearing the first creak and tear of the fabric before it suddenly gave way and her gown and petticoats slithered down to lie at her feet.

She was naked. He could sense it. He could feel her warmth. He could smell the jasmine scent again, fainter now, transmuted into something different, sweet and hot, on her skin. He remembered the sensation of her breasts against him and reached for her, but suddenly the blade of the dagger was at his throat and he fell back a step and she put her hand against his chest and pushed. His thighs came up against the edge of a bed. The blade pricked harder and he allowed himself to fall into the softest, widest, most comfortable mattress he had ever known.

She ripped the shirt from him then and straddled him, her thighs pressed tight against his side. With one hand she freed the buttons on his pantaloons and allowed his shaft to spring free into her hand. He tried to tumble her beneath him, but the blade at his throat warned him to be still. It traced an idle path down his chest, over his breastbone, farther down the line of his stomach until the flat of the blade kissed the tip of his straining shaft. At the same time, she squeezed him in her palm.

Christ, she was quite mad. And he too was about to lose his mind.

She tossed the dirk aside and came over him, sliding down to take him inside her body. His mouth opened on a shout at the heat and warmth and slickness of her, but she swallowed his cries in a kiss. She rocked, deeper and deeper, tighter and tighter and his mind splintered and he grabbed her hips hard, grinding her down on him as he came violently, desperately, calling out.

She rolled off him and lay by his side. Above the harsh pants of his own breathing he could hear the quick gasp of hers. Despite the shocking wantonness of the entire coupling, Jack felt as though something was missing, something he did not understand.

He turned his head to look at her, foolishly since he could see nothing of her in the oppressive dark. Suddenly, though, he had the certainty that she was about to run. He felt it in the flicker of movement through her body, heard it in her intake of breath.

His hand shot out and grabbed her wrist just as she started to move. He pulled her back against him, tucking her into his side, holding her still.

"Don't you know it is bad manners to run out on a man so soon after having him?" His whisper teased her hair. He felt it brush his lips.

After a moment she laughed and he felt her body soften against his. She said nothing, though.

"What is your name?" He wanted to talk to her, wanted it quite desperately, in fact, as though the physical connection between them simply was not enough. Odd, when previously he had never wanted more from a woman than the simply physical.

"Rose." There had been the very slightest hesitation in her voice before she had spoken. Not her name, then.

"I'm Jack." He did not deal in lies, half-truths or evasions. It was not his style.

She rubbed her hand gently over his bare chest in acknowledgment. She might be a woman of few words, but she made up for it in other ways. His blood was tingling from that small touch.

"I want to see you."

"No." Her response was instant and with a note of panic in her voice.

"Why not, sweetheart?" In deference to the fear, he kept his own tone light, brushing the tangled hair away from her face, his fingers a gentle caress against her cheek.

She shifted slightly in his arms as though she was uncomfortable with both the endearment and the gentleness. He knew she was rejecting the intimacy. It was odd when they had just shared the most intimate experience possible.

"I don't want any light." Now there was an unconscious command in her voice. A woman accustomed to giving orders, then. That made her all the more intriguing.

"And what if I do?"

"You will have to be satisfied with touch."

She took his hand and placed it over her breast. It was a gesture intended to stop conversation. He realized that. Yet he still succumbed. He felt her nipple harden against his palm and felt his blood heat in response. He toyed with her breasts with fingers, lips, teeth and tongue, allowing himself to be distracted, taking pleasure from her gasps and the way she arched to his touch. She urged him on in broken whispers, begging him to nip and suck harder to a point where pleasure turns to pain. He was painfully erect again by then and she spread herself for him and pleaded for him to take her hard, then harder still, her hands gripping the wooden headboard tight as he plunged into her. It was wild and wicked and he felt as though he were in a hot, dark dream, but even as he ravished her he felt the touch of a shadow on him as though something, somewhere was wrong. It almost felt as though she was asking to be punished, as though each stroke of his body into hers, each nip of his teeth at her breast, was penance.

Through the long night she let him do whatever he wished to her; she was his plaything and it was spectacular, unimaginably exciting, and he felt exhausted, satiated, but he couldn't quell that stubborn instinct that something was missing. The final time he made love to her slowly, languorously, trying to anchor the intimacy between them in something deeper, trying to capture and hold her. Jack had no idea why he wanted that connection when he was by nature a man who wanted only the most superficial of love affairs. Perhaps it was the challenge; he was unaccustomed to a woman who held something back. Normally they were the ones pushing him into a closeness he did not want.

By now her skin was flushed and damp, slick against his. She moved with him on the same dark tide of desire and pleasure, she came for him when he demanded it, her body was his, and yet somehow it felt as though she still eluded him in all the ways that mattered. Afterward she slept but he lay awake listening to her breathing, his mind alert. At one point she cried out. He pulled her into his arms and held her and she calmed, but he felt tears on her cheek where it was pressed against his chest.

Eventually the warmth of her in his arms lulled him

into sleep too, only to awake hours later when the sun was high in the sky and the room was bathed in light.

Jack knew before he opened his eyes that she would be gone.

IT WAS STILL dark when Mairi woke. For a moment her mind felt empty, light and free, and her body felt supremely ripe with pleasure, satiated and satisfied. A second later the desolation swept in, dark, cold and lonely as a winter's night, banishing the light.

It was always like this when she woke up. There was an all too brief period of blissful peace and then she fell into the dark. Grief and loss crouched in the shadows, waiting to spring. This morning the misery was sharper than usual, painful as a whetted knife. She had sought to drown her unhappiness in sensual pleasure and had only made matters worse.

She slipped from the bed and immediately missed Jack's warmth. He had been lying on his side, with one arm draped across her in casual possession, drawing her close in to the curve of his body. She was not sure how she had been able to sleep like that, in the arms of a stranger. It seemed wrong, impossible to accept when she rejected any sort of intimacy with anyone. Odd that she could give her body to him wholly and completely, holding nothing back, and yet the act of sleeping together afterward was something she regretted.

Shivering, she dragged on her underclothes, then tiptoed to the chest and took out a plain gown and shawl. Her hands shook as she tried to tie the fastenings. She could not see what she was doing. She tiptoed to the door, slippers in her hand. Light was starting to creep through the shutters now. She did not want to look back, but something compelled her to turn.

Jack was lying in the center of the big bed, in the midst of all the crumpled sheets and tumbled blankets. The covers rode low over his hips, revealing the broad expanse of his muscular chest dusted with golden hair. Tawny hair several shades darker fell over his forehead, a contrast to the stubble shadowing his chin. His eyes were closed, the lashes thick and black. The strengthening light skipped across the lean planes of his face, a long nose and resolute chin. It was a strong face, handsome enough to cause any woman to catch her breath, but that was not why Mairi gasped.

She felt a pang of shock, then a pang of horror, sharper, stronger, almost violent in its intensity.

Jack Rutherford.

It could not be.

She put out a hand and grabbed the bedpost for support. No. It was not possible. She had deliberately chosen a stranger, picked him out at a masquerade ball. She had seen him across the ballroom in his black domino and mask, and there had been something about him that captured her interest. She had thought he looked a little dangerous, a little wild, unknown to her, perfect for her purpose. They had not even spoken; they had had one dance and she had been so aware of him, burning with the need that possessed her, that at the end of it she had taken him by the hand and brought him here, to the secret little house she owned in the back streets of the Old Town of Edinburgh. She had wanted the entire experience to be a secret, but unfortunately she had chosen a man who was not a stranger at all.

Jack Rutherford. She supposed that the clue had been

in his name, but she had not even registered it last night. There were plenty of men called Jack. She had not recognized his voice either, but they had spent so little time in each other's company of late that it was no wonder.

She felt shaken, completely confused. She did not even *like* Jack Rutherford. He was arrogant, self-assured, deplorably confident, all too well aware of his charm and the effect it had on every woman he met. They had been thrown into each other's company when her sister had married Jack's cousin three years before. Jack had suggested they should get to know each other better, intimately, in fact. She had rejected his advances with an icy disdain. After that they had barely spoken and held fast to an intense mutual dislike.

She tightened her grip on the wood until her fingers hurt. The blood was pounding in her ears. She simply could not understand why she had been drawn to Jack the previous night. All unknowing, she had chosen the one man she should never have gone near. They were bound by marriage and mutual acquaintance. She had no idea how she could keep her identity secret from him now.

A cold draught scuttered across the floor, setting her shivering again. She already had regrets enough about the night. She had wanted to lose herself in a world that was entirely physical, to escape the unhappiness that clouded her mind, if only for a little while. No matter how spectacular the sex had been, she had found there was no escape.

Jack stirred in his sleep and sighed as he turned over. Mairi felt another pang of fear. He must never find out that she was the woman he had spent the night with. Inevitably he would have questions, questions she did not want to answer. She would have to make sure she never saw him again. Yet with the ties between their two families, that would be almost impossible.

She rubbed her forehead in frustrated fury. It was almost as though she had deliberately chosen him, and that was a thought that disturbed her very much indeed.

She would close the door and walk away and forget all about him. She would pretend this had never happened.

She risked one last glance. Jack was a man with a hard edge, a ruthless man, but he had shown her tenderness tonight. The thought made her feel vulnerable. It was very difficult to equate the Jack Rutherford she had thought she knew, all arrogant charm and brash swagger, with this man. She felt off-kilter as though all her assumptions about him had been overset, challenged by his gentleness as a lover. He had wanted to know her, not simply know her body. That confused her.

She turned away, suddenly raked with misery, and closed the door. She had plunged them from barely civil acquaintance into profound intimacy. Now she had to turn back the clock.

Frazer materialized from the steward's room as soon as she stepped into the hall. She wondered if he had slept.

"No need to look so disapproving," she said. "You're not my father."

The steward's expression remained, as ever, completely inscrutable. He had a dark, closed face, austere and secret. Truth was, Frazer was old enough to be her father and was in fact father to the host of handsome young men she employed as footmen and grooms. He had worked for her for ten years, ever since her marriage. Frazer was a servant, yet somehow Mairi felt she was the one who had to work for his good opinion. This morning she suspected she had lost it once and for all.

"Can I get anything for you, ma'am?" Frazer was exquisitely polite. "Would you like the maid to draw a bath for you?"

"Just the carriage, if you please," Mairi said. She would not delay a moment. She fidgeted with her gloves. "If you could tidy the bedroom—"

"Of course, ma'am." The steward's voice was arctic.

"The gentleman is still asleep," Mairi said.

"Would you like me to wake him? Give him a shave? Breakfast?" Mairi was sure she could detect sarcasm in Frazer's voice now. She looked at him sharply. He looked blandly back at her.

"Let him sleep," Mairi said. She could feel herself blushing at the implication. "Then show him out. Oh, and, Frazer—" She hesitated. "If he asks any questions…"

Frazer nodded. "Of course, ma'am. Not a word."

"Thank you." Mairi's throat felt rough. Tears pricked the back of her eyes. Frazer might disapprove of her behavior, but she still held his loyalty. Four years now since her husband, Archie, had gone and she could still feel the pain of his leaving squeeze her heart like a vise.

Outside in Candlemaker Row the wind was sharp. A pearl-white sky was unfurling over the city of Edinburgh. Mairi drew the shawl more closely about her. By the time she reached the Royal Mile the carriage was waiting, one of Frazer's handsome sons standing ready to open the door for her. She climbed in and set off for her house in Charlotte Square, for a bath and for clean clothes. She ached so much. Her body ached from the pleasure, but her heart ached more.

She closed her eyes. Despite the extraordinary intimacy of the night, she felt lonelier than she had ever felt in her life.

CHAPTER TWO

July 1815

"YOU LOOK BLUE-DEVILLED." Robert, Marquis of Methven, threw down his cards and viewed his companion with amusement in his narrowed blue eyes. "Money troubles, is it?"

"Why do you say that?" Jack Rutherford placed his own hand slowly on the table and reached for his cup of coffee. It was rich, warm and exceptionally good and it did nothing to soothe his spirits. What he really wanted was brandy but these days he never drank it. He had had an unhappy relationship with alcohol in his youth and he had no intention of ever letting his drinking get out of control again.

"You've been playing as cagily as a spinster aunt betting a shilling at whist," Methven said cheerfully. "Your mind is elsewhere. And it cannot be a woman who's spoiling your game since you never let them get to you—"

Jack shifted edgily. Some coffee spilled. He looked up to see his cousin laughing at him.

"Damn you, Rob," he said, without heat.

"Never seen you like this before," Methven said. "I suppose it had to happen sometime. Who is she?"

Jack paused. The club was three-quarters empty and

wreathed in silence, which was good since he did not fancy rehearsing his romantic disasters to an audience. It was a situation he seldom if ever found himself in. Usually he was fighting women off rather than pining for their company.

"I don't know," he admitted, after a moment.

Methven raised a quizzical brow. "No name?"

"We didn't talk much."

His cousin sighed with weary acceptance. Robert knew him well. "Description?" he said.

"She was tall," Jack said. "She was slender and she had long hair. I don't know," he repeated. "It was too dark to see."

Methven almost choked on his brandy. "Devil take it, Jack. Where did this…uh…encounter occur?"

"At a masked ball," Jack said. "At least that was where it started. It finished…" He shrugged. "Elsewhere. Somewhere in the Old Town."

Methven was laughing now. Jack supposed it was funny in a way; he had a reputation for leaving women before the sheets were cold, and here he was, craving a woman who had used him and discarded him with a ruthlessness that stole the breath. It had not happened to him before. He did not like it. He was always the one to walk away first.

Yet that was not why he wanted to find her. He felt unsettled, distracted. Three months. It was ridiculous. He should have forgotten her two months and twenty-nine days ago. Yet her memory lingered. Only the previous day he had let a business deal slip through his fingers because he was not paying attention and someone else had undercut him with a better offer. Women had never come between him and his work before, and the fact that this one had done so frustrated him and made him angry.

"What *do* you know about her?" Methven was asking.

Nothing much that he wanted to discuss, Jack thought. He knew she was lovely and lissome, with skin that smelled of jasmine and was as soft as silk. He knew her hair curled deliciously. He had traced the contours of her face and knew it was fine-boned with a straight nose and a haughty little chin. He knew she had high, rounded breasts, small but perfect, and that her stomach curved in a way that made him ache to have her again and that the skin of her inner thighs was the softest of all.

He knew he was getting an erection merely through thinking about her and that if he did not find her soon he would run mad. He was sure his determination to track her down was no more than a physical compulsion, driven by lust, and that it would burn itself out once it was satisfied. But until he could find her he remained very unsatisfied indeed.

"She was a lady," he said, remembering the cut glass accent and the note of command. Not a virgin, for surely a virgin would not have been so utterly without inhibition. And yet for all her apparent experience, he had sensed her vulnerability. And she had been sad. He remembered the way she had cried out in her sleep and the tears on her cheek, and felt a sharp, unwelcome pang of protectiveness.

"Forget her," Methven was saying. "You know what Edinburgh society is like. She is probably a bored wife or a predatory widow. You will only be one of many. It sounds as though you both got what you wanted."

He raised a shoulder in a half shrug. "Don't spoil the memory, Jack."

It was good, if unpalatable, advice. Jack did not flatter himself that his mystery seductress had bedded no one but him. The anonymous black carriage and the luxurious love nest both argued against it. He was probably only the latest in a long line of conquests. He had experienced a night of unbridled passion with absolutely no commitment given, wanted or required, the sort of night many a man would kill for. He should be grateful. And he should walk away. Most certainly he should not make a fool of himself a third time by returning to the house in Candlemaker Row in a vain attempt to find her or to persuade the steward, tight as a clam, to reveal even one tiny detail that might help him in his search.

Methven pushed the coffeepot toward him. "She must have been good," he said. "Or bad in the best possible way."

Jack did not reply. His mouth tightened. Oh yes, she had been good, very good indeed. He had never known a woman like her, never been so lost in carnal pleasure, never felt this ache of longing.

"Have you tried bedding a harlot for the sake of a cure?" Methven asked. "Replace one whore with another—"

Jack was already half on his feet, his hand going to his sword, before he realized what he was doing. He saw his cousin raise his brows in laconic amusement, realized that he had been set up and wondered what on earth was showing in his eyes.

"I apologize," Methven said swiftly. "I did not realize it was like that."

"It isn't," Jack growled. He subsided into his seat

with a sigh and splashed some more coffee into his cup. "I don't know…" He stopped. He did not know why he had reacted so badly when his cousin had, in all likelihood, been correct and the woman had probably been a high-class harlot. Except that somehow he knew she was not. And for some reason it mattered.

"She wasn't a whore," he said stubbornly.

"Have you been back to the place you met?" Methven said. His blue eyes were steady and watchful now, measuring Jack's reaction. Jack kept his expression studiously blank.

"I have," he said. The masked ball had been held at Lady Durness's town house in Charlotte Square. The house was closed now for the summer and the butler had been less than helpful on the subject of her ladyship's guest list. The anonymous black carriage had had no family crest. The house in Candlemaker Row, so opulent, had given no clues.

He had to accept that she did not want to be found, and as he was not a man who forced his attentions on unwilling women, that was the end of the affair. He was left with nothing but frustration, anger at having been used and a sense of thwarted lust.

"It doesn't matter," he said. He summoned up a smile. "Was there something in particular you wanted, Rob? Your note mentioned a favor."

His cousin nodded. He was staring thoughtfully into the middle distance in a way that made Jack feel uneasy. Then he raised his eyes to meet Jack's gaze. "You know that Ewan is to be christened at Methven in a month's time?" he said. "We would like you to be present."

Robert had married Lady Lucy MacMorlan three years before and they already had two sons, the second baby having been born two months previously. James, the heir, had been baptised at a grand occasion the previous year. Now it seemed that the spare would be getting the same treatment.

"I suppose this will be another of your grand clan gatherings," Jack said.

Robert played with the stem of his wineglass. "The christening will certainly be a formal occasion," he said at last, "but the house party is a family event."

Jack tried not to groan aloud. He hated family occasions, formal or informal, and this one would no doubt prove even more uncomfortable than the last. Traditionally the Methven and the MacMorlan clans had been enemies. Some members of the family still seemed to think that they were.

"Surely your marriage should have been sufficient to heal the rift between the clans?" he said. "Must you do more?"

Robert's blue eyes were amused. "Yes, I must. Lucy and I have not seen Lachlan and Dulcibella since they eloped. They had the tact to stay away from James's christening last year."

"Well, you are not missing anything," Jack said. "Don't invite them. Grandmama can't stand them. No one can. You had a very lucky escape there, Rob."

Robert's eyes warmed and Jack knew he was thinking of his wife. Three years previously Robert had been betrothed to marry Miss Dulcibella Brodrie when she had eloped with Lucy's brother, Lachlan. Robert, Jack thought, had been immensely fortunate; Lucy was charming, clever and beautiful and loved him to distraction. Dulcibella was spoiled, shallow and spiteful and loved no one but herself. There were already rumors of a rift in her marriage to Lachlan.

"I have to be on good terms with Lachlan," Robert said. There was an edge to his voice now. "Now that Dulcibella has inherited the Cardross estates, we are neighbors. I don't want any border disputes." He leaned forward, resting his elbows on the table. "There was something else, Jack. We wondered... Will you stand as godfather to Ewan?"

The atmosphere changed; silence settled. Jack could find no words. He felt cold to his bones at what his cousin was asking. To be a godfather he would have to embrace family ties, family responsibilities. He would need to be a real active presence in his godson's life. God forbid that anything might happen to Robert and Lucy, but if it did he might even be required to act as both boys' guardian, a role for which he was supremely unfit. Jack repressed a shudder.

"You don't need me," he said lightly. "Ewan has a whole clan of relatives far more suitable than I."

Robert's eyes narrowed. "Jack," he said, "should anything happen to Lucy or I, I would want you to stand as guardian to both James and Ewan."

Cold fear seeped through Jack's body. It was impossible.

"Rob—" he said, with difficulty.

"Lucy and I would like it very much," Robert said gently. "If you feel able to accept."

Jack did not look at him. He kept his gaze fixed on the dregs of the coffee that swirled in his cup.

"I am not exactly an ideal role model," he said, striving for a light tone. "Ewan deserves better."

"On the contrary," his cousin replied evenly. "Ewan

could not do better." Then as Jack remained silent, his
tone quickened with impatience. "Jack, for God's sake,
give yourself some credit. I know what you are thinking,
but you did what you thought was best for Averil—"

Jack cut him off with one swift gesture. He never
talked about his sister and he was not going to start now.
"I left her to rot in that terrible school, Rob," he said. "I
did nothing for her."

There was silence, heavy with unspoken comment.
Then Robert sighed. "Very well. I respect your frank-
ness and I do understand." He shifted in his chair. "You
will still come to Methven for the christening, though?"

"That's not really a question, is it?" Jack said. "You
are ordering me."

Amusement gleamed in Robert's eyes. "I can do no
such thing, as you are well aware." He allowed a moment's quiet. "Grandmama would appreciate it. She
has been in poor health lately, as you know. Seeing you
would cheer her."

"I don't respond well to blackmail," Jack said mildly.
He let out a long sigh. "Oh, very well. As long as she
has no further plans to marry me off."

"It would make her happy to see you wed," Robert said.

"You're looking shifty," Jack observed.

His cousin sighed. "Grandmama may—and I only
say *may*—have invited a number of eligible ladies to
Methven for the house party—"

"Like a cattle mart," Jack said. His mouth twisted.
"You're not selling this to me, Rob."

"Now that you have the estate at Glen Calder, you
must surely be thinking of the future," Robert said
mildly.

"My future does not involve a wife and family," Jack said, his voice hard. "Not every man wants such things." He gulped down a mouthful of coffee, and another. It was not what he wanted. What he wanted—what he needed—was the fierce burn of brandy. It was not often these days that he thought of drinking himself into oblivion, but tonight the prospect was tempting. Too tempting. He knew his weaknesses, knew how little it would take. He pushed the bottle further away. He wished Robert was not drinking brandy but it was not his cousin's fault. Robert had offered to take coffee with him and Jack had refused and ordered him the spirits. He hated anyone pandering to his weakness.

"Jack, you should not blame yourself," Robert said. He cursed under his breath. "You should not have to bear the weight of your parents' mistakes."

"Let us not speak of it," Jack said. His throat felt rough, his voice strained. He could hear his cousin's words, but they could not touch him. He did not believe them because the truth was that he had failed. As the only son, he had had the duty to protect his mother and his sister after his father's death, and he had failed them both shamefully.

He eyed the brandy bottle. His fingers itched to reach for it. He could feel the compulsion creeping through him like a dark tide.

It was better that he should be alone. That way there was no danger he would fail anyone but himself. He slid a hand across the table, reaching for the bottle.

"...Lady Mairi MacLeod," Robert said.

Jack stopped, his head snapping round. "I beg your pardon?"

"I said that I would like you to escort Lady Mairi

MacLeod to the christening," Robert repeated. Then, when Jack did not immediately respond, "I know that you dislike her, but she is my sister-in-law. It would be a courtesy."

Jack groaned. "Must I?" he said. Just when he had thought that the evening could not become worse, it had done so.

Dislike did not even begin to encompass his feeling for Mairi MacLeod. When he had first met her three years before at her sister's wedding he had thought her fascinating, cool, beautiful, self-contained, a challenge. He liked rich widows and they tended to like him in return. He had wasted no time in suggesting to Mairi that she should become his mistress. She had told him in no uncertain terms what he could do with his proposition and after that had treated him with the utmost indifference. Jack was not accustomed to rejection, and it annoyed him that even after so clear a refusal he was still attracted to Mairi MacLeod with a powerful dark strain of awareness he could not dismiss. A week in her company escorting her over bad roads on the long and arduous journey to the Highlands would make him want to alternately strangle her and make love to her and neither option was possible.

Robert gave an exaggerated sigh. "I fail to understand your antipathy."

"Then let me enlighten you," Jack said. "Lady Mairi is proud and haughty. She's too rich, too beautiful and too clever."

Antagonism stirred in him again. It infuriated him that he could not be indifferent to Mairi MacLeod. Not even his night of outrageous passion with his mystery seductress had been able to break her spell. In fact, oddly it seemed to make the craving worse. Now there were two women he lusted after and could not bed.

Robert was laughing. "Does she have any other faults you wish to share?" he murmured.

Jack ran a hand through his hair. "I would rather not escort her," he said. "Why can't she travel with her family?"

"Because they are at Forres and Lady Mairi is at her home just outside Edinburgh," Robert said with unimpaired calm. "It's a courtesy, Jack. As I said, we are trying to heal the breach between the clans." He shrugged. "If Lady Mairi dislikes you as much as you say, then she will refuse your escort."

"She might accept simply to torment me," Jack muttered. He gave a sharp sigh. "Oh, very well. But you owe me a favor."

"I really do not think so," Robert said dryly.

"Five minutes," Jack said. "It will only take me five minutes to ask and for her to refuse." He would spend no longer than that in her company. He would go to Ardglen, he would invite Mairi to travel with him to Methven, she would refuse and then he would be gone. Once at Methven for the christening, they could cordially ignore each other.

He sat back, the tension easing a little from his shoulders. He and Mairi MacLeod could surely manage to be civil to each other for so short a time. Five minutes and then it would be done.

"TELL LADY MAIRI MACLEOD that Mr. Rutherford wishes to see her."

Mairi had been in the drawing room when she heard the door knocker sound with a sharp rap that was both arrogant and commanding. A moment later there were voices in the hall and one, a deep drawl she now recognized with every fiber of her being, made her jump so much that she almost snipped off her own fingers rather than the long stems of the roses she was arranging. Laying the secateurs softly on the table, she tiptoed across to the half-open door and stood poised, aware of the tension seeping through her body. The heavy scent of the roses seemed to fill the air, stifling her breath. The blood beat hard in her ears. She gripped the door handle tightly and closed her eyes as the world spun too fast.

Time had lulled her into a false sense of security. She had left Edinburgh the same morning that she had left Jack sleeping off his excesses in her bed. She had come to her country house and had dropped out of society in the hope of avoiding him. She had begun to think she was safe.

Yet here he was.

She tried to steady her breathing, to tell herself there was no danger. Even if Jack had identified her, she did not have to confront him. She had told the footmen to admit no one, and they were very well trained. Even now she could hear one of them politely refusing Jack access to her with a smooth and well-practiced rebuttal.

"I'm sorry, sir, but Lady Mairi is not receiving guests at the moment."

"She'll see me," Jack said briefly.

Mairi drew back, but it was too late. Perhaps Jack had seen the flicker of her shadow across the black-and-white marble floor of the hallway. Perhaps he sensed her presence. She had only a few seconds' warning and then Jack was striding into the drawing room and facing her. There was both authority and an easy grace in the way he moved across the floor toward her. She felt all the breath leave her body in a rush, felt the shivers chase across her skin. She realized that she was shaking and knitted her fingers together to still the betrayal.

The first thing she noticed about him was the elegance of his tailoring. He had certainly gone to a lot of trouble in his dress before he called on her. She was not sure how to interpret that. Jack always dressed well, but today he looked spectacular; his clothes were expensive and beautifully cut, the linen pristine white, the boots with a high polish. He carried it off well too, casually but with supreme elegance. So many men looked ridiculous in their fashions, impaled on high shirt points, their jackets stiffened with buckram. Jack Rutherford did not need any artificial aids in order to look good. The jacket of green superfine fit his broad shoulders without a wrinkle. His pantaloons were like a second skin, molding his muscular thighs.

Mairi felt awareness spark and flare deep inside her. Her breath caught beneath her ribs, and her heart started to race. Jack looked a little bit dangerous, more than a little handsome with the tousled tawny hair tumbling over his brow and those narrowed laughing eyes, his face chiseled and clean-shaven. The impossible intimacies they had shared made her consciousness of him so fierce that she was not sure she could hide her reaction to him.

She was staring. She chided herself for it and took a deep breath to steady herself.

He executed a perfect bow. "Lady Mairi."

There was no apology for interrupting her, no reference to the fact that he had explicitly ignored her desire for solitude. In Edinburgh she had been the one who had driven their encounter. Now that seemed absurd. Jack Rutherford was far too forceful to be anything other than in control. His easy charm cloaked a will of steel.

"Mr. Rutherford," Mairi said, matching his indifference with a chilly civility of her own.

His gaze brushed her face. There was no recognition at all in his eyes.

He did not know.

Relief weakened her knees and she almost had to grab the table for support. Disturbingly, beneath the sense of reassurance were other emotions. She identified disappointment and realized that everything that was feminine within her wanted him to remember her.

Madness. She should be happy to have got away with it. She should be grateful and relieved, anything but this vain and foolish dissatisfaction.

"How do you do, sir?" she said. "I hope you are well."

Jack's mouth twisted as though to suggest that he knew the words were no more than a commonplace courtesy. He did not even trouble to reply.

"I understand that you will be traveling to Methven for the christening of your nephew," he said. His gaze was moving about the room as though he had no particular desire to look at her. "I am here to offer my escort."

He was here about Ewan's christening. Mairi felt simultaneously relieved to understand the reason for his visit and deeply irritated that his offer had been made in such an offhand manner.

"How kind," she said. Then, stung to sarcasm by his indifference: "I had no notion you desired my company so much."

His gaze came back to her, cool hazel, remote. "The offer is made is at my cousin's request, madam, rather than my own inclination."

"Of course," Mairi said. "I knew it would not be your choice." She smiled at him, equally cool. "Please tell Lord Methven that I appreciate his thoughtfulness but I will make my own arrangements."

Jack nodded. She could tell he was not going to try to persuade her to change her mind, presumably because escorting her to Methven Castle was the very last thing on earth that he wanted to do. Everything about his demeanor suggested that he wished to be gone from her drawing room and preferably her life. She could understand that. While she could think of nothing but their wicked night together, Jack still thought of her as a woman who had rejected his advances and treated him with disdain, a woman he was unfortunately bound to through their mutual relatives.

If only he knew. The irony of it almost made her smile.

"Goodbye, Mr. Rutherford," she said. "It is fortunate that Methven Castle is large enough that we need see little of each other during our stay."

She picked up the secateurs again, gripping the cool metal tightly against her hot palm.

In a moment he would be gone.

Jack's gaze fell on the roses with their deep red petals. They looked rich and vibrant against the sun-warmed wood of the table. The sunshine slanted light and shadow across his face, accentuating the high cheekbones and the hard jaw. Mairi felt her heart skip a beat. He looked up and met her eyes, and her heart jolted again for fear that she could not hide her reaction to him.

"My grandmother would like those flowers," Jack said, surprising her. "She adores roses. Do you grow them here?"

"In the walled garden," Mairi said. She touched the petals lightly. "These were cultivated specially and named after me—Mairi Rose…" She stopped, catching herself, remembering that in Edinburgh that night she had told him her name was Rose.

Jack did not appear to have noticed. His head was bent as he considered the flowers. He did not move.

After a second Mairi's breath came more easily. She walked toward the door and put her hand on the knob again, pulling it wider in a clear signal that it was time for Jack to leave.

"Good day, sir," she said sharply.

Jack looked up and met her eyes.

Her heart stopped at what she saw there. The cool indifference was gone. In its place she saw incredulity and anger and a fierce heat that made her breath catch.

"Rose," Jack repeated, very softly.

The tight, breathless sensation in Mairi's chest intensified. The doorknob slipped against her damp palm. She felt a craven urge to make a dash for the stairs, to run, to hide. Except that there was nowhere to hide.

"I believe," she said, and her voice was now no more than a thin thread of sound, "that you were leaving, Mr. Rutherford."

Jack's eyes narrowed, his gaze intensifying on her. She felt another shiver chase down her spine. Then he smiled.

"Actually," he said, still very quietly, "I don't think I was."

He came across and leaned past her to place a palm against the drawing room door and closed it very firmly.

CHAPTER THREE

JACK WATCHED MAIRI walk away from him. Each step was a deliberate move to put distance between them. She looked composed, elegant, every inch the aristocratic lady.

His gut instinct was confirming what his mind was still refusing to accept. This was the woman with whom he had spent the most explosively passionate night of his entire life. This was the woman he had been seeking for the past three months.

He felt a blinding rush of fury. He had felt angry and frustrated enough when he had imagined that his mystery seductress was a complete stranger to him. To realize that it was Mairi MacLeod who had used and discarded him was breathtaking. Clearly she had had absolutely no intention of ever revealing her identity to him. It had probably amused her to reject his advances and then pick him up as though he were for hire. The only surprise was that she had not left payment when she was gone in the morning.

The knowledge that he had been a fool as well as a dupe did not soothe his fury. He should have recognized her but he had been so bound up in lust that he had missed the clues to her identity. He felt another sharp pang of anger, made all the more acute by the sudden and devastating knowledge that he still wanted her. She might be amoral, spoiled and deceitful, but he wanted her very much indeed.

She crossed the room toward the wide marble fireplace and turned back to face him. The afternoon sun struck through the long windows with their filmy drapes and spun a soft golden glow about her. Her gown of palest blue was a shocking, ethereal contrast to the striking dark auburn of her hair. She stood bathed in a gentle light, but there was nothing gentle about her beauty and Jack felt an equally fierce pang of response. He wanted to dislike her. He had every reason to dislike her. Strange, then, how the discovery that she was the passionate wanton of his dreams suddenly made her the most fascinating woman he knew.

He looked at the tender line of her neck and the way that the loose curls of red-gold hair caressed her nape and he was instantly transported back to the house in Candlemaker Row, the twisted sheets and the hot darkness, the intimate slide of her skin against his. He felt his body harden into arousal.

"You are Rose," he said. "You spent a night with me in Edinburgh three months ago." He knew it had been her. He had seen the truth reflected in her eyes a moment before, but he wanted to make her admit it.

She turned to look at him. Her expression was guarded, betraying no hint of emotion. "I am," she said, "and I did."

Jack was reluctantly impressed. Nine out of ten women would have denied it, claiming that they did not know what he was talking about. But perhaps Mairi was so brazen when it came to taking lovers that she did not care about protecting her reputation with lies.

"I expected you to pretend not to understand me," he said.

Mairi raised one shoulder in a shrug. "That would have been a tedious conversation when we both know the truth," she said.

She sounded indifferent, but there was a tension in her slender body that told Jack that she was nowhere near as cool as she seemed. That pleased him. She had been in control on the night she had seduced him. Now it was his turn.

"Mairi Rose," he said. "How convenient to have an alias when you require it."

Her lips tilted upward in the parody of a smile. "I have three names," she said. "Mairi Rose Isabella."

Jack raised his eyebrows. "Even better," he said. "A choice of aliases."

"I didn't want you to know who I was," Mairi said. She spoke dismissively, as though it were a matter of little importance that she had deceived him. Jack felt his temper catch. It was a novel sensation to be treated as though he was of no account, and it was not one he cared for.

"That," he said, "was obvious. The plain black carriage, the army of silent retainers, the anonymous—if luxurious—tenement house hidden away down the back streets…" His anger was still simmering and he wanted to provoke her. "I can only assume that you have had a great deal of practice when it comes to selecting and seducing your lovers, Lady Mairi."

If the barb hurt she ignored the sting.

"I apologize if you feel I used you," she said sweetly. "A man of your reputation is surely accustomed to casual encounters."

"I would still prefer to know the identity of the

woman with whom I am making love," Jack said cuttingly.

She smiled. "I do not believe you complained at the time, Mr. Rutherford."

She laid emphasis on his title, as though deliberately drawing attention to the fact that she outranked him, a duke's daughter and he nothing more than the younger son of a baron.

Well, hell. She might be proud; she might pretend to be above his touch, but she was still an amoral wanton and he still desired her.

"I'm not complaining," Jack said. "I cannot deny that I enjoyed having you." He had been deliberately crude and he saw the color come into her face. He felt no remorse; it was the least she deserved having flaunted her brazenness in his face.

"I might have preferred that you admit to your desires honestly," he continued. "But the sex itself was very pleasurable. I like that you allowed me to do whatever I wished to you. A woman without inhibitions is a rare thing."

He saw her expression harden into hauteur. She did not like being treated with such disrespect. Well, now she knew how he felt.

He strolled toward her across the room. As soon as he got close she turned away from him. He had the impression that given half a chance she would simply walk out on him, but as he was now between her and the door, he had cut off her escape. Which was good, because he had not finished with her yet, not by a long chalk.

He circled behind her. She kept her head bent so that all he could see was the sweep of her lashes dark against the curve of her cheek and the pure lines of her jaw and throat. She looked impossibly delicate. Her air of vulnerability was most deceptive. "Why did you choose me that night in Edinburgh?" he asked, his voice hard. "There must have been a reason. What was it?"

She looked directly up at him then. "I am sorry," she said. "You appear to be laboring under a misapprehension, Mr. Rutherford." Her blue eyes, dark as midnight, mocked him. "When I picked you up at the ball I did not even know it was you." She paused just long enough for the insult to sink in. "You could have been anyone."

Jack felt a rush of pure, primitive fury, impossible to deny, difficult to explain. She was taking blatant shamelessness to a new level in claiming that any man would have sufficed as her lover that night. And instinct told him she was lying.

He grabbed her arm and jerked her close to his body. At such close quarters he could smell the sweet elusive fragrance that had haunted his nights. He could hear her breathing. It was not quite steady.

"I don't believe you," he said. "You must have known it was me. You chose me deliberately. I believe you have wanted me from the first time we met and your protestations of virtue were nothing but a sham." He was not sure if it was pride or stubborn instinct that forced him to press the matter, but he was sure she was not telling the truth.

If she was a liar, though, she was a damned fine one. Her eyes were very candid. She shrugged. "Whether you believe me or not is your choice, Mr. Rutherford," she said. Once again there was a touch of mockery in her voice. "Perhaps you have too good an opinion of yourself to wish to accept that I did not recognize you. My observation of you over the past few years suggests that your arrogance is such that you assume every woman must find you irresistible."

Touché.

She had his measure. If Jack had not been so angry, he would probably have found it amusing that Mairi MacLeod knew him so well.

He eased his grip on her arm, sliding his hand down to her elbow. Her skin was smooth and warm beneath his touch, the lace edge of her sleeve just brushing his fingertips.

"But you did find me irresistible, Lady Mairi," he said. "Whether or not you knew my identity."

He drew her closer so that her skirts were touching his thighs. She was rigid with tension now. He could feel it thrumming through her body and see the pulse that beat in the hollow of her throat. Awareness crackled between them as hot and sudden as a flame catching at tinder.

"I believe you chose me because you wanted me," Jack continued softly. He leaned closer; spoke in her ear. "Perhaps it was instinct, perhaps you did not realize what you were doing, but you wanted me as your lover."

Now, for the first time, he saw a different expression in her eyes and knew at once that this was precisely what she feared; that some deep and powerful compulsion had driven her to pick him out from all the men at the masked ball that night. For a split second she looked frightened, but then disdain smoothed the emotion away and her defenses were firmly back in place.

"I did not have you down as a romantic, Mr. Rutherford," she said lightly, "and I hesitate to shatter your illusions once again, but I do not believe in some sense of recognition that binds people together. That is nonsense."

"You don't believe that desire is a powerful enough force to draw people together?" Jack questioned mockingly.

"The only thing that is powerful here is your imagination, Mr. Rutherford." Mairi's tone was chill now, all emotion locked away. She released herself from his grip and stepped away from him very carefully, the pale blue silk of her gown brushing his leg as she passed.

"I was not imagining that night in Edinburgh," Jack said. "You were completely abandoned in my arms, without restraint or shame. Although by your own admission you respond like that to any man who beds you."

Mairi spun around, cutting him off with a decisive chop of the hand. At last he had provoked her beyond tolerance. There was high, angry color in her cheeks, and her eyes were a glorious stormy blue. "Enough, sir," she said. "You are insulting and your observations on my character and behavior are of no interest to me. It is time you left."

Jack held her gaze. "You cannot have it both ways, madam," he said. "Either you are a harlot who spreads her favors indiscriminately or you are attracted to me specifically and should drop this pretense of indifference. I do not believe that you have said a single honest thing to me this afternoon. Be honest in this one thing at least and admit that you want me."

Their gazes locked, his fierce with heat, hers defiant. He had never known a woman quite so guarded. He had never felt so strong a compulsion as he did now, wanting to smash her defenses and force her to admit to her desires.

He raised a hand and brushed the loose tendrils of copper-colored hair away from her neck. The minute he touched her, she froze. He let his fingers slide gently down to the base of her throat, dipping in to the hollow there. He felt her tremble. It was a tiny but betraying gesture and it made his blood surge. Her skin was heating now beneath his touch, a pulse beating against his fingers. She felt soft and warm and tempting.

He leaned in closer so that his lips were a mere inch from hers. Her eyes were a hazy slumberous blue now, half-closed. He brushed his lips across hers in the lightest of kisses. She gave a gasp; he felt her breath on his lips and was suddenly possessed with the most ravenous hunger to drag her into his arms and kiss her senseless.

Instead he ruthlessly reined in the urge and kissed her again, a little deeper, a little longer. Her lips parted, clung to his, betraying a truth she had refused to put into words.

"You want me," he said.

The ache in his groin was intense now. In a second he remembered being in the carriage on that helter-skelter ride across Edinburgh, remembered the anticipation and the driving need. He kissed her for a third time and she tasted as sweet as he recalled; he ran his tongue along her lower lip and dipped it inside her mouth, tangling with hers, the kiss deepening into blatant demand. Another kiss, hard and insistent this time, and he was within a few ragged steps of losing control, pushing aside the spray of roses that lay on the polished table and taking her on it.

He felt the prick of a blade at his throat.

"These secateurs are sharp as any dirk," Mairi said. Her voice was a little husky. "Step back, Mr. Rutherford."

It took Jack several seconds to process the words, and during that time the blade only pressed harder, so he thought it wise to obey. He brought a hand up, running his finger against the cutting edge. It was, as she had said, fiercely sharp. As was the look in her eyes.

"I could disarm you," Jack said. With a twist of the wrist it would be easy enough, but he suspected that Mairi MacLeod probably had another weapon concealed somewhere about the place, and she looked as though she would be very glad to have an excuse to use it on him.

"You have lost the element of surprise," she said pleasantly. "You have also overstayed your welcome." She walked across to the door and opened it for him. "Goodbye, Mr. Rutherford," she said.

No fewer than three black-clad footmen came forward in a phalanx to escort Jack to the front door. Evidently they had been waiting to burst in and rescue Mairi if she had given the signal. Their expressions were threatening, especially the man who had failed to prevent Jack from entering in the first place. He looked as though he felt he had something to prove.

Jack, who had taken on far more intimidating men in far more intimidating places than Lady Mairi MacLeod's drawing room, stifled a smile. He briefly weighed the merits of causing a mill and regretfully decided against it.

"You employ a private army," he said, allowing his gaze to travel back from the row of black-clad retainers to Mairi's face. "What is it that you are afraid of?"

He thought for a moment that she was going to refuse to answer and would instead have him thrown out on his ear on the gravel without any further conversation.

"I am a rich widow," she said, after a long moment. "A very rich widow. There have been…" She hesitated. "Threats of kidnapping, of forced marriage. I employ an entourage for my own protection since I have absolutely no desire to wed again."

"I pity the poor fool who would try to force *you* into marriage," Jack said. "You seem very handy with a weapon." The look he gave her was insolent, sweeping from the top of her head to the tips of her toes, and he saw the hot color sting her cheeks at his impudence. Her chin came up.

"I shall be tempted to wield one again," she said, "if you do not leave my house immediately."

Jack grinned. "You have nothing to fear from me, sweetheart," he said. "I am even richer than you are and I do not intend ever to wed you, only to bed you. Again."

He flashed her a mocking smile before strolling in his own good time down the front steps. He almost expected to feel her dirk thudding between his shoulder blades. Instead he heard the door slam shut behind him. Another black-clad groom was waiting on the gravel, holding his horse for him. Through the archway to the mews, he could see a traveling carriage being prepared, not plain black this time but with the crest of the Duke of Forres and the arms of MacLeod entwined. It was the last word in luxury, fast and well sprung, sufficient even to deal with the state of the Highland roads. Lady Mairi was indeed making her own travel plans and they did not involve him.

Once they were at Methven, though, she would not

be able to avoid him. The castle was huge, but the nature of a house party was such that the participants were thrown together no matter their wishes. Jack was suddenly aware that he was looking forward to the visit with a great deal more enthusiasm than he had felt the previous night. A house party also gave ample opportunity for intimacy and he wanted to rekindle his affair with Mairi, wanted to taste again the heat and the passion of their night together. He wanted *her,* her fragility and her strength, the fierce emotions she hid beneath that cool exterior. He knew she desired him too. She had betrayed herself when she had kissed him. She might lie, but her body's response to him did not.

He was also still very angry with her for pretending indifference to his face and then seducing him secretly, for spending one night with him and then dismissing him like a paid lover. He recognized the anger and it interested him. He was not generally an introspective man, but something about Mairi MacLeod had him examining his reactions and his emotions like a poet or a philosopher. It was bizarre and he did not like it. But the anger was unusual. He did not generally bear grudges. He was not interested in revenge. Usually he forgot, moved on. It appeared that with Mairi MacLeod he had not moved on.

He shrugged. That was easy enough to solve. Another night of rapture, this time on his terms, and he would be ready to forget her. It had always worked before. His interest in a woman seldom outlived the intimate knowledge of her.

He encouraged his horse to a canter that raised the dust on the road. Lady Mairi MacLeod might be faithless and amoral, but then so was he. In that they were well suited. He was certain it would not be long before he was in her bed again.

CHAPTER FOUR

MAIRI SAT AT her desk with the household accounts spread in front of her. Jack Rutherford had gone, but the air still seemed to hum with his presence, fierce and elemental. It was impossible for her to concentrate. The columns of figures blurred before her eyes, and all she could see was Jack's face and all she could feel was the touch of his lips against hers. She had wanted him very much and she knew he knew it.

Damn him.

She could not really blame Jack for being angry with her. Nor could she blame him for thinking her a whore when she had deliberately told him that any man would have done as a lover that night. That had been the literal truth, but no man could hear that without thinking her a shameless harlot.

With a little sigh she laid her pen aside and pinched the bridge of her nose to ease the headache behind her eyes. She could not understand why she was attracted to Jack. He was the complete opposite of her husband, Archie, who had been gentle and kind. Yet from the moment that Jack had walked into the drawing room, she had been acutely conscious of him, of the vitality and energy he brought with him, of the confident swagger in his step and the muscular perfection of his body beneath the close-fitting and beautifully tailored clothes.

She did not want to want him. Yet it felt as though he had in some way imprinted himself on her so that her senses craved him, the taste and the touch of him. She disliked intensely the feeling that she was so vulnerable to him, but she could not escape it.

In Edinburgh she had used Jack shamelessly to drive out her feelings of loneliness and melancholy. She had sought out a man that night in order to forget for just a little while the huge weight of responsibility she carried and the secrets she kept. And for a time it had worked; she had forgotten everything in the bliss of Jack's touch and the shocking, exciting sensations conjured by her own body. She had had so little experience of sex. She had had no idea, no notion at all, that it could be so delicious. It bore no resemblance to the mortifying fumbles she had endured at the start of her marriage to Archie MacLeod when they had barely managed to consummate their union.

Well, she had certainly made up for that inexperience now. She could barely believe that she had acted with such brazen lack of restraint when she had been with Jack. So much of her knowledge had been theoretical before, gleaned only from the books in her father's library.

Even now the memory of Jack's lovemaking made her feel very hot and slightly faint. She put her head in her hands and groaned. She hungered for Jack now. She wanted to know again that wicked pleasure she had felt at his hands. It was impossible. It could not happen.

Two blackbirds squabbling on the terrace outside roused her with their noisy calls. Shaking her head impatiently, Mairi turned back to the file of papers on the desk. This was mainly correspondence that Murchison,

her secretary, had already filtered and deemed important enough for Mairi to see. Archie MacLeod had not
been an elder son, but he had inherited a huge fortune
from his nabob godfather at the age of one and twenty.
There were the two houses in Edinburgh, the country
estate outside the city where Mairi was currently living and Noltland Castle in the eastern Highlands near
the town of Cromarty. There was money in bonds and
investments. There were endowments to charity and a
dozen other business and philanthropic ventures. The
entire inheritance had come to Mairi at Archie's be-
quest.

Today's crop of correspondence included reports
from the trustees of all the various charities that Archie had set up. While his inheritance had been rich
beyond the dreams of avarice, his generosity had been
equal to it. He had been desperate to use the money to
do good; there were almshouses for the indigent elderly,
an orphanage, a cholera hospital, so many good deeds
and good works that Mairi's head swam whenever she
tried to keep track of them all. She was the custodian
of Archie's inheritance now, though, and she had to be
worthy of it. She had to continue his good work.

At the bottom of the pile was one last letter, written
in terse legal terminology. It was from Michael Innes,
the heir to the MacLeod barony. Mairi read the letter
through once a little carelessly and a second time with
a growing sense of irritation. It stated that Innes was
bringing a case to court to prove that Mairi was an unsuitable chatelaine of the late Archibald MacLeod's estates. He claimed to have evidence of her lax financial
management and her personal immorality. He would

be laying this before the courts and petitioning for all the late Archibald MacLeod's holdings to pass to him.

Mairi allowed the letter to drift down onto the desk. It was not the first time that Michael Innes had threatened to take her to court. He had resented Archie's inheritance from the first and had always insisted that it should have been subsumed into the main MacLeod estate because he believed it was impossible for a woman to administer such a huge inheritance without a husband's guidance. Mairi knew he was motivated by spite and greed. Now, though, a line at the bottom of the letter caught her eye and she paused to reread it for a third time.

You may be sure that I will not hesitate to expose all the old scandals in the pursuit of truth.

A ripple of unease passed down Mairi's spine. She rubbed her eyes. They felt dry and gritty. Her head felt heavy as though it were full of sand. She tried to think.

I will not hesitate to expose all the old scandals…

Her father-in-law had worked very hard to make sure that those scandals would never be revealed. Mairi could not believe that Michael Innes knew anything of them. No one did. Only she and Lord MacLeod knew the truth in its entirety. Or so she had thought. But that was the trouble with secrets. You could never be completely sure that they were safe.

Mairi's head ached suddenly, so sharply she bit her lip. She did not know what to do. There was no one to share her burden but Lord and Lady MacLeod. Archie had wrought devastation on their lives as surely as he had torn hers apart and there was not a moment when she did not seek to make up for that.

She sat irresolute for a minute and then picked up

her pen. She knew she had to write to her father-in-law to tell him of this latest threat. He could not be left in ignorance. She felt sick as she started to write the letter. The old laird was too frail and too ill to be troubled with such matters these days, but she needed his wise counsel and there was no one else she could trust.

A moment later, there was a knock at the door and Frazer entered with a large dish of tea on a silver tray. Mairi moved her papers aside and Frazer placed it carefully on the desk. All Frazer's movements were precise and ordered.

"I thought you might require some refreshment, madam," he said.

"Thank you," Mairi said, smiling at him. "I do. These accounts make my head hurt."

"I meant as treatment for the shock, madam," Frazer said.

"Ah," Mairi said. Her smile broadened at Frazer's austere expression. The steward was a strict Presbyterian and he never hesitated to make his disapproval known. She suspected that he considered it a part of his duties to try to keep her on the straight and narrow. "I collect you are referring to Mr. Rutherford," she said. "I fear my sins have found me out."

"Quite so, madam," Frazer said, with no flicker of a smile. "I am sorry that Murdo and Hamish and Ross were obliged to hear the gentleman refer to the sensual excesses he shared with you."

"Elegantly put, Frazer," Mairi said. "However, since Murdo drove the carriage the night I picked up Mr. Rutherford and Hamish and Ross acted as grooms, I am sure they are already aware of my morally reprehensible ways. Thank you for the restorative tea," she added. "You are most thoughtful."

Frazer's expression eased a fraction. "Murdo asked me to apologize, madam," he said. "He is exceeding sorry for his failure to prevent Mr. Rutherford's ingress."

"Murdo is not at fault," Mairi said. She stirred honey into her tea, then laid the spoon down thoughtfully. "I suspect Mr. Rutherford always does as he pleases."

"Indeed," Frazer said. "A dangerous man, madam." He bowed and went out, shutting the door with exaggerated care.

Mairi took her teacup in her hand and walked across to the long windows. They stood open onto the shallow terrace. Beyond that a small flight of steps led down to the gardens, and beyond that Mairi could see the silver glitter of the sun on the sea. The July day was hot; only the slightest of breezes stirred her hair. If the weather held for a few weeks, it would be beautiful for the christening at Methven. It would also be awkward to be obliged to see Jack Rutherford again, but she would ask Lucy for a room as far away from Jack's as possible. It was common knowledge that she and Jack disliked each other. Lucy would not think there was anything odd in such a request.

She drained her cup. Her thoughts were drifting to family matters now and she wondered if Lucy was enceinte again. If Lucy and Robert produced an enormous brood of children, there might be years of such trips to Methven for family occasions such as christenings, birthdays, even marriages in time. Mairi shuddered. She hated family reunions, hated the reminders of her own solitude and most of all hated her status as a childless widow. She had desperately wanted a family of her own. The lack of it was like a hollow space in her life, a painful barrenness that she could ignore but that would never heal.

She set her cup down with a clatter on the little cherrywood table by the door. In the fullness of time, Jack would probably bring a wife and family of his own to future events. Despite his denials, a man wanted a wife or at least an heir. She felt an empty, yawning sensation in the pit of her stomach. There was no child to inherit Ardglen, or Noltland or any of Archie's fortune even if she could keep it safe from Michael Innes's grasping hands.

To distract herself she stepped out onto the terrace and went across to lean on the sun-warmed balustrade. The air was full of the scent of roses and honeysuckle. The sun felt hot on her face. There was silence but for the faint jingle of harness and the sound of distant voices from the stables.

For a second it felt as though time had slipped back and any moment she would see Archie coming toward her, smiling as he strode across the gravel of the parterre in his ancient gardening clothes, burned brown by the sun, dusting the soil from his hands. She had always teased him that he employed several gardeners and yet preferred to do the work himself. He had never been happier than when he was outdoors.

The silence stretched, sounding loud. Nothing moved in the quiet gardens. It was a waiting silence, as though someone was watching, as though something was about to happen. Mairi felt odd, as light-headed as though she had had too much sun.

The loneliness ambushed her so suddenly and viciously that for a moment it seemed as though the sun had gone in. She could no longer feel its warmth or the roughness of the stone beneath her palms. It was terrifying.

"Madam?"

Mairi had not heard Frazer coming out onto the terrace until he cleared his throat very loudly. She turned, trying to pin a smile on her face. It felt forced, wobbly, and the tears stung the back of her eyes and closed her throat. She fought desperately for control.

"Hamish asked me to tell you that the carriage is prepared for your departure to Methven in the morning, madam," Frazer said. "We will all be ready to leave as soon as you are."

The words were commonplace, but for a second Mairi struggled to understand them. "Thank you," she said. Her voice sounded husky. "Please tell Hamish I shall be ready by seven."

"Of course, madam." Frazer bowed. "And Mr. Cambridge is here to see you," he added.

Damnation.

Mairi blinked. It was so inconvenient that Jeremy Cambridge was here now when she felt as wrung-out as a dishcloth. If she were not careful she would cry all over him and that would be a disaster on many levels.

"Shall I tell the gentleman you are indisposed?" Frazer spoke delicately, hovering by the terrace door.

"No." Mairi cleared her throat. "No, thank you. If I am to leave for Methven tomorrow, there will be no time to speak to him. But, Frazer—" She raised her chin. "Pray give me a moment."

The steward nodded.

As soon as he had disappeared, Mairi made a beeline for the pier glass that hung to the left of the fireplace and checked her reflection. It was not as bad as she had thought, though her eyes looked strained and bright and there were lines at the corners she could have sworn were new. With a sigh she tucked a stray curl back beneath her bandeau and turned to face the door.

When Jeremy Cambridge was announced she was standing behind her desk. She found she needed the physical barrier. Not that she needed protection against Jeremy. There was nothing remotely threatening about him. Jeremy's father had been estate manager to Lord MacLeod, but he had had ambitions for his children to rise in society. He had sent Jeremy to university and his sister Eleanor to finishing school. Jeremy was now a respected banker in the city of Edinburgh and was among other things the MacLeod family's man of business. He was large, solid and reliable. Steady. Safe. Mairi found herself thinking that he was the opposite of Jack Rutherford in every respect. He had nothing of Jack's restless spirit or air of danger.

"Lady Mairi." They had known each other for a number of years, but Jeremy was never less than respectful. He held out a hand to shake hers. "I was passing by and called on the off chance that you might be at home. I hope I find you well."

"I am in very good health," Mairi said. "No need for formality, Jeremy. Would you care for a cup of tea?"

She saw him relax. His gray eyes warmed. "Of course, if you have the time to spare. Frazer tells me you leave for Methven tomorrow. Will you call on Lord and Lady MacLeod on your journey?"

Mairi nodded. "I intend to. I hope Lady MacLeod will be well enough to see me." Lord MacLeod would have received her letter by then. She paused, toying with the idea of confiding in Jeremy about the latest threat from Michael Innes, then decided against it. She needed to speak to the laird first. Jeremy did not know anything of Archie's secrets, and it would be better if it remained that way. Besides, she had her vanity, and while she knew Jeremy well, she would not relish discussing with him what Innes referred to as her moral turpitude.

She waited while Frazer, who had evidently anticipated her order, maneuvered the tea tray into the room and placed it at her elbow on the table beside the gold-striped sofa. Mairi sat. Jeremy, who had been waiting for her to be seated first as a gentleman would, sat down opposite, his body angled toward her most attentively. Mairi's lips twitched. Jeremy was so devoted. She had never been quite sure, though, whether he admired her or her fortune. Another face rose in her mind, strong, dark, not remotely a gentleman. She could feel the clasp of Jack's fingers about her wrist, hear the low timbre of his voice and feel the touch of his lips. Her fingers shook. The teaspoon rattled against the side of the pot as she stirred.

"Is all well?" Jeremy asked.

"Of course." Mairi could feel her face heating. She kept her gaze averted from him, making a little performance of pouring the tea, adding milk and passing it to him. "Is there any news of interest?" she asked. "I have been at Ardglen so long I have heard none of the latest gossip from the outside world."

Jeremy's face fell as though she had asked the one question he had been hoping to avoid.

"There isn't a great deal of news," he said evasively.

"Nothing from Edinburgh?" Mairi said.

Something moved and shifted in Jeremy's eyes again. His gaze slid away from hers. "There's nothing much to tell," he muttered.

Well, that was odd. There was always news from Edinburgh, even in the summer when society was quiet and many people were at their country estates. Mairi waited, but Jeremy said nothing else, merely draining his cup in one gulp. He had ignored the cook's homemade Abernethy biscuits, and now he looked as though he could not wait to leave.

It was the mention of gossip from Edinburgh that had wrought the change in him. Mairi felt a vague flicker of alarm. She wondered if the talk had been about her. Normally she was not so vain as to assume that everyone was talking about her, but taken together with Michael Innes's threatening letter, it left her with a bitter taste of fear in her mouth.

Had Innes learned somehow of her night with Jack? Did everyone know?

She added more honey to her tea and drank it down, trying to calm the flutter of panic. The MacLeod heir had made such wild threats before. There was no reason to suppose that he had any more evidence now than he had had in the past.

She looked at Jeremy. He was staring evasively at the pattern on the Turkey carpet. The tips of his ears were bright pink and he looked as though he were sitting on pins.

He knew. Mairi was sure of it. And if Jeremy had heard the gossip, so must everyone else. Her heart did a little sickening skip. She would apologize to no one for the night that she had spent with Jack Rutherford, but she did not want it to be the talk of Edinburgh. That would be beyond embarrassing. As a widow she was allowed a certain latitude in her behavior, but it was demeaning to feel that her reputation was besmirched and that everyone was dissecting her behavior. It had never happened to her before.

But perhaps she should have thought of that before she had thrown caution to the winds and enjoyed a night of wild passion with Jack.

"More tea, Jeremy?" she asked, reaching for the pot. She could only hope that the gossip would die down while she was out of the city. Her absence would surely starve it of fuel. Or so she hoped.

"No, thank you." Jeremy leaped to his feet. She had been right; he was suddenly desperate to leave. She put out a hand, caught his and held it tightly. He was too much of a gentleman to wrench it from her grip, so he stood there like an abashed schoolboy in the head-master's study.

"Jeremy," Mairi said. "You would tell me if there was something I should know?"

He looked shifty. There was no other word for it. The expression sat uncomfortably on such a fair, open face.

"Are people talking about me?" Mairi asked.

Jeremy did not answer directly. "It's nothing," he said. His throat bobbed as he swallowed. "I can see…" He cast a look at her, quick and furtive. "I can see that it's nonsense."

"What is?" Mairi said, mystified.

This time Jeremy eased a finger around his collar. "It's nothing," he repeated. "All nonsense."

Most unsatisfactory, but short of torturing the news out of him, Mairi knew she could not make him talk.

She sighed. "Then I wish you a safe journey home, Jeremy, and I shall hope to see you soon."

Jeremy looked relieved. His gaze softened as it rested on her. He took her hand again. "And I hope you have a good trip to Methven." He hesitated. "Once the christening is past, though, I think that perhaps you should return to Edinburgh."

Mairi raised her eyebrows. "Do you? I had thought to go to Noltland first."

Jeremy's jaw set stubbornly. "Edinburgh would be better. You need to be seen in society rather than appear to be hiding out in the country."

He kissed her hand this time with rather more fervor than she was expecting. "Lady Mairi—" he said. There was a great deal of repressed emotion in his voice.

"Jeremy?" She hoped to goodness he was not going to make her a declaration. She did not wish to hurt his feelings, but she could never look on him as anything other than a friend. Guilt gripped her; she had leaned heavily on Jeremy after losing Archie. She hoped he had not interpreted her friendship as something stronger.

"Goodbye, dear Jeremy," she said, and stood on tiptoe to kiss his cheek. "You know how much I value your friendship."

Jeremy blushed endearingly and almost tripped over the edge of the Turkey rug on his way to the door. Stammering that he would see her in Edinburgh in a month's time, he let himself out into the hall, where Mairi could hear Frazer furnishing him with his outdoor clothes.

Silence washed back in. Soon Frazer would return to collect the teacups and her maid, Jessie, would come to discuss packing for her trip. She should not have left it this late really, not when she would be away for at least four weeks. The journey itself would take more than a week; Methven was on the northwest coast and she was making a number of calls along the way.

A part of her would be sorry to leave Ardglen just as the roses were coming into bloom. They always reminded her of Archie. He had been her friend since childhood and she missed him very much. She wandered out onto the terrace again and walked slowly down the mossy steps and along the neat gravel path to where the rose garden slumbered within its mellow brick walls.

The other part of her, the part that shrank from the loneliness, wanted to leave for Methven directly, but the shadows were lengthening and the afternoon was slipping into evening. It would be better to wait until the morning and make an early start. Once the christening was over she would travel to Noltland—no matter what Jeremy advised—and then back to Edinburgh for the winter season and then to her father's home at Forres for Christmas. She liked to have plans. She needed them. They gave structure to her life, a life that sometimes seemed dangerously empty no matter how much work there was associated with Archie's inheritance. She had to keep moving, keep traveling, keep occupied, to drive out the darkness.

CHAPTER FIVE

IT WAS EVENING by the time the traveling carriage drew into the courtyard of the Inverbeg Inn on the shores of Loch Lomond. Mairi had been on the road for twelve hours and was tired and travel-sore. She was glad to see the lanterns flaring at the inn door and to know that Frazer had booked ahead to secure her a room and a private parlor.

When the steward came hurrying to assist her from the carriage, however, it was clear that there was a problem.

"Forgive me, my lady," he said, "but there is only one private parlor and it is already occupied."

Mairi raised her eyebrows. "By whom?"

"By your husband, ma'am." The landlord, a thin, nervous fellow with a sallow complexion and shifting gaze, had followed Frazer out and now stood at the bottom of the carriage steps. "He arrived but a half hour ago and asked for the private parlor. When I said it was reserved for you, he assured me there was no difficulty as he was your husband, traveling ahead of you on the road. He ordered the best food in the house."

Her *husband*.

Mairi had little trouble in guessing whom she would find in the private parlor. Jack Rutherford. She felt a prickle of antagonism along her skin. Jack had a damned nerve in assuming the role of her husband. He could only have done it to provoke her because she had refused his escort to Methven or because with even more breathtaking arrogance, he had assumed that they would resume their affair on the journey. Either way she was going to put him straight.

The landlord was looking from Mairi to Frazer's set face. "I'm sorry, madam. If there is a problem—"

Frazer cut in. "There is no difficulty, landlord." He turned to Mairi. "If you would be so good to wait in the carriage, madam, I will go and deal with the gentleman."

Mairi gathered up her skirts in one hand and stepped down. "I'll deal with him myself," she said.

Frazer looked alarmed. "But, madam, this could be dangerous—"

Mairi smiled at him and patted his arm. She paid Frazer and his sons to protect her, but she wanted to confront Jack on her own.

"Rest easy," she said. "I doubt there is any danger. You may wait out in the passage and I will call you if I need some strong-arm tactics."

The landlord looked affronted and muttered that there was no call for fisticuffs and that he kept an orderly house. A word from Frazer and the gleam of silver coin quieted him and he led them inside.

The inn was blessedly warm and very noisy. From the taproom came a roar of voices. A fug of tobacco smoke wreathed beneath the door, and the smell of ale was strong, overlaid by the delicious scent of roasting meat. The landlord led Mairi down a narrow stone-flagged passageway whose whitewashed walls were decorated with a motley collection of dirks and claymores. They might come in useful if Jack proved difficult.

The door of the private parlor was ajar and there was the murmur of conversation from within. Mairi pushed the door wide.

Jack Rutherford was sitting in a big armchair, feet up on the table, toasting his boots before the fire. He had removed his jacket and loosened his stock, and in the golden firelight he looked tawny and lazily handsome and every inch a chaperone's nightmare. A plate on the table by his side bore the remains of some venison pie. A serving girl with an extravagantly large bosom displayed to advantage in a thin and low-cut smock was topping up his glass. She was standing very close to him and giggling as she poured. Some of the liquid splashed onto Jack's sleeve, and the girl started to dab ineffectually at his clothing with her apron, giggling all the harder. Jack was watching her through half-closed eyes that held a gleam of laughter.

The draught from the open door stirred the fire to hiss and spit and the candle flames to waver. Jack looked up. The laughter died from his eyes and they narrowed to an unnerving green stare. He swung his legs to the floor and got slowly to his feet, sketching a bow. Mairi supposed she should be grateful that he had the manners to do even that. She walked forward into the center of the room, stripping off her gloves and laying her reticule in the seat of the chair opposite Jack's.

"Ah, my errant husband," she said coldly. "Already looking to set up a mistress while you wait for me."

Jack smiled, a wicked smile full of challenge. He sat down again. "If the welcome I got from you was warmer, sweetheart, maybe I would not need to look elsewhere."

"You would always look elsewhere," Mairi said. "You are a rake, sir. I wouldn't look for fidelity from you. If I wanted that I would get a dog." She tried to erase the bitterness from her tone, but she knew she was too late. Jack had heard it. His gaze had narrowed on her thoughtfully.

The serving wench now barreled forward to claim Jack's attention. Quite evidently she preferred to be center stage.

"You didn't tell me you were married," the girl said accusingly. She was twisting her hands in her apron, a maneuver, Mairi was quick to see, that pulled the neck of her smock even more dangerously low. Jack, however, seemed to have no difficulty in keeping his gaze from the heaving bosoms that were on a level with his eyes. He was dangling his half-empty glass from his fingers and watching Mairi with a speculative expression. He did not take his gaze off her for a single moment.

"It slipped my mind," he murmured.

"Strange," Mairi said acidly, "when you had told the landlord only a half hour before that we were wed."

"My tiresomely lax memory," Jack said.

"It is a match for your tiresomely lax morals," Mairi agreed sweetly. She glanced around the room with its deep chairs and velvet curtains drawn against the night, then back at Jack, lounging comfortably in his chair. "Let's cut the pretense, sir," she said. "Was the taproom too shabby for you? Or are your pockets to let? Was that why you decided to pretend we were married, so that I would pay your bills?"

"It was all for the pleasure of your company, my love," Jack said. His eyes gleamed mockingly. "I enjoy your conversation so much. It is so very astringent."

Mairi loosed her cloak and laid it over her arm. The room was hot and she was feeling more heated still beneath Jack's cool green gaze. She felt as though he could strip away all the defences she had cultivated so carefully over the years. There was something keen and watchful in his eyes. He saw more than she wanted him to see.

She turned a shoulder to him and addressed the landlord instead.

"I would like some of your beef stew and a glass of wine, please." She flicked a glance at the table. "I will finish this bottle my *husband* has started—" She shot Jack a look. "Unless he wishes to have it all to himself."

"I am drinking water," Jack said, "but you are welcome to share if your taste runs to it."

"Water?" Mairi stared at him, her antagonism briefly forgotten. It was so incongruous. She would have had him down as a man who drank nothing but the best claret and brandy.

Jack shrugged. There was an element of discomfort in his demeanor. "Riding is thirsty work," he said. He spoke dismissively and yet Mairi had the impression that there was a great deal more behind the words. More that he was not prepared to disclose. After a moment he raised his brows in quizzical enquiry and she blushed to realize she was still staring.

"Landlord," she said hastily, "I would like to be taken to my room, please, and to have some hot water sent up for washing." She paused as an unwelcome thought struck her and she spun around to face Jack again. "I trust you have not moved into my bedchamber as well, sir?"

A devilish light sprang up in Jack's eyes. "It was tempting," he drawled, his voice dropping several tones so that it rubbed across her senses like rough velvet, "but I was waiting for you to invite me, darling."

A wholly inappropriate wave of heat washed over Mairi, rushing through her veins. Her knees weakened and she almost slumped into the armchair, remembering only at the last moment that they had company in the room and that she should be slapping his face—not falling into his arms.

"You'll have a long wait, then," she said. "I suggest that you should have your own chamber. Then there will at least be space in there for you and your vastly inflated opinion of yourself." She gave him a cool little smile. She was proud of that smile. It was diametrically opposed to the way she was feeling inside.

"I would like you gone from here when I return, if you please," she said. "Frazer—" She turned to the steward. "If you could escort Mr. Rutherford to the part of the inn that is farthest away from me…"

"No need for an escort," Jack murmured. "I can find my own way." He stood up, grabbing his jacket from the back of the chair and slinging it over his shoulder. He sketched her a bow that had nothing of deference in it. "Your servant, madam."

The landlord, scratching his head over the eccentric ways of the aristocracy, led Mairi up the inn's wide stair to the landing and indicated the third room on the right. It was big and well appointed, and Mairi's traveling bags were already standing waiting at the side of the bed. Her maid, Jessie, a small dark girl who was the youngest of Frazer's ten children, was busy unpacking and shaking out a gown for the following day.

Mairi sat down abruptly on the side of the bed. She realized she was trembling a little and she was not quite sure why. She could deal with Jack Rutherford. She could deal with most things. That was one thing her marriage and its scandalous aftermath had taught her.

Jessie was chattering, which was a good thing because it distracted her. Unlike her father, Jessie was not in the least silent and austere. "It's no' that bad, this inn," she said. "Leastways it's clean and comfortable."

"The clientele leaves something to be desired," Mairi murmured.

"I hear there's a fine gentleman staying." Jessie was full of the news. "Cousin to Lord Methven. Rich and handsome, they say. The kitchen girls are all hot for him."

"I'm sure he'll be delighted to hear it," Mairi said.

Jessie stood staring mistily into space, Mairi's gown forgotten in her hands. "They say he made a fortune in India," she said. "Trading in spices and the like."

"It was Canada," Mairi said, sighing. "Trading in timber." She did not know much about Jack's background, but she did know that he had made his first fortune before he was five and twenty and his second after he had returned to Scotland, importing luxury goods through the port of Leith.

"*They* say that he is a master swordsman and a dangerous rake—" Jessie rolled the word around her tongue with fervor. "And that he owns a huge estate over Glen Calder way."

"All of which makes him nigh on irresistible," Mairi

said sarcastically. "Is that my yellow muslin you are crushing in your hands?"

Jessie looked down. "Och, yes. I'll have it pressed for you before tomorrow, madam."

"Thank you," Mairi said.

By the time she went back down to the parlor, the fire had been built up and a glass of claret poured for her. The same maidservant, sulky this time, brought in a plate of beef stew. Of Jack Rutherford there was no sign. Mairi knew she should have been glad, and she was. But she also felt a tiny seed of disappointment, and it was this that disturbed her more than anything.

She did not linger after her meal but went out into the passageway intent on retiring to her chamber to read. Her head was a little fuzzy from tiredness and from the good red wine, and at the bottom of the stair she paused, clutching the newel post for support. The door to the taproom was open a crack and she peeped in. Through the fug of smoke and the crush of people, she could see Jack Rutherford. He was sitting at a table to the left of the fire, playing cribbage with three other men, a tankard on the table in front of him. Mairi wondered whether it contained more water or if Jack had moved on to something stronger.

As she watched, there was a roar from the crowd as Jack won the game. Several men slapped him on the back and he grinned, lifting the pewter cup to his lips. Mairi watched his throat move as swallowed, slamming the empty tankard down and calling for another round for everyone, largesse that was greeted with another roar of approval. There was a pile of silver coin by his elbow that was considerably larger than the pile at the side of any of the other players; as she watched Jack scooped up a handful of silver and passed it over to the landlord in return for the new tankards of ale that even now were overflowing onto the table. It was a raucous, good-humored gathering and Mairi felt a small pang of envy. Jack was welcomed into the easy camaraderie of the taproom and not just because of his money.

One of the inn servants passed her with a murmured word of apology; the taproom door creaked a little on its hinges and Jack looked up from his game. For a moment their eyes met; then a spark of mockery came into his and he raised his glass to her in mocking toast. Mairi shot away up the stairs, furious with herself for being caught staring.

She saw no more of Jack that night and fell asleep quickly, lulled by the quiet lap of the waves on the shore of the loch. By the time she arose for breakfast, Jack had already set out on his journey to Methven. Mr. Rutherford was riding, the serving girl said, with his luggage following on behind. It meant that he would be a great deal quicker than Mairi was on the road and she could only be grateful to be spared an endless procession of nights staying in the same inns as Jack was.

When Frazer came out to the carriage, he had a face as long and dark as a wet day in Edinburgh.

"What on earth is the matter?" Mairi asked, as the steward stowed his purse in the strongbox beneath her seat.

Frazer's mouth turned down even farther. "The landlord would take no money for our stay," he said. "The entire bill had already been settled."

He handed her a note.

Mairi had never seen Jack Rutherford's writing, but

she had no difficulty now in identifying the careless black scrawl as his.

"A gentleman always pays," the note ran.

Mairi dropped the letter on the seat beside her. She remembered taunting Jack the previous night when he had appropriated her parlor. She remembered she had said he wanted the comforts that only money could buy. She also remembered that he was one of the richest men in Scotland and had no need to beg those comforts from her.

"Everyone thinks you are his fancy piece now," Frazer said sourly. "And that I am some sort of pander who delivers Mr. Rutherford's women for him as and when he wishes. The landlord congratulated me on such a profitable job. He promised his discretion."

"Oh dear," Mairi said. She knew she should feel exasperated, but she could not help her lips twitching. It was so obvious that Frazer was more annoyed to have been mistaken for a procurer than he was for the damage to her reputation. As the carriage rolled out onto the road to Achallader, Mairi reflected wryly that Jack's had been a clever revenge. She had turned him down, but despite that he had given everyone the impression she was his mistress.

JACK REINED IN his horse when he reached the summit of the track above Bridge of Orchy. The view was spectacular: the great sweep of the mountains painted in green and gold, the glint of sunlight on the water below. There was an ache in his chest, a knot of nostalgia. He had not traveled this way in years. He was not really sure why he had ridden up here today when the road to Methven should have taken him along the wide glen below.

Nothing he had seen in Canada or beyond could surpass the peerless beauty of this land. He had turned his back on Scotland over ten years before, but eventually it had called him back. When Robert had returned to take up his title and estates, Jack had thought of staying on. Unlike his cousin he had no particular reason to return to his ancestral land, but in the end he had sold his business at vast profit and taken ship for home.

Below him on the road to Achallader he could see something that resembled a royal progress, a line of four traveling carriages rumbling along in convoy. Lady Mairi MacLeod was on the move. His mouth twitched into a smile. She was making such a grand statement of wealth and status with the carriages and the servants, the endless baggage train. He wondered how she had felt when she had discovered that he had paid her shot at the inn. Damned annoyed, he would imagine. She did not appear to have much of a sense of humor, and for that reason alone it had felt irresistible to provoke her.

He wondered suddenly if Mairi ever rode out as he was doing this morning, free of all the trappings of luxury, alone with nothing but the wide sky overhead. He doubted it. She was hedged about by so much protocol and protection. She had probably forgotten what it was like to be alone. But perhaps she was wise. She was fabulously wealthy and it was not so many years since rich widows in these parts had been kidnapped and forced into marriage.

Marriage, he suspected, was not on Mairi MacLeod's agenda, and why should it be when she had everything she could desire and the freedom to take lovers as she pleased? He did not particularly resent her refusal of him the previous night. They were playing the game;

she knew the rules as well as he did, and it would not be long before she succumbed. She desired him, and waiting only made the anticipation sharper and sweeter.

He frowned a little, remembering the bitter tone in Mairi's voice the previous night when she had dismissed him as a rake. Rakes made the best lovers if not the best husbands, but perhaps that was where her antipathy arose. He had never met Archie MacLeod and had heard nothing but praise for the man, but perhaps there was something he did not know. Perhaps MacLeod, extraordinary as it seemed, had kept a harem of mistresses stashed across Edinburgh.

The carriages disappeared from sight, and the dust settled on the road. It was early morning and the air was cold and fresh. Silence enclosed Jack, pierced only by the song of a skylark as it rose higher and higher into the blue arc of the sky. The isolation was almost eerie, poised on the edge of loneliness. Jack urged the horse to a walk and headed on down the track into the next glen.

As the road wound downhill he passed a scattering of white-washed crofts at the side of the track. They were empty, the walls starting to crumble, ruined chimney stacks pointing to the sky. A little farther there was a tiny kirk, foursquare and gray, with its bell still hanging from the tower.

Jack paused. Memory was pressing close now. He could almost feel the ghosts at his heels. This had been one of his father's livings though the Reverend Samuel Rutherford had not been a particularly devoted minister of the church. As the son of a baron, he thought it was his right to collect rich livings as he might silver or porcelain. They were an adornment to his status, but he had little interest in the congregations for whom he had a responsibility. Jack's mouth twisted wryly. He had often thought that his obsession with work was a direct rebellion against his father's deplorable laziness.

He tied the horse to the railings around the old churchyard and walked slowly up the path. This was where his parents were buried. His father had built a grand manor a quarter mile down the road, a house that Jack had taken great pleasure in abandoning to wrack and ruin. When he had returned from Canada and was looking for an estate of his own, Black Mount was the very last place he would have considered.

The dew was still fresh on the grass, though the sun was hot and would dry it soon. Jack paused by the graves of his parents. There was a ludicrously ornate mausoleum for his father, which was completely out of place in the stark simplicity of this country churchyard. His mother's stone was less elaborate: "Beloved wife of Samuel Rutherford…" Those words, Jack thought, hardly did justice to the all-consuming love that his parents had felt for each other.

He felt chilled all of a sudden, though there was no cloud covering the sun. His parents' love for each other had been exclusive, violent and in the end utterly destructive. When he was a child, it had been something he had not remotely understood. As an adult, he could see how dangerous love had proved to be for them.

He went down on his knees in the grass. Here, overgrown with strands of dog rose and bramble, pink and white, was a simple stone engraved with the name Averil Rutherford and the dates 1791–1803. He brushed the undergrowth aside. Suddenly his hands were shaking.

The harsh call of a black grouse made him jump. A

shadow had fallen across the path. Looking up, he saw a man in black cassock and white collar, his father's successor, perhaps, in this remote spot.

"Can I help you?" the man said, but Jack shook his head. Suddenly he was keen to be gone.

"No," he said. "Thank you."

He felt the man's eyes on him all the way down the path, but he did not look back. He unhitched the reins and threw himself up into the saddle without bothering to lead the horse over to the mounting block, and kicked the stallion to a gallop. He knew he could not outrun the memories.

And he knew that no one could help him.

CHAPTER SIX

MAIRI STAYED THE second night of her journey with Lord and Lady Gowrie at Lochgowrie Castle near Kinlochleven. It was nice to be in a private house rather than an inn, to eat well, to have good company, hot water and a bed the size of Dunbartonshire. As she took a bath before dinner to wash away the aches and pains of the journey, she reflected that she was in all probability spoiled. Wealth and privilege tended to do that to a person even when that person was as aware as she that the privilege came with a very high price.

Maria Gowrie was a friend of hers and fellow member of the Highland Ladies Bluestocking Society. They dined quietly together, just the three of them, for Maria said rather plaintively that their neighbors, the Duke and Duchess of Dent, had refused their invitation since they too had a guest.

"The cousin of the Marquis of Methven," Maria said. "Jack Rutherford. I did ask him if he would like to join our party here, but he is so in demand. He already had three invitations."

Mairi rolled her eyes. Even here it seemed impossible to escape Jack. If he was not actually present, then people were still talking about him.

"I asked the Dents if they would all care to join us

for dinner, but Anne Dent wishes to keep Mr. Rutherford for herself," Maria continued.

"Probably has him in mind as her next lover," her husband grunted, signaling to the footman to serve more beef. "I hear Dent isn't up to much these days."

"I hear Jack Rutherford is the best lover in all Scotland," Maria said.

"I hear he's a fine fly fisherman and a first-rate shot," her spouse countered.

"And I hear far too much about him," Mairi said. She felt irritated. It seemed that people could not get enough of Jack, whereas she had already had far too much of him.

"May we speak of something else?" she said. "Do you anticipate good sport on your salmon rivers this summer?"

The conversation turned from fishing to the series of scientific lectures that were taking place in Edinburgh later in the year and from there to a variety of other topics, but much to Mairi's annoyance when she retired to the cavernous bedroom, taking a Highland terrier with her for warmth, she found she could not sleep. The dog's snores rose to the ceiling, but Mairi lay wakeful, thinking of Jack Rutherford. It was not that she wanted to think about him. In fact, it annoyed her immensely that she could not seem to stop thinking about him. And when she finally fell asleep, it was to dream about Jack too and all the vivid, heated detail of the night they had spent together. In her dreams the loneliness she felt was banished and she was loved. It was intense and overwhelming and wonderful, but then she woke and realized that she was alone and the sense of isolation almost crushed her. She hugged the dog tightly. It was hardly the same, but its warmth was comforting.

She felt tired and heavy-eyed at breakfast, and not even the sparkle of the sun on Loch Leven and the softness of the Highland air could lift her spirits. It seemed as though she felt every jolt and jerk of the carriage that day. She pressed straight on at Fort William and finally stopped for the night at the Cluanie Inn long after the sun had dropped behind the mountains and the thick blue shadows of dusk were gathering over the glen. The inn was quiet; from behind the parlor door came the low murmur of voices and the clink of glasses, but Mairi was too tired to wish for anything but supper in her chamber and the comfort of a well-sprung bed.

"Mr. Rutherford is staying here tonight," Jessie said, bringing in a steaming ewer of hot water. "Only fancy the coincidence!"

Mairi groaned aloud. In truth, it was not much of a coincidence. There was only one route to Methven, and there were not many inns along the way, but it irritated her that Jack was making the same journey at the same time she was.

"As long as he does not think to share my parlor tonight," she said.

"The landlord says he dines with the lord lieutenant and some military gentleman," Jessie announced importantly as though she had made it her life's work to study Jack's social diary.

While Jessie took one of her gowns to be pressed for the next day's journey, Mairi slipped down the stairs to make sure that Frazer and the men were comfortably accommodated for the night. They had rooms over the stables, as the inn was small. The cobbled yard was quiet and the sweet scent of hay mixed with the more pungent smell of the dung. Only one of the boxes was open and a fine bay stallion poked his head inquisitively over the door as Mairi walked past, nudging at her for a stroke on the nose. He was very powerful—Mairi was a strong rider herself, but she was not sure she would be able to control him—and he was beautiful too with the rising moonlight gleaming on his coat and reflecting in his dark, intelligent eyes.

Mairi jumped as a man pushed open the tack room door and strolled out into the yard, whistling under his breath. It was Jack, his shirtsleeves rolled up to the elbows, a bucket in his hand. He had not seen her in the shadows; he moved across to the pump, put the bucket down on the cobbles and splashed the water over his head and neck. The droplets glittered in the darkness, the water running down the strong line of his throat to soak the linen of his shirt. He looked damp and disheveled and thoroughly delicious, and her throat dried to see him and her heart gave an errant thump. It was annoying, this effect he had on her, even if it was no more than a physical reaction. She could have done without it.

She must have made some movement because Jack turned quickly, his hand going to the knife that was stuck in his belt.

"Interesting reactions," Mairi said, "for a man who lives in these peaceful times."

Jack laughed, his teeth showing white in the darkness. "It's always best to be prepared, Lady Mairi, peacetime or not. I beg your pardon if I startled you."

"Not at all," Mairi said. "I carry a knife too."

"I remember," Jack said. There was something in his voice that made Mairi wish she had not reminded

him, something of their previous intimacy when she had
given him her dirk and let him slice through her laces.
She shivered to remember the raw desperation that had
driven her then. She felt her cheeks warm and was glad
that it was too dark for Jack to see. She did not want
him making her blush as though she were a debutante.

"What are you doing here at Cluanie?" she said. "Are
you following me?"

Jack's smile mocked her. "There is only one road
to Methven," he said, "so forgive me for using it at the
same time as Your Ladyship."

He came over and leaned on the stable door, stroking
the velvet nose of the stallion, speaking softly to him.
His shoulder was turned to her and it felt as though he
was pointedly excluding her.

"He's a beautiful horse," Mairi said. "Do you tend
him yourself?" She was not sure why she was prolong-
ing the conversation with him when it was clear he had
no particular desire to speak with her. Perhaps it was
the darkness that was hovering at the corners of her
mind, so much blacker and more suffocating than the
Highland night. It stalked her, this depression of spirits, waiting until she was alone and vulnerable, and just
now she was afraid to be on her own in case it swarmed
in to claim her.

"Unlike you, I do not travel with an army of servants," Jack said dryly. He closed the stable door and
started to roll down his sleeves. "I prefer it this way,"
he said. "I have always worked for a living one way or
another. I would be lost with nothing to do."

"Your implication being that I live a life of idle luxury," Mairi said. The criticism stung her. He had no
notion how hard she worked.

Jack gave a half shrug. "If you like."

"I don't." Mairi said. She felt a flash of temper that he should judge her so carelessly. "You have no idea what I do with my time."

Jack straightened up, propping his broad shoulders against the doorjamb, and looked at her unsmilingly.

"I know that you seduce men at masked balls," he said.

"No, you don't," Mairi said. Her anger burned a little brighter. It felt good, warming, making her feel alive. "You know only your own experience of me," she said. "You have no idea how I behave with other people. You are basing your judgment on a sample of one."

This time Jack smiled, and dipped his head, conceding the hit. "You *are* a bluestocking," he said. "Are we going to have a philosophical discussion about probability? About the likelihood that I was not the first?"

Their eyes met, locked. "I don't think so," Mairi said. "I prefer not to explain myself to anyone."

"No," Jack said. His lips twisted into a bitter smile. "You simply prefer to control everyone."

Mairi felt startled. She realized it was true. She also realized that no one had put it into words before. It was odd that Jack Rutherford, who knew her so little, could apparently read her so easily—odd, and disconcerting.

"I have been on my own a long time," she found herself explaining after all. "It breeds independence."

"Four years since your husband died," Jack said.

A lot longer than that....

The words seemed to hang between them even though she had not spoken.

"Do you miss him?" Jack sounded abrupt.

"Of course." She had to be careful. There was danger here. Everyone thought that she was the archetypal merry widow who hid her grief beneath a mask of gaiety. They thought her brave and stoical, her flirtations a distraction from the grief of loss. And to a large extent that was true. Except that it was not a husband that she grieved for.

"He was my best friend," she said.

She felt Jack shift beside her. "An interesting choice of words," he said. "Not your soul mate, or—" He sounded mocking. "Your love?"

The word lacerated her with its irony.

"We were childhood friends turned—"

"Lovers?"

"Husband and wife," she corrected.

And even that was a lie.

She could sense Jack looking at her through the gathering darkness.

"No passion, then." He was quick, too quick. She felt vulnerable, unmasked already. "I see."

He waited for her to contradict him, to issue some conventional denial, but the words were locked in her throat and she could not force out the lie. She stared at him whilst the shadows gathered more deeply about them. He put out a hand and touched her sleeve quite gently, but suddenly it felt as though the slight contact scalded her. She felt it again then, the lightning flash of attraction and the awareness that was exciting and terrifying at the same time. She trembled.

No, there had been no passion between her and Archie, but now, here with Jack, she was shaking with the force of it.

She started to walk across the cobbled courtyard, heading for the inn door. If she could only make it into the light, where there was noise and people, she would be safe from this dangerous temptation. But Jack kept pace with her effortlessly, within touching distance. She only had to reach out and she knew she would be in his arms, and she wanted to kiss him, she wanted *him,* with a hunger that was even fiercer than before.

"I hear you stayed with the Dents last night," she said. Her voice sounded thin even in her own ears. She was trying to think of anything to distract herself now from the urge to kiss him. She felt dizzy. Her head buzzed. She had never known physical attraction and certainly had not realized that it could feel as though she had drunk too much too quickly.

"You seem very interested in my movements," Jack said, "for someone who claims to want nothing to do with me." He sounded amused, assured. He was making no effort to touch her and yet she felt like prey. She shivered and quickened her pace.

"I heard that *you* stayed with the Gowries," Jack said.

So he had been asking about her too. Mairi felt a quick flicker of pleasure even though she knew she should not. If it was as easy as this for Jack to seduce her again, she should be ashamed.

"Dinner was good," she said. "You missed some fine salmon. But I understand you were too busy to join us. So many people competing for the pleasure of your company."

Jack grinned. "It's a constant problem for me."

"I'm sure," Mairi said tartly. She was starting to feel a little steadier, and the inn door was only twenty feet away now.

"Don't you find the same?" Jack asked. "When you

are rich beyond the dreams of avarice, Lady Mairi, the world wants to be your friend."

"No," Mairi said. "I don't find that. But then I am not as cynical as you are, Mr. Rutherford. Or perhaps I just have nicer friends. We tend to attract the friends that we deserve."

Jack laughed. "Touché," he said. "Where do you find yours? Do you pick them up at masked balls, as well?"

Mairi just managed to repress a gasp. "Very seldom," she said. "That usually ends badly."

"Do you think so?" Jack said. "I thought it ended rather well."

"It ended," Mairi said. "That is the point."

"Are you sure about that?" Jack said softly. "Your continued interest in me rather argues the reverse."

Mairi smiled. "Unfortunately my interest in you will always be a pale imitation of your fascination with yourself. You don't really need any other admirers, do you, Mr. Rutherford?"

She reached for the handle of the door and stepped inside. Instantly light, warmth and sound enveloped her. She felt ridiculously relieved as though she had escaped some sort of danger. Foolish. She had probably imagined it all, the flare of attraction, the leap of desire and that troubling but exciting undercurrent of antagonism, as though he had not quite forgiven her for deceiving him.

"Please don't pay my shot here like you did at Inverbeg," she said. "And preferably spare me the pleasure of your company again until we reach Methven."

She saw Jack smile. He shut the door very quietly behind them.

"You are trying to take control again," he said. He looked at her, his gaze thoughtful. "I don't take orders."

Without warning he stepped closer to her, narrowing the gap between their bodies to nothing. In the small flagged hallway, there was nowhere to go. Mairi could not breathe for the smell of his skin, the mingled scent of sweat and fresh air and leather. It went straight to her head again like champagne, and like champagne it also made her knees feel weak and her toes curl in her shoes.

Jack brought up his hand to stroke the curve of her cheek very gently. "All I want," he said, "is to have you in my bed again."

Mairi gasped. She was trembling even more now. His gentleness confused her, mixed as it was with such stark desire. The confusion kept her still for a moment, enabling him to move the last foot to take her in his arms.

He kissed her, his lips moving against hers with a possessive demand that stole both her breath and her resistance. When he finally drew back, her emotions felt so shaken up that she could feel the tears prickling her throat. It was essential that she protect herself before Jack saw how vulnerable she was. Panic clawed at her. She felt so exposed. He could not know how he had made her feel.

"We are going over old ground," she said. "Good night, Mr. Rutherford."

She stepped back and saw his arms fall to his side. Saw the expression in his eyes dissolve into blankness. She turned and hurried up the stairs. She was still shaking when she reached the safety of her room. She wished Jack Rutherford had not come back into her life.

THE SHEEP'S HEAD alehouse in Edinburgh's Candlemaker Row had seen its fair share of miscreants over the years, and when a tall, dark man clad in a ragged jerkin and trews slid inside at close to eleven on a rainy night, no one spared him a glance other than to growl out an order to shut the door and be quick about it. The newcomer brought with him a strange mix of scents: fresh rain-washed streets, the smell of tobacco and the stench of prisons, but that too was not unusual in the Sheep's Head. The landlord cast him a sharp look and jerked his head toward a door at the back of the taproom. The man nodded and slipped through it, silent as a ghost.

"Cardross."

The gentleman who was waiting for him did not stand to greet him, nor did he extend a hand, which was a sign of how far the former Earl of Cardross had fallen. His title stripped from him, his estates confiscated, the fugitive former earl was a shadow of the fine lord he had once been. He knew it and he resented it fiercely, but feral cunning prompted him to play this hand carefully. It was the only one he had.

"Do I know you?" Cardross asked, taking the chair opposite the other man and resting his elbows on the battered table. He appraised his companion. An ordinary-looking man, large, fair, not remotely dangerous in appearance and probably all too easily underestimated as a result.

"No," the man said. "Though we have…friends… in common."

Cardross grinned. "Was it your friends who sprang me from the jail?" he asked.

"Perhaps," the other man said.

Cardross waited, but it seemed that silence was a

quality his companion was comfortable with, for he said nothing else, merely letting his gaze, pale and thoughtful, rest on Cardross's face. After a moment he snapped his fingers and a servant, lurking in the shadows, brought a tankard of ale and a plate of cold mutton pie. Cardross fell on them like the starving animal he was while once again his companion was silent, watching him eat.

"Do you want revenge, Cardross?" the man asked idly. He toyed with his empty glass as he watched Cardross's face.

Cardross felt a flicker of cruelty gleam within him and then fade. It was not that he had lost his appetite for viciousness, far from it. It burned as hungrily as ever. But revenge, while a tempting concept, was also ultimately a pointless one. Revenge would not give him back his lands or his title. The king had taken those when he had been attainted for treason, and they were gone forever.

"I want no revenge on that whey-faced little bitch who stole my lands," he said. His voice was harsh. "Crushing little Dulcibella Brodrie would be a waste of time. Aye, and that man milliner she calls husband."

The other man's mouth twitched into a smile. "I like that about you, Cardross," he said. "You see a bigger picture." He pushed the ale jug toward the other man, then sat back and watched as Cardross slopped the contents into his tankard.

"If not revenge," he said softly, "then what do you want?"

"Money," Cardross spat out. He wiped his mouth on his filthy sleeve. "Money to buy a new life."

The man nodded. "I can help you there."

Cardross's lip curled. This man was no benefactor. There would be a price. "What do you want in return?" he said.

His companion smiled, shifting in his chair. He did not answer at once. His gaze was fixed on the fire. Then he raised his eyes and Cardross felt his body jolt in recoil from what he saw there. Hatred. Bitterness. A violence that was so sharp and cruel he had seen nothing to match it before.

"I want your cousin, Lady Mairi MacLeod," the man said. "She has something that belongs to me by right. When I have Lady Mairi—and her fortune—you'll get your cut. Enough to buy a new life."

Cardross stared at him hard. "You want to *wed* Mairi?"

"I didn't say that," the other man said easily. His gaze was shuttered now. That flash of unspeakable ferocity had vanished.

A queasy curiosity stirred in Cardross's veins. He felt no loyalty to his cousins. Mairi's sister Lucy and her husband, Robert Methven, had been instrumental in bringing about his downfall. Yet there was something about this stranger with his soft ruthlessness that was utterly chilling.

"You're not the only one who wants Lady Mairi," Cardross said. "Or her fortune."

"So I hear," the man said. "Michael Innes wants the money." He shrugged. "He's a lawyer, not a fighter."

Cardross laughed, harsh as grating metal. "Innes will still fight dirty in the courts. I hear rumors he'll raise old scandals as well as traduce Lady Mairi's reputation."

The other man's gaze was suddenly razor-sharp, all indolence fled. "You heard talk of that even in jail?"

Cardross shrugged, draining his tankard, banging it down on the table and letting out a long belch. "Prisoners talk," he said. "Jailers talk. Everyone says Michael Innes will claim Lady Mairi is a whore. He'll swear black is white if it means he gets his hands on Archie MacLeod's money."

He saw the other man relax infinitesimally. "And the old scandals?" he questioned idly.

"Something to do with Archie MacLeod." Cardross was annoyed that he did not have more information to trade, but there was no point in pretense. He shrugged again. "Some say there was a grand scandal years back and the old laird of MacLeod hushed it up. I know no more than that."

"Let us hope no one else does," the other man said thoughtfully, "including Michael Innes. Or I might just have to kill him."

There was an odd silence, skin-prickling in its intensity. Cardross found himself staring again. The other man's light eyes were completely empty of emotion.

He repressed a shudder. Not many things scared him these days, but this soulless executioner made him feel slightly sick. He had no doubt, not a shadow of it, that the man had killed before and would do so again.

He cleared his throat. "So you want Mairi," he said, "and I am to bring her to you?"

The other man nodded. "She is traveling to Methven for her nephew's christening. There should be ample opportunity for you to abduct her on the road before she gets there. You set out tonight."

Cardross looked wary. "She has people to protect her."

The other man shrugged. "Frazer's clan. An old man

and some pretty boys. They'll be no match for you with the men I have found for you." He leaned forward, suddenly urgent. "She is not to be hurt, Cardross. Do you understand me?"

That took the fun out of it. Cardross gave an exaggerated sigh. "Not even a little?"

"Not even a little or the deal is off."

Cardross drove his hands into his pockets, sitting back. "Why should I trust you to keep the deal anyway?"

"You can't," the other man said. He shrugged indifferently. "Take it or leave it. There are soldiers out there looking for you even as we speak. You know that. I can get you out of the city, hide you in places they'll never find you."

Cardross thought about it. It was not much of a bargain and there were no guarantees, but the alternative was to skulk in low taverns and tenements for the rest of his life. He'd be running, hiding from the law, with no money and no future, and the certainty that one day someone would sell him to the authorities for no more than the price of a loaf of bread.

He nodded. "If I need to contact you—"

"I'll find you."

That, Cardross thought, was scarcely reassuring.

He nodded again. "And should I fail…" He was not sure even why he asked other than that some touch of fear breathed down his neck. Failure was not an option.

The other man smiled for the very first time. "Don't," he said.

CHAPTER SEVEN

MAIRI HEARD JACK leave early the following day and was glad that he was now ahead of her on the road. There were no other routes to Methven through these wild mountains, and she did not particularly want to stay overnight in the same inns as Jack for the rest of the journey. She was far too aware of him, far too vulnerable to him. She needed to keep her distance. Not that it was likely that they would come across each other again now; on the dark bay stallion Jack was a great deal faster on the roads than she and anyway, she had planned to spend the next couple of days at Dornie Castle, where the Highland Ladies Bluestocking Society were holding a meeting. She had been a member of that exclusive club for ladies since she had first been wed, and though she had missed most of the meetings in the past three months, she was keen to attend this one where the program included lectures on botany and mechanics according to the Newtonian method. There were also some decidedly less cerebral entertainments planned. The Highland Ladies met every month in a different location and they prided themselves on the variety of their repertoire. They were readers and writers, open to new intellectual interests, and very proud of their achievements in a world dominated so frequently by men.

The weather was fine again, a pale blue sky arching overhead, scattered with little white clouds amid the bright sunshine. Mairi watched the scenery unroll beyond the window. It was comfortable to travel like this, but for the first time on her journey she felt dissatisfied as though the carriage were a box, a luxurious prison but one in which she was locked up all the same. She wondered suddenly what it would have been like to ride with Jack over the high mountains and to splash through the streams. A longing locked in her chest to throw aside all the rules that trammeled her life. Jack encouraged a wildness in her that was unfamiliar, but it was very seductive.

It was past luncheon when they arrived at Dornie, and she found the castle abuzz.

"Lady Mairi!" Lady Dornie, elegant in figured red silk and diamonds, came forward to grasp Mairi's hands as soon as she arrived and to draw her into the group of ladies chatting among the ferns and statuary of the orangery. "How glad we are that you were able to attend our meeting today," she said. "You have been absent from society so long that we were all starting to be concerned for your health." Her gaze flickered to Mairi's stomach, making her implication crystal clear. "I do hope," Lady Dornie added, her tone heavy with curiosity, "that you have not been in poor spirits?"

Mairi felt a quiver of alarm. More than one lady was casting her sideways glances and a few, like Lady Dornie, were staring with more curiosity than courtesy at her stomach. The inference was plain.

They thought that she was pregnant.

If this was the gossip that Jeremy had alluded to, it was a great deal worse than she had feared.

Lady Dornie was watching her, a slightly malicious

smile curving her thin lips as she waited for Mairi's response. Mairi pulled herself together with an effort.

"My health has never been more robust, thank you," she said. She accepted a glass of champagne from a footman. "I had a problem with the drains at my house in Charlotte Square," she added. "A putrid smell. So I retired to Ardglen for a while until it was fixed."

"Ah, the drains," Lady Dornie said. "Of course. Such a nasty problem." She glided away to welcome another newcomer, leaving Mairi to survey the crowd. It was an entirely female gathering. The Highland Ladies was a clandestine society whose meetings were private and whose interests were a closely guarded secret. Men were not permitted to attend unless giving an expert lecture or providing some sort of entertainment.

"Mairi, my dear!" Lady Kenton, a distant relative and godmother to Mairi's sister Lucy, was hurrying toward her, wreathed in smiles. "How charming to see you here," Her Ladyship said, beaming. "I was not certain whether you would already be at Methven for Ewan's baptism."

"I am on my way there," Mairi said. "You will be joining us?"

"Alas, I cannot," Lady Kenton said. "My niece is to be married next weekend in Edinburgh." She grasped both Mairi's hands and stood back to look at her. "I am so glad I saw you, though. You are looking very well, my love, and very thin."

"No more than usual," Mairi said. She was starting to feel irritated. There was an undercurrent of gossip in the room; fans flickered, the ladies smiled at her as she passed, but their eyes were cold. She had thought that she was among friends, but there was something spiteful edging the chatter. She would have hoped for better from the Highland Ladies.

"You were quite fat at the MacAlmonds' Ball in April," Lady Kenton said. "More than one of us remarked upon it."

"I am fatter at certain times of the month than at others," Mairi said dryly. "It is a common affliction for ladies, so I understand."

"Of course, of course." Lady Kenton was looking at her, a little frown between her eyebrows. She took Mairi's arm and drew her across to where a couple of chairs were placed in an alcove beneath a laden lemon tree. The faint sweet smell of citrus scented the air.

"Now we can have a private coze," Lady Kenton said, settling herself amid a jangle of clashing bracelets and a sparkle of emeralds. She leaned forward, fixing Mairi with her wide blue eyes. "I cannot tell you how delighted I was at your sister's marriage. As Lucy's godmother, I consider it my greatest achievement."

Mairi narrowed her eyes. She knew Lady Kenton well enough to know that this apparent change of subject was no such thing. Lady Kenton had a bee in her bonnet and would return to it soon enough.

"I had not realized that you played so great a part in bringing Lucy and Robert together, ma'am," she said. As far as she recalled, Lady Kenton had been anxious for Lucy to marry their cousin Wilfred Cardross, and that, Mairi thought, would have been a match made in hell rather than heaven.

But Lady Kenton had conveniently rewritten history, at least in her own mind. She waved a hand to dismiss Mairi's comment.

"Oh, as soon as I saw Lucy and Robert together, I

ing her tune. "Dear Mairi, of course! And there is no question of you being ruined by this. You are not a debutante. You are a widow and more importantly you are the daughter of a duke. Your status alone ensures that people would never give you the cut direct. And you are rich. Which means that no one will ever speak of you as more than an outrageous flirt."

"An outrageous flirt," Mairi said. "How charmingly euphemistic. And all over something so minor it hardly merits mention." Jack, she thought, would not like to hear his lovemaking dismissed so carelessly. Not when ~~he~~ ~~thought he~~ was the best lover in Scotland, and for all

knew they were meant for each other," she said. Her eyes were misty. "And look how well the matter has turned out. Two children already and wed less than three years. Your dear mother would have been so proud." Her gaze sharpened and fixed on Mairi's face. "But what about you, my love? I wish you could find the same happiness. I hear rumors, unsavory ones, I fear." Lady Kenton fidgeted with her glass. "There is no getting away from the matter, Mairi, my love. You are considered at best to be a fast widow and at worst…" Lady Kenton paused, dabbing at her lips with her handkerchief. "Well, people are saying…" She broke off, clearly uncomfortable.

"Please be frank, ma'am," Mairi said. She felt another chill ripple of anxiety. Her night with Jack had been private, and for it to be picked over by the gossips felt intolerable. She wanted to believe this was only because it had been a terrible mistake. Yet the hollow feeling beneath her breastbone did not only stem from dread of what the gossips were saying. It felt disturbingly as though they were trying to cheapen something that had been important to her.

Madness. That was complete madness. There had been nothing special about her night with Jack. She swallowed hard and tried to concentrate on what Lady Kenton was saying.

"It started with that wretched girl Dulcibella," Lady Kenton said. "Oh how I wish your brother had not eloped with her! She is quite the most unpleasant creature, all smiles and sweetness on the surface and as vicious as a snake underneath!" Lady Kenton glared at her champagne glass. "She has always been jealous of you and she commented to Lady Dornie a few months ago that you were looking rather plump."

"I remember the occasion," Mairi said. "It was a fancy dress ball. Those Roman drapes billowed a great deal in the wind."

"Indeed they did," Lady Kenton said. "And then there was the wrap-over pelisse you wore at the Grahams' supper. The colors were divine, but the cut made you look as though you were hiding an entire family of orphans beneath your skirts."

"I can see where this is taking us," Mairi said a little grimly. The hollow sensation in her stomach was spreading. "There was also that huge muff I carried during the snow in March. I did like it and it was in the height of fashion—but it was immense."

"Sufficient to conceal a bump," Lady Kenton lamented. "Then…" She fidgeted. "Well, there was Lady Durness's masked ball."

A chill shiver touched Mairi's skin.

"You left with a gentleman," Lady Kenton whispered. She leaned forward, dropping her voice still further. "You were *seen*."

It was the cardinal sin. Discretion was all. Mairi knew she could be as licentious as she chose as long as she did not get caught. And she had been, fair and square.

Hell and damnation.

"I'm not sure he was a gentleman," she said.

Lady Kenton gasped. "You mean the gossip was true? All of it? The affair? The pregnancy? The *child?*"

Mairi stared at her in disbelief. "Of course not—"

"You have been out of town for three months," Lady Kenton hissed. "You were seen in an *intimate situation*

with a man. You were getting fatter. And now you thin. First fat, now thin!" She fixed Mairi with a pl tive gaze. "You can imagine what everyone is sayii my love. They imagine an affair that has been goin on for some time, they have seen you with a lover an they are sure you have borne a child to him!"

Mairi gulped down some champagne. This was all far, far worse than she had imagined. She needed time to think. Most of all she needed time away from the spiky glances and the scandalous tongues, but there was no chance of that, not in Lady Dornie's orangery with all the members of the Highland Ladies Bluestock-ing Socie

...ety waiting to pounce on any scrap of information. That was the trouble with bluestocking writers. If there was a gap in their knowledge, they would simply fill it with fiction.

"People have too much imagination and too much time to gossip," Mairi said. "To have built so much on so little." She looked at Lady Kenton, who was cravenly avoiding her gaze. "Dear ma'am," she burst out, "surely you cannot believe this nonsense?" Then as Lady Kenton did not immediately reply: "What else are they saying? That I gave the baby away?"

Her voice was rising with anger, but inside she felt a wash of desolation. She would have given anything to have a child. The very last thing she would ever have done would be to give her baby away.

She saw Lady Kenton cast a swift glance around and gesture her to be quiet.

"It's nonsense," she said again, this time keeping her voice discreetly low. "You know it. I might have spent the night with a lover, but that is all."

"Of course," Lady Kenton said, effortlessly chang-

she knew, he probably was.

"You know how it is with rumors, my dear," Lady Kenton said unhappily. "They take on a life of their own. The truth becomes irrelevant and even the smallest transgression…" She let her voice trail away.

Transgression. Mairi supposed that her night with Jack had been more than just a small mistake. The timing had been bad, the fact that she had been seen leaving the masquerade with him, worse. Jack had been a monumental error and now she was paying for it.

"There has been comment in the scandal sheets, some of it very nasty," Lady Kenton said unhappily. "They refer to your *energetic* social life and everyone knows that is code for running a stable of lovers. And of course that ghastly girl Dulcibella has stoked the fire by saying you had quite retired from society to somewhere more private in order to indulge your interests."

Mairi resolved to throttle her sister-in-law the next time she saw her. That should enliven the family gathering at Methven.

"I had not realized," she said. "I've seen no papers since I left Edinburgh."

She tapped her fingers on the table, an irritable tattoo. The rumors about her romantic life had run ahead of her ever since Archie had died. She had disguised her loneliness and misery well under a veil of hedonistic excess, a whirl of parties, balls and flirtations. It was no wonder if her reputation had suffered. And she had not really cared what people were saying. She had been too cocooned in unhappiness to care. The irony of it was that she had never once taken a man to her bed until that night with Jack Rutherford, when she had been so lonely that she had sought to forget her despair for a short while. And now people were talking and she was swamped in lurid rumors and she felt utterly miserable. For a second she felt the same despair sweep through her that had overwhelmed her at Ardglen. She felt so very alone.

"Of course a woman has certain needs," Lady Kenton was saying, sipping delicately at her second glass of champagne. A flush had come into her cheeks. "I do understand that. A lusty man in her bed…" She took another mouthful of champagne, her eyes glittering with a combination of wine and prurience. "Tell me, my love…" She leaned forward conspiratorially. "Who was he?"

"My lips are sealed," Mairi said. If that was one piece of information the scandalmongers did not possess, she was not going to supply it. And not out of loyalty to Jack, but out of sheer annoyance.

Lady Kenton, however, was made of sterner stuff. "Was he…good?" she whispered, eyes gleaming.

"Exceptional," Mairi agreed, straight-faced. "Lusty, vigorous and very talented."

Lady Kenton made frantic fanning gestures with her hands. "Oh my!" She seemed to remember that she was supposed to be taking the role of wise adviser and took a deep breath.

"Well, that is nothing to the purpose. It seems to me that it would be better for you to wed again. That would put paid to the rumors. I had already thought of Lord Donaldson as a bridegroom for you. He would be quite complaisant if you had…other interests."

"How thoughtful of him," Mairi said. She sighed. "Dear ma'am, I *have* no other interests! I have almost lived like a nun since Archie's death. That incident at the ball was—" She shrugged. How to describe Jack… "A mistake," she said. "And now I am apparently the most notorious woman in Scotland."

"Oh well, that *is* bad luck to get caught out the only time," Lady Kenton agreed. "What a pity! You could have been having no end of fun." She tapped Mairi's arm. "Be sure to bear my advice in mind, though. And should you wish an introduction to Lord Donaldson, I shall be happy to oblige. He still has all his own hair and most of his own teeth."

"It's a wonder he has not been snapped up before now," Mairi said. "I know you only have my best interests at heart, ma'am," she said, "but I am sure I can live the scandal down since there *is* no actual scandal."

"That is all very well," Lady Kenton said, "but what about Michael Innes? He is sure to try to take advantage of this. You know he feels that dear Archie's fortune should have come to him as heir, and not to you. And he is a lawyer." Lady Kenton was wringing her hands now. "He is well connected in the legal sphere. You cannot afford to give him this chance."

A cold, cold shadow brushed Mairi's heart. She remembered the letter she had received at Ardglen. She had tried to dismiss it as just another of Innes's threats, but it had had that nasty undertone of gloating. Perhaps this was what he intended to use against her. In his hands these rumors would be given the worst possible construction. She would be presented as immoral and corrupt, as a woman who had betrayed the memory of the husband who had entrusted her with his estates, a completely unsuitable and unworthy chatelaine. And if Innes started digging into scandal, there was no knowing what he might find. Archie's past might be exposed, he would be vilified, his parents destroyed, and the past would reach into the present and annihilate other lives. Lady Kenton was also right that Innes was a lawyer with extensive contacts in the legal world. He was unscrupulous enough to use every last one of them to his advantage.

"I do believe," Lady Kenton said, watching her face, "that you should give serious consideration to my suggestions. A betrothal would protect you from further slurs on your reputation—"

"I protect myself!" Mairi snapped. "I always have done so." She stopped and clamped her lips together tightly. It was true but Lady Kenton did not know the secrets behind her marriage to Archie MacLeod and was far too conventional to be told.

"I beg your pardon, ma'am," Mairi said, seeing Lady Kenton's distress. "I did not intend to snap. I am upset." She squeezed Her Ladyship's hands in an attempt to convey apology and comfort. "Be sure I shall consider your advice. And thank you. I am grateful."

Lady Kenton had brightened, a smile now lighting her face again. "You are a good girl, Mairi, and those people who say you are headstrong do not realize how good you are."

"Thank you, ma'am," Mairi said ruefully. She bent to kiss Lady Kenton's cheek. "Now please excuse me. I must go and prepare for our first lecture."

"It is botany and Chinese art this afternoon," Lady Kenton said, "and mud bathing this evening. It's medicinal, you know. Frightfully good for the skin."

"Of course," Mairi said. She had heard all about Lady Kenton's medicinal treatments from her sister Lucy. Some confusion over a massage treatment at a gathering of the Highland Ladies Bluestocking Society a few years ago had led to Lucy being hopelessly compromised by Robert Methven. It seemed to Mairi that mud bathing might prove equally dangerous.

She enjoyed the lecture on botany and then chose to spend her time curled up on the window seat in the extensive library at Dornie reading old copies of the *Quarterly Review.* As soon as the dinner gong sounded and she joined the ladies in the salon, though, she was again aware of the swirl of gossip and rumor. It was so marked that she was tempted to cry off and drive away to find an inn for the night, but she knew this would only fuel further speculation.

She also knew that in time another scandal would come along and people would forget all about her in the excitement of another reputation to rip to shreds. Michael Innes, though, was not so easily dismissed. He was a vengeful, grasping man who would take any opportunity to try to seize her money and lands. She tossed and turned all night, trying, through broken sleep, to think of a way to prevent everything she had tried to protect from being destroyed.

CHAPTER EIGHT

"THIS IS VERY good of you, Mr. Rutherford." Lord Mac-
Leod shook Jack's hand. His grip was firm but his hand
cold, the skin paper-fragile. He had insisted on standing to greet Jack when he was announced, but Jack
was rather afraid that his host would collapse before
he made it back to the chair before the fire. Lord Mac-
Leod moved slowly to his seat, as though each step
pained him, but there was also something defiant in
His Lordship's stance that absolutely forbade any help.
Jack respected that.

A footman fetched refreshments. Wine was offered
but Jack chose coffee. He wanted to keep a clear head.
He had no notion why the laird of MacLeod had summoned him. They were barely acquainted. But he suspected that MacLeod wanted something and he also
suspected he would not like what it was. As a general
rule he seldom did favors for people unless there was
some very substantial benefit to himself. It was a rule
that served him well. Arguably it was also selfish and
dishonorable, but he cared little about that.

"My wife apologizes that her health is too poor today
to permit her to see you." Lord MacLeod had settled
himself back into his chair, a glass of claret at his elbow.

"My best wishes to Lady MacLeod," Jack said. "I
am sorry to hear that she is indisposed." He shifted in

his chair. He felt uncomfortable. The room was too hot; the fire was fierce even though the sun shone outside, sparkling on the waters of Loch Carron and softening the jagged edges of the mountains. In such a light even the high peaks looked a little less forbidding. He could not imagine, though, that the dour walls of this ancient castle could do much to cheer its occupants. There was an unhappiness that weighed on the air and dampened the spirits. He was the least superstitious of men, but even he could feel the chill of it.

He had met Lord MacLeod's heir, Ruraidh MacLeod, during his time in Canada and done some business with him. They had watched each other's backs in some wild territory. MacLeod had been only one of a number of Scots adventurers out to make a fortune as Jack had done himself. Jack had had no notion that MacLeod was heir to a barony, still less that he was brother-in-law to Lady Mairi MacLeod. The man had been dour to the point of silence and had never spoken of his home and family. Jack had assumed that like so many of them, MacLeod had come to the New World to start a new life. It was an unwritten rule that you did not ask questions.

It was only when MacLeod had died of a fever and Jack had undertaken to return his effects to the family that he had visited Strome Castle and met Lord and Lady MacLeod, gallantly attempting to hold their lives together in the face of the heartbreaking loss of not just one but of both their sons. He had visited them a couple of times since, understanding that they had wanted to talk about Ruraidh to someone who had known him and to learn something of their son's life in Canada. It seemed little enough to do. Jack sensed that Lord and Lady MacLeod were painfully lonely while hiding their grief behind a valiant display of strength. He admired their refusal to surrender to despair.

This morning Jack sensed, however, that Lord MacLeod wanted something more than to reminisce over his son's time abroad. There was something even more keen and watchful than usual in the old laird's gaze as it rested on him. They exchanged pleasantries on the weather and the state of the roads. Jack refilled His Lordship's glass of claret and declined the offer of more coffee.

Lord MacLeod shifted in his chair, moving away from the shaft of sunlight that pinned him in its glare and into the shadow. He was toying with his glass as though reflecting on a decision. Then he squared his shoulders, looked Jack in the eye.

"I need your help, Mr. Rutherford."

Jack felt an instinctive sense of withdrawal, exactly as he had done when Robert had asked him to stand as godfather to his son. The ties that bound other men were not for him. He almost said as much, but then he saw the bleak desolation in MacLeod's eyes. The old laird had no one else to ask.

"Sir?" Jack said.

His reluctance must have been all too apparent because once again he saw that disquieting gleam of amusement in Lord MacLeod's eyes. The laird of Strome might be old, but there was nothing frail about his wits.

"It concerns my daughter-in-law," Lord MacLeod said. "Lady Mairi, widow of my younger son."

Jack's mouth turned dry. He swallowed hard. He and Lord MacLeod had never discussed Mairi. Her name had never once been mentioned between them. Now he had a curious sensation of guilt and fear as though he were a seven-year-old boy once more in his father's study—on the rare occasions that his father had actually noticed his existence—and was about to be soundly berated for some sin he had committed. In Mairi's case his sin was fairly obvious: lust.

"You are acquainted with Lady Mairi, I believe," Lord MacLeod continued.

"Yes," Jack said. Acquaintance was not really the right description for his relationship with Mairi, but in this context it was all he was prepared to admit. "We have met."

Lord MacLeod nodded. "I thought you must know each other as she is kin by marriage to your cousin Lord Methven."

He paused as though expecting Jack to make some observation about Mairi. Jack remained prudently silent. Lord MacLeod smiled slightly.

"Lady Mairi is very precious to my wife and to me," he said. "We owe her a very great deal." A shadow fell across his eyes, as though he were looking far back into the past. "She could not have been more of a daughter to us if she had been our own flesh and blood."

Jack hoped his surprise did not show on his face. He had not imagined that Lady Mairi MacLeod had much of a softer side. No matter. This was one situation he was most definitely not getting involved with. While he might be interested in getting to know Mairi better in the purely physical sense, he most certainly did not want to get embroiled in the MacLeod family affairs.

"I am sorry to hear that there are difficulties, my lord," Jack said carefully, "but I do not think that I am the right man to help you." He could feel the sweat prickling his collar. His cravat felt too tight.

I am not the man you think me.

MacLeod shifted a little in his chair. Jack, watching, could see how the movement pained him. That pain was etched deep in the lines on the old laird's face, and yet he did not betray it with a single word or glance. He kept his eyes on Jack's face until Jack started to feel ashamed, his refusal unworthy and lacking in courage. The sensation astonished him. Not one man in a hundred had the power to intimidate him. It was annoying that the laird of MacLeod did.

"I am sorry to hear that, Mr. Rutherford," MacLeod said at length. His voice was dry. It crackled like old parchment. "I believe you to be an honorable man. Allow me to make my situation explicitly clear. Allow me to appeal to that honor." He pinned Jack in his fierce dark gaze. "I am turning to you, Mr. Rutherford, because I have no son of my own now. Indeed, I have no close relatives other than my wife and my daughter-in-law. Under normal circumstances I would not dream of so importuning an acquaintance. But these are not normal circumstances."

"You have an heir, my lord," Jack said with increasing desperation.

Do not appeal to my honor. I have none.

MacLeod smiled. There was no humor in the look. "It is my heir, Mr. Michael Innes, who poses the problem, Mr. Rutherford. He is a distant cousin, untrustworthy and devious. My title and estate are entailed to him, but that is not sufficient to satisfy him. He wants more. He has started to make threats."

Again there was a silence. Lord MacLeod's gaze was

as sharp as a blade on Jack's face and it did not waver, but behind his steely composure Jack could see a man who would give all he had to regain his strength and be able to defend what was left of his family with his own sword.

"I am honored by your confidence, my lord," he said, "but I fear I cannot—"

"The threats are against Lady Mairi," Lord MacLeod interrupted bluntly. "I have heard that my heir seeks to take my late son's estate from her. He will blacken her name in any way he can in order to do so. He will take her to court and attempt to ruin her."

Jack felt a flare of protective fury that shocked him. Had Michael Innes been present at the moment, he would very likely have taken the man apart. His reaction threw him completely. It was a matter of complete indifference to him if Mairi MacLeod got herself into trouble. In fact, the way she behaved was all too likely to get her into trouble, and he was not the man to get her out of it again, absolutely not.

"I cannot imagine that Lady Mairi is easily intimidated by any man," he said. "She should tell him to go to hell."

He thought of the army of retainers with which Mairi surrounded herself. That private army made a great deal more sense now. It was not simply a rich woman's whim or an example of her self-importance.

Mairi was afraid.

Again he felt that odd sensation: anger, protectiveness. He did not wish to feel protective of Lady Mairi MacLeod. It made an already complicated situation infinitely more complicated. He pushed the thought away. He was reading entirely too much into his responses.

Lady Mairi was beautiful and he desired her. That was not complicated. It was very simple.

Lord MacLeod was smiling. "It seems you know my daughter-in-law well, Mr. Rutherford. I imagine that would be her initial response. She is not easily frightened. But there is more to this than a threat against Mairi's reputation." His fingers gripped the head of his cane, the knuckles showing white. "If my heir is trying to dig up scandal, he may stumble upon old secrets that would destroy all of us." He fell silent, staring into the red heart of the fire.

"What is the nature of these secrets?" Jack asked. He could think of nothing that could be so scandalous that it would warrant such a description. Yet the laird of MacLeod was not a man to scare easily, and his thin face was bleak with fear as well as anger.

MacLeod's gaze came back to him. "I cannot tell you," he said. "Should you choose to accept my commission, it will be Mairi's decision as to whether she entrusts the truth to you. It is your choice, Mr. Rutherford." He was staring into the distance with the faraway expression of a man whose mind was focused on times long past. His hand shook as he reached for his glass. He brought his gaze back to Jack's face and suddenly he looked tired, withered and worn. "I cannot act." He gestured down his body. "I am an old man, racked with illness. But you—you could help my daughter-in-law. You could give her your protection and…persuade… Mr. Innes that it is not in his interests to threaten her."

The answer was obviously no. Jack did not even have to think too hard about it. He was not in the business of helping either old men or beautiful women out of trouble. This was nothing to do with him. The inappropriate sense of protectiveness he had felt toward Mairi faded and the hard carapace settled once more about him, reassuringly cold and unemotional.

"It is my cousin, not I, whom you should be approaching, my lord," Jack said. "As Lady Mairi's kinsman, Lord Methven would, I am sure, be willing to offer his help."

Robert would curse him, he imagined, for involving him in someone else's disputes, but he was a man who took his family duties very seriously. While Jack was not. Not at all. Suddenly he longed for a glass of brandy and, equally strongly, to be free of Strome Castle and its dark secrets and the sense of responsibility that Lord MacLeod was trying to place upon him.

Lord MacLeod nodded. "I thought of asking Lord Methven, but I imagine it would be more difficult for him to keep this matter private. Whereas you—" He smiled. "You are a solitary man, are you not, Mr. Rutherford, accustomed to keeping secrets?"

He paused, giving Jack the opportunity to feel uncomfortable. MacLeod was right, of course. He was a loner by inclination. Which made him all the more disinclined to embroil himself in other people's problems.

"My lord—" he said again.

"It would not prove difficult for you to help us," the old laird continued as though he had not spoken. "Besides—" Lord MacLeod looked up, directly at him. "The assistance I have in mind cannot be provided by Lord Methven. I had it in mind that you should become betrothed to Lady Mairi."

Jack almost choked on the dregs of his coffee. For a moment he thought he had misheard, but the laird was still smiling gently at him as though he had made him a particularly tempting offer that Jack surely could not refuse.

Jack put his cup down gently and cleared his throat. His neck cloth felt even tighter now. He resisted the urge to loosen it and thereby show quite how shaken he was.

"My lord—" he said for a third time.

"As Lady Mairi's fiancé you would able to give her the protection she requires and have the right to deal with the threat posed by my heir," MacLeod continued, quite as though he had not heard Jack's strangled objection. "Find out what he knows. Persuade him to withdraw his lawsuit. Once that threat is removed you would be free, of course, to end the engagement should you wish to do so."

Jack took a deep breath. "Sir, I am honored you consider me a suitable fiancé for Lady Mairi, but I fear you have the wrong man," he said. "It would do nothing to help her reputation were she to be betrothed to me. On the contrary, it would probably sink it without trace."

Lord MacLeod's gaze was shrewd. "I appreciate that you are not a man whose natural state is in wedlock, Mr. Rutherford, but that is not what is needed here. What is needed is a man who is strong enough to protect Lady Mairi and ruthless enough to deal with Mr. Innes. You are both of those."

Jack knew flattery when he heard it, but he was also obliged to admit that Lord MacLeod had a point. He was most certainly not intimidated by the thought of a lawyer who intended to destroy Lady Mairi MacLeod's reputation. But it was impossible that he should get involved. It simply was not something he would do. Even now he was wondering why it was so difficult to give a simple refusal.

"Does Lady Mairi know of your plans, my lord?" he asked. "I hardly think she will welcome your suggestion."

MacLeod smiled. "Mairi will not be pleased at my interference, but as head of this clan I still have the right to order her marriage."

Mairi, Jack thought, would be absolutely furious to be so manipulated. Knowing her penchant for independence and for controlling her own life, he was willing to bet that she would be outraged that the head of her clan sought to interfere.

It would almost be worth agreeing just to see her face.

Silence fell again but for the soft hiss and spit of the fire as the wood fell apart with a shower of sparks. Outside, the day was still bright. Jack could see little ripples of breeze ruffling the surface of Loch Carron. In the distance an elegant black traveling carriage turned off the road to Achnasheen and started up the drive toward the house. Jack recognized it at once.

"I see that your daughter-in-law visits you on her way to Methven," he said.

"Lady Mairi always calls on us when she is passing Strome," Lord MacLeod said. "I was hoping to have your decision to place before her."

He put his empty glass on the table with a soft click and made absolutely no attempt to persuade Jack further to his point of view.

Jack watched the coach as it rolled along the lime avenue toward the castle. He allowed himself to consider, just for a moment, the merits of Lord MacLeod's plan. Shocking as it was to admit it, there were aspects of the commission that tempted him. Life had been tame lately. When he had returned to Scotland from Canada he had seen the purchase of his estate at Glen Calder as his next challenge, but as soon as that was running efficiently he had felt the same restlessness of spirit possess him again. He could never settle. He thought he never would. Business could occupy him for a while—he had invested in ironworks, engineering and ship building, in luxury imports for the thriving New Town of Edinburgh—but he always felt as though there was something lacking in his life. If he agreed to help MacLeod, it would at least fill a few idle hours. After the christening at Methven he could seek out Mr. Michael Innes, discover the man's plans and persuade him in the nicest way possible to desist from them.

Then there was Lady Mairi. He wanted her very much and he was sure she could be easily persuaded into rekindling their affair. Her incendiary response to him the previous night proved it. Accepting Lord MacLeod's commission would place him close to her, acknowledged as her fiancé in public. He could take advantage of that public respectability to be her lover in private. Just the thought of it was sufficient to cause his body to harden into arousal. It would be dishonorable of him to use the situation to gain Mairi as a mistress, but then acting with such ruthlessness had never troubled him before.

There was the crunch of carriage wheels on gravel outside, the slam of a door. It was time to decide.

The library door swung open.

In the moment before she realized that he was there, Jack saw a very different Mairi MacLeod from the one who had treated him with such prickly disdain. She did not wait for the butler to announce her but hurried for-

ward toward Lord MacLeod smiling, her hands out-
stretched. She was wearing a yellow traveling gown.
The color clashed gloriously with her hair and made
her look like a flash of sunlight in the shadows of the
room. There was such luminous happiness in her face
that Jack felt something shift inside him, an odd, hollow sense of loss he could not understand.

Lord MacLeod was smiling too as he pulled himself
to his feet and inclined a cheek for her kiss.

Then Mairi saw Jack and stopped. The sun was still
shining, but to Jack it felt as though the temperature in
the room had plummeted by several degrees. He saw her
eyes narrow and in that moment he knew she was wondering what on earth he was doing there and whether
her father-in-law knew anything of the true nature of
their relationship.

Her chin came up a notch in the resolute way Jack
recognized. She did not look intimidated or scared. She
looked him directly in the eye.

Jack smiled blandly at her. He had no objection to
keeping her guessing as to his business at Strome Castle.

"Mairi, my dear," Lord MacLeod was saying, "I believe you know Mr. Rutherford? He has kindly agreed
to act on my behalf and deal with Michael Innes."

Mairi looked comically taken aback. She also looked
deeply disapproving and made no attempt to hide it.
"Are you sure, my lord?" she asked. "I cannot conceive
of Mr. Rutherford doing anything so chivalrous."

Jack made his decision.

"I would be delighted," he said promptly, bowing.

The suspicion and doubt deepened in her eyes, chal-
lenging him to honesty. "Would you, indeed, sir?"

Jack smiled. "Of course. And in order to strengthen my hand in dealing with the gentleman, your father-in-law and I have agreed that you and I should become betrothed."

Mairi's mouth fell open. She closed it with a snap. "I beg your pardon? You and I should *what?*"

"We are betrothed," Jack said. He came across to her and took her hand in his. He kissed her, a light respectful kiss on the cheek, and smiled as she pulled away from her as though he had bitten her.

"Gently," he murmured, his breath stirring her hair. "You don't want to upset your father-in-law. He is very pleased with his plan."

At such close quarters he could see the golden flecks in the stormy blue of her eyes and the furious line of those lush red lips so close to his own. His body stirred.

"One of us is clearly insane," Mairi said, "and I do not believe it is me." Her glorious blue eyes narrowed on him. "Tell me, Mr. Rutherford," she said. "Before I smash this plan to smithereens, what could possibly induce you to agree to a betrothal with me? What would you gain?"

Jack smiled and drew her the last quarter inch so that his lips rested against her ear.

"You," he said.

CHAPTER NINE

A HALF HOUR later and Jack was sitting in the drawing room at Strome with a fresh pot of coffee and a three-day-old newspaper to peruse. Lady Mairi was still closeted with her father-in-law in the library, presumably in the throes of trying to persuade him to abandon his plan. Jack had no objections to the wait. He was enjoying himself far more than he had ever imagined he would. He was also certain that Mairi would not prevail. The laird was old but he had a will of iron.

He heard a door slam and the sound of running footsteps. A moment later, Mairi erupted into the drawing room. She looked infuriated. Her cheeks were pink, her blue eyes bright with anger. Jack found he liked her like this, with her elegant facade rubbed away by real raw emotion. She had been hiding herself before but now those barriers were down and he felt a leap of response through his entire body. He cast his newspaper aside.

"Meeting not go well?" he inquired.

Mairi gave him a contemptuous look. "My father-in-law," she said, "has heard that as there are certain rumors going around that I have indulged in sexual profligacy—" she spat out the words "—and considers that it would be in my interests to gain the protection of your name immediately."

Jack grinned. "Sexual profligacy? Sounds interesting. Tell me more."

"I don't need to tell you more," Mairi flashed. "You were there!" She ran her hands through her hair, scattering the diamond-headed pins on the polished floor of the drawing room, where they winked in the sun. "This is all your fault."

"That is a little unfair," Jack said mildly, "given that *you* seduced *me* rather than the other way around."

Mairi cast him another furious glance, but she did not contradict him. "Damnation," she said. "The only time—" She broke off.

"You've never been caught before?" Jack said.

Again that sharp blue gaze skewered him. "I've never indulged in sexual profligacy before, Mr. Rutherford." Her tone was caught somewhere between exasperation and despair.

Jack was rather pleased to hear it. He suspected she was telling the truth. She was far too controlled, far too careful, to take such a risk. Which made it all the more interesting that she had taken that risk with him.

"Damnation," she said again, softly this time. She rubbed her forehead. More pins fell from the enchanting confection of curls held in place by her yellow bandeau, and her hair tumbled around her shoulders, making her look deliciously ruffled. "I cannot believe how they have built a monstrous scandal out of next to nothing."

"Not a particularly flattering description of our night together," Jack said.

She smiled reluctantly at that. "Your confidence can take it," she said. "It is completely intact, unlike my reputation." She tapped her fingers irritably on the table. "Normally I would not regard it," she said. "Gossip will always fade and I am a widow, so I have some license. But with Michael Innes sniffing around for scandal, this could not have happened at a worse time."

"So I understand," Jack said. "Lord MacLeod said that Innes was intent on slandering you in the courts in order to gain possession of your fortune."

Mairi shot him a sideways glance. "Was that all he told you?"

"No," Jack said. "He told me that if Innes dug too hard for scandal he might expose old secrets that would be dangerous even now. Secrets to do with your late husband."

On reflection he was not sure that he wanted to do anything to preserve the memory of the sainted Archibald MacLeod. Jealousy was not an emotion that he was particularly familiar with, but he was tolerably certain he was feeling it now because he wanted Mairi MacLeod. He wanted to take her to his bed and make her forget that Archie had ever existed, and soon he would do precisely that.

He saw Mairi close her eyes briefly. When she opened them he was shocked at the naked despair he saw there. The laird evidently had not exaggerated. This was a powerful secret. Which strengthened his hand since Mairi would be prepared to do anything to keep it hidden. He had no compunction about exploiting the situation. This was business, the business of seduction, and if Mairi needed his protection, then he would drive a hard bargain in return.

"I cannot conceive," Mairi said, "how my father-in-law could have chosen so inappropriate a man as you to help us, Mr. Rutherford. I am still waiting for you to explain how that came about." She was leaning both palms on the marble-topped table now. The position was enticing, thrusting her breasts forward against the flimsy muslin bodice of her gown while the skirts skimmed the curve of her buttocks and thighs. Clearly she had no idea of the picture she presented. The train of Jack's thoughts was inevitable, so much so that she had to repeat herself before he even registered that she was speaking.

"I beg your pardon?" he said.

She frowned as though he were a simpleton. "I am waiting for you to explain your connection to Strome and the MacLeod family. Are you not attending?"

"I am," Jack said, allowing his gaze to appraise her most thoroughly, "but not to your question."

She straightened up with a huff, folding her arms across her chest, her cheeks blazing. "Mr. Rutherford! Just answer the question."

"I knew Ruraidh MacLeod in Canada," Jack said. "I call on his parents occasionally."

Mairi looked startled. "Do you?" she said. "I would not have expected you to be so thoughtful."

"Don't mind my feelings," Jack said.

"I don't." She was looking at him as though she suspected him of keeping something back. "I suppose that might explain why Lord MacLeod would turn to you for help," she said grudgingly, "though why you would agree…"

"I've explained that, as well," Jack said. "I intend to work this situation to my advantage."

She shot him another glance, sharp and intensely blue. "You mentioned that earlier," she said. "Since I am no naive virgin, I can only assume that the price of your help is that I become your mistress." Her voice dripped contempt. "You have an odd idea of the privileges of a fiancé. In all the books of conduct I have read, a betrothed gentleman may fetch a lady a glass of lemonade and dance with her three times at a single ball. That is as daring as it gets."

"I think," Jack said, "that you will find my interpretation of the role a great deal more enjoyable." He wanted her already, wanted her here, now. She was so deliciously tempting and the awareness between them blazed like fire.

She dropped into the seat opposite his, pressing her palms to her burning cheeks. "Can I not appeal to your honor?" she said softly. Her eyes were a candid blue. She looked sincere. Jack sighed. He was getting a little tired of people asking him to exert a quality he simply did not own. Why they should assume he possessed integrity just because he was the son of a gentleman was a mystery to him. It was not that he did not have his own code of ethics; he did. But when it came to seducing a woman he was attracted to and who he knew wanted him too, he would not hesitate.

"I'm afraid not." He spoke gently. "Self-interest is the basis of all my relationships."

Mairi shook her head slightly. She was frowning. "That cannot be so. You and Robert are close. You must be. You have worked with him for the past ten years."

"It has always been to my advantage to do so," Jack said.

Mairi looked horrified as though she had cherished some sort of illusion about his family relationships. "I thought you were to be godfather to Ewan—"

Jack cut her off with a shake of the head. "I refused. Responsibility without profit is not to my advantage."

He saw the look of withdrawal come into her eyes. Yet it seemed she could not quite believe him to be so callous. "Then what about your grandmother?"

A memory unrolled in Jack's mind, unwanted, unbidden, of the jail door swinging open and his grandmother standing there, her silk and lace so incongruous amid the dirt and the squalor, the shouts of the drunks and the screams of the madmen. He remembered being fiercely ashamed of the state he was in, the stench of the alcohol on his clothes, the blood and the filth. She had taken him away from that and had forced him to make something of his life. But she had not been able to undo the rest of the damage. It was too late for that. He had failed too many people. He had known there and then through the shame and the humiliation that he could never allow himself to care again, never allow himself to *love,* because he would lose, he would fail again, and that could never happen.

This time he cut Mairi off with a chop of the hand.

"Take it from me that I have no finer feelings," he said. "I may be a gentleman by birth, but by nature I am a man who drives a hard bargain. Your presence in my bed is the price I will extract for my help. Take it or leave it."

Mairi jumped to her feet. "Somehow I do not believe you discussed that part of your plan with my father-in-law," she said. "He believes you to be honorable." She gestured toward the door. "I should go back in there and tell him exactly what sort of man you really are."

Jack grabbed her wrist. "But you won't, will you?" he said softly. "Because you need my help. You need me quite…desperately. We must preserve your…spotless…

reputation, in public at least so that your late husband's secrets may remain hidden."

Their eyes met. He saw anger and contempt in hers, but also something close to desolation. She was trapped, and she hated it. For a woman like Mairi MacLeod who was so accustomed to taking command, he could see it was the most frustrating thing in the world to be so powerless. She would hate to have to submit, and yet if she did not she stood to lose all she cared for.

"You are quite intolerable," she said.

"Agreed," Jack said. "And yet you will have to tolerate me somehow if you want my help."

Mairi shot him another glance from those smoky blue eyes. This one he felt in the groin.

"Under normal circumstances," she said, "you are the very last man on earth I would agree to be betrothed to, but unfortunately there is no one else."

"Thank you," Jack said.

"If there was any other way—" Mairi said.

"We'll take that as read," Jack said.

She inclined her head. "As soon as it is possible, I will jilt you," she said. "Thoroughly and with considerable satisfaction."

"Not before I have made love to you," Jack said. "Thoroughly and with considerable satisfaction."

Her eyes were huge, shadowed with emotions he could neither read nor understand. He put out a hand and touched one of the auburn curls that had escaped from her bandeau. It was soft and it wound trustingly about his fingers like a silken noose. He cupped her cheek. Her skin was soft too; in a flash he was remembering the tender curves and hollows of her body and he was plunged into a sexual need so acute and primitive he almost dragged her into his arms.

Instead, exerting extreme self-control, he slid his hand to the nape of her neck and drew her forward a little until their lips were only a couple of inches apart.

It was like igniting a fire. When his thigh brushed the material of her gown, she gave a tiny gasp. Her eyes darkened to smoky, slumberous dark blue. Her lips parted.

So she felt it too; he had known she had, known from the moment he had kissed her at Ardglen that the attraction between them was both mutual and raging hot. But this confirmation, the evidence that she was as close to the edge of control as he, was almost enough to push him straight over that edge.

"Surrender to me," he whispered. "Last time you took what you wanted. This time it's my turn."

His mind was full of the images of the previous night they had spent together, her body slick and heated against his, over his, beneath his.

She put a hand against his chest. He could almost imagine that that felt hot too, that her touch branded him.

Then, as though from a vast distance he realized that she was holding him off, not drawing him to her. They were still very close, almost touching.

"You're a blackmailer," she whispered, her lips moving against his. "You seek to take advantage of my weakness. You are no better than Mr. Innes."

Jack smiled. "I think you'll find that I am a lot better than Mr. Innes," he said, "or indeed anyone else." He changed the angle of his head slightly, seeking to deepen the kiss. His tongue touched the corner of her mouth, then slid across her lower lip. She opened to him at once, as though she could not resist. She tasted of strawberries and sunlight and he felt a rush of raw sexual need.

"Well?" he said as he released her.

"I can't—" Mairi said.

"I think you probably can," Jack said. He ran his thumb over her lower lip and felt her quiver in response.

"I don't respond well to blackmail," she said.

"On the contrary," Jack said. "You just did."

She shook her head slightly. He was not sure if she was disappointed in him or in herself. If her poor opinion was for him, that scarcely mattered, but he found that he did not like her being disappointed in herself. Which was odd, as he had no idea why he should care.

"Tell yourself you have no choice," he advised, "if you wish to pretend you are virtuous."

Her eyes were full of disillusion. "There is always a choice, Mr. Rutherford. If I become your mistress, I am not going to deceive myself that it was anyone's choice but my own."

Jack smiled at her formal use of his name. "If you are going to become my mistress," he said, "you should call me Jack. Since we are betrothed it is perfectly acceptable for you to use it publicly—Mairi."

She looked shocked. A woman who had given her body to him without inhibition looked shocked when he addressed her by her given name. That amused him.

"You take liberties," she said stiffly.

"I've barely started," Jack said.

He kissed her again. There was resistance in her, and indecision and a tumult of other emotions that he could sense and not understand, but when she opened her lips to his he forgot everything and lost himself in the driving need he had for her. When he released her, her eyes were blank with shock and she pressed her fingers to her lips.

"I can't believe how I feel," she whispered. She sounded confused, doubtful. She also sounded very young and inexperienced, and it gave Jack an odd pang of doubt. He wondered if he had misjudged her and all her sophistication was nothing but a facade.

"How do you feel?" he asked. He did not expect her to answer. She was too guarded in her emotions to be open with him. Yet now she looked at him with a dawning sense of wonder that, had he not been a complete cynic, might have made him feel like a god.

"I feel hot and dizzy and a little bit drunk," she admitted.

Jack smiled. He could not help himself. So her sainted husband had evidently not been perfect at all. He had clearly been perfectly useless when it came to sex.

"You sound like a debutante after her first kiss," he said, then regretted his words as the soft light vanished completely from her eyes.

"There is nothing of the debutante about me," she said crisply.

"That's true." He caught her hand and pulled her around to face him. "When I asked you about that night in Edinburgh," he said, his voice a little rough, "you said you did not know that it was me. Was that true too?"

Her lashes flickered down. He felt her tremble. "Yes," she whispered.

Jack felt a savage disappointment. He had been so sure she had been lying, but by her own admission she had brazenly set out that night to seduce a man, any man. The vulnerability he had sensed in her just now had been a product of his imagination. He had seen it because he had wanted it to be so.

He was not sure why he felt so disappointed. He had no interest in anything other than possessing her.

"I wanted to forget everything that night," she said. He saw her throat move as she swallowed convulsively. "I was looking for oblivion."

Jack remembered her tears. Without a doubt she must have been missing Archie MacLeod, with whom she had shared a marriage, a relationship far deeper than a mere affair. He tried to find some compassion, but all he was able to feel was a fierce pang of jealousy— jealousy for her loyalty to her husband and an even less admirable fury that she had set out to drown her grief in the arms of any man who served her purpose. Some- one other than he might have taken her; she would have made love with someone else the same way she had done with him, with heat and passion and abandonment.

"Well," he said harshly, "next time you will be in no doubt that it is me." He kissed her again. He still felt angry and he let it show in the way he took her mouth, took it and plundered it until she was gasping.

He loosed her, but only so he could look down into her eyes. "You need to understand," he said harshly. "If you agree to be my mistress, then I want everything. Everything I ask you must give me."

She was trembling, but not from fear. She nodded.

"Say it," Jack said.

"I agree," she whispered, and he felt again that flash of vicious triumph.

He released her. "I'll travel with you," he said coolly.

"As we are betrothed. One of your men can ride my horse."

He saw her bite her lip. Her dislike of him taking control was a tangible thing. He could feel the antagonism coming off her in waves. Still, antagonism so often made the conquest all the sweeter. She had used him. Now it was his turn.

MAIRI HAD NEVER been more aware of a man in her entire life. He sprawled on the seat opposite, totally at ease, totally in command, his broad shoulders resting against the cushions, his long legs stretched out in front of him and casually crossed at the ankle. He was indecently handsome. In confined quarters the effect those spectacular good looks had on her was most uncomfortable. There was a dangerous heat spreading slowly through her body, and her heart bumped hard in her chest. He was not looking at her, but it felt as though he was. It felt as though he was thinking about all the things they were going to do together—all the wicked, wanton, exciting things she craved and yet feared at the same time. She did not understand why she was so attracted to Jack Rutherford and she did not like it, but she was at a loss to know how to prevent it. There was no point in pretending that she had been coerced into this situation. Jack had made an indecent proposal and she agreed, not just for the protection of his name but because ever since that night in Edinburgh her senses had been thirsting for more. She felt as though she had been living in flat black-and-white and Jack had given her not only color but taste and texture too.

Their eyes met briefly and Mairi felt a tug of sensual awareness. She shook her head sharply. All she seemed able to think about was Jack and that moment he would choose to enforce her side of their bargain. Perhaps even here, now, in the carriage… Her eyes flew to his face and she realized that he was looking at her. In fact, he was laughing at her. He had read her thoughts.

"I have more finesse than that, I assure you." His words were a low, amused drawl. "Though sex in a carriage can be a stimulating experience. Have you tried it?"

"No." She turned her face away, very aware that she was blushing. It was odd that when she had picked him up in Edinburgh she had felt so brazen and confident yet now she was quite the reverse. She looked back on that night as something she could not quite explain, something shocking. She had felt so lonely and bereft, so very alone, that she had acted in a way she barely recognized. She did not want to explain that to Jack, though. Such a confession would lead inevitably to questions about her relationship with Archie, and that was not something she ever wanted to discuss, least of all with Jack. The painful secrets that were Archie's legacy weighed down on her. She could not trust Jack with the truth. She trusted no one.

She stared hard at the passing scenery, not really seeing it through the sheen of tears in her eyes. Confusion was not an emotion she was familiar with. From the earliest age she had taken control of her life, of her marriage and then of Archie's estates and her inheritance. Everything had been clear and ordered and she had been the one ordering it.

She felt hot and disturbed, and she did not want Jack to know. She might give him her body as the price of his protection, but she was never going to allow him into her mind.

She turned her thoughts toward Michael Innes and the danger he posed. The thought of him taking her to court filled her with a cold dread. It would be shameful enough to have her own life held up to scrutiny and criticism—demeaning, painful and embarrassing for her family. But that was as nothing compared to the damage Innes could do if he discovered and disclosed the secrets of Archie's past. Lady MacLeod's health was even more fragile than her husband's, and the shame of the disgrace would destroy her. Their daughter, Eleanor, the only child the MacLeods had left, would be tainted by the scandal too, left with no hopes of marriage. Innes would take the money and the land and undo all that Archie had tried to achieve. Archie had relied on her to keep his estates and his people safe. She could not bear to fail him and betray his trust.

She glanced at Jack. His face was set and dark as though his thoughts were far away. He looked hard, uncompromising. She knew from the little her sister Lucy had told her of Robert and Jack's business dealings abroad that he could be ruthless and determined. In truth, she would have known that about him anyway. Beneath the elegance and charm, Jack Rutherford was as hard as nails. She wondered suddenly what had made him so. She knew nothing of his past. She knew very little of him at all other than that he was Robert's cousin and the Dowager Lady Methven's grandson. People spoke of his business interests and his fortune and his estates but never of the man or his background.

She wondered what on earth the Dowager Lady Methven would have to say when she heard about the betrothal, Robert and Lucy too. She did not want to lie to her family, yet she could hardly tell the truth.

She thought about Jack touching her with casual possession, the intimacy of his use of her name. She would be obliged to tolerate his behavior without complaint when he treated her as though she were his betrothed. It felt like a great deal more than she was prepared to give. Then she thought of what else she would have to give him, her body, without reservation or restraint. Her stomach dropped at the thought and a mixture of apprehension and wicked anticipation spiked through her. She pressed her fingers to her hot cheeks.

"We will be stopping at the Kinlochewe Inn soon," Jack said. "I thought we could stay there tonight."

It was the last stop before Methven. Mairi half wanted to press on to their destination, but it was another couple of hours on bad roads and at the end of it there would be too many explanations. Her head ached again, fiercely. She put a hand up to her forehead and rubbed it absentmindedly.

Jack was watching her. "What is the matter?" he said.

"My head hurts," Mairi said shortly, "and I am very tired. I would appreciate some privacy this evening—unless you insist on claiming me as your mistress immediately."

A wicked smile tilted the corner of Jack's lips. "The prospect of making love to a woman with a sick headache does not really appeal to me," he drawled. "Besides, anticipation adds an edge to desire."

Mairi turned her face away again, but she could feel her already hot cheeks heating even more. The carriage clattered through the gateway into the inn yard. Jack helped her down, holding her against him for a moment as her feet touched the ground. His hand was in the small of her back and he held her still while he kissed her. He took his time. Mairi's face was flaming when he let her go. She knew he had made sure that everyone saw. Jack Rutherford had claimed her and everyone would know it.

CHAPTER TEN

JACK COULD NOT sleep. Normally he slept well, but tonight he was restless. He tossed and turned, knotting the sheets in a tourniquet about him, throwing the covers off, pulling them on as the chill of early morning settled on the room. The reason for his discomfort was not far to seek. She was about four feet away through the thin wall.

Prior to that evening he had not been aware that he had a conscience. He had done plenty of things in his life of which most men would be ashamed, and yet he had never felt a hint of regret. He prided himself on his ruthlessness and his ability to take what he wanted, using whatever means were at his disposal. He had thought that this was no different, that he was entirely justified in driving a hard bargain and demanding from Mairi the one thing he wanted. She had used him. Now it was his turn. Yet he felt no triumph. He felt nothing but a sort of emptiness.

This was not how it was meant to be.

Jack stared at the ceiling, at the play of the shadows across the peeling white paint and the cobwebs gently swaying from the beams. He knew Mairi wanted him with a hunger that matched his own. He had felt it in every kiss; she had admitted as much. Yet he also knew that blackmail was not the way to achieve what he wanted. It was not worthy of him. More importantly he wanted Mairi to give herself to him of her own free will.

He was going soft in the head. It was inexplicable.

With a vehement curse he threw back the covers and wandered across to the table, where he poured water from the jug into the bowl and splashed it on his face. He crossed to the window. It stood ajar and he pushed the curtain back to look out over the mountains. A pale mist hung between them as light as gossamer. The sun was rising. It was going to be another beautiful day.

The beat of hooves on the road caught his attention. A lone rider was coming in fast from the west. Early in the morning or late at night, such an arrival usually indicated an urgent message. Jack shrugged himself into his jacket and reached for his boots.

The horseman galloped into the yard below. Looking out, Jack saw Methven livery. He slid out of the bed-chamber door, taking care not to wake the rest of the inn's occupants, but as he made for the stairs someone moved in the shadows. His hand went instinctively to his sword and then he recognized the glimmer of light on her face. It was Mairi. Her hair was down in a cloud of dark auburn. Her feet were bare beneath the lace trim of her nightgown. She wore nothing else but a shawl about her shoulders, and in the flat morning light she looked pale and so vulnerable that Jack's heart gave a strange jolt. With a soft oath he let his blade slide back into its sheath.

"I saw the messenger from Methven," she said. "I'm coming down with you."

"Looking like that?" Jack said. "One glance and he will forget the nature of his message." His gaze slid over her. One curl had slipped beneath the delicately embroidered neckline of her nightgown and was nestling in the valley between her breasts. He could see their rounded shape beneath the fine cotton and the darker outline of her nipples rubbing against the material. His gaze dropped lower to the shadow at the juncture of her thighs. Suddenly all tenderness in him fled, replaced by desire. He felt his body harden into arousal. His eyes met hers, dark and hot, and he saw there the same flare of primitive need. It was like the previous time, only much more fierce.

He took a step toward her, all thoughts of the messenger and his letter forgotten, but in that instant he saw Mairi's body stiffen. She stepped back, twitching the shawl defensively about her shoulders, clutching it tight in her fist. The gesture made Jack's heart jolt again. Instead of wanting to rip the nightgown from her and take her against the wall, he found he wanted to wrap her up tightly and protect her. The switch from predator to protector threw him completely. He cursed under his breath.

"I'll come and tell you the news as soon as I've spoken to him," he said abruptly.

For a moment he thought Mairi was going to insist on accompanying him, but then she gave a nod that was equally abrupt and backed toward her bedchamber door. "Thank you," she said. Then she spoiled it. "See that you do," she added sharply.

Grinning, Jack went downstairs, where the yawning landlord was pulling back the bolts in response to the messenger's knock. Ten minutes later the man was taking breakfast to set him up for the journey back to Methven and Jack was climbing the stair again, letter in hand, and knocking on the door of Mairi's chamber.

"Come in here," he said, gesturing to his own room next door. He did not want her maid interrupting them.

In the time he had been gone, she had taken the hint and now she was completely swathed in a red velvet cloak. Not an inch of bare skin was visible other than her face. Strangely Jack found that there was something mysterious and seductive about her even when she was fully covered. The red velvet rippled sinuously around her slender body and clashed vividly with the red hair that still tumbled about her shoulders. She looked glorious. He found himself transfixed by the shimmer and flow of the velvet and by the knowledge of what lay beneath the rich material.

Hell. His concentration was shot to pieces and all because this woman seemed to be able to command his responses simply by existing. It was a novel experience for him to find himself so much at the mercy of his emotions and he did not like it at all, but there was not much he seemed able to do about it. He allowed her to precede him into the room and shut the door behind her.

She turned, waiting for him to speak, her eyebrows arched in imperious demand. When he did not her expression dissolved into anxiety.

"Is something wrong?" she asked. "Lucy—the children—are they quite well?"

There was so much concern in her voice that Jack cursed himself for worrying her.

"Everyone at Methven is well." He saw her expression relax at his words. She smoothed the cloak; her fingers were shaking.

"Thank God," she said.

"Rob was sending a warning, though," Jack said. "Your cousin, Wilfred Cardross, has escaped from

Edinburgh Jail. Rob wanted us to be aware in case Cardross should spring an attack."

Mairi was frowning. She sat down on the edge of her bed. "You think that Wilfred might attack us on the journey? And so close to Methven?"

"Since he bears a grudge against both our families," Jack said dryly, "I would not be at all surprised." He and Robert had sprung the trap that had captured Wilfred Cardross three years before. Mairi's brother, Lachlan, was now master of the Cardross estates through his marriage to Dulcibella. There were more than enough reasons, Jack thought, for Cardross to bear a fierce resentment.

"Dismiss your men and ride with me this morning," he said. "Cardross will be expecting you to be traveling in the coach. It is a sitting target. You'll be safer with me."

He saw temptation gleam in her eyes, saw a quicksilver flash of excitement before it faded and died. Earlier in the journey he had found himself wondering whether all spontaneity had been ironed out of Mairi's life by her formidable control. Now he could see that beneath those layers of restraint there was still a spark of wildness. He wanted to strike that spark to a blaze.

"Do it," he said. His voice was rough. "You know you want to."

Her head was bent and she would not meet his eyes, but he could feel the indecision in her like a thread pulled taut. For a moment he thought she was going to accept and his heart surged, but then she looked away and shook her head.

"That would be foolish," she said, "and dangerous. I'll be safer in the coach."

Jack came toward her. "What are you afraid of?" he asked softly. "I've told you I will protect you."

He heard her breath catch, a tiny sound. He was so close to her now that he could see the way that her breasts rose and fell with the quick shaky breaths she took. Once again she would not meet his eyes.

"Look at me," Jack said.

She looked up then. Her blue eyes were dark and wide, full of shadows.

"What are you afraid of?" he repeated.

"I'm afraid of being alone with you," she whispered. "I'm afraid of how you make me feel."

Suddenly they were not speaking of the ride to Methven or the danger posed by Wilfred Cardross and he had never wanted a woman so desperately in his entire life.

His fingers captured her chin and turned her face up to his. Despite the raging need he had for her, he waited, gave her time to move away. Instead she pressed a little closer to him, unconsciously, instinctively. The red velvet cloak rubbed sensually against his body.

Raw lust exploded in him and he kissed her. He had wanted to be gentle at first, but hunger overrode tenderness and instead he kissed her hard and felt her instant response. It was a response that threatened to push them both over the brink too soon, too quickly. Jack felt as though he were sliding into an abyss. There was an edge of desperation in him that he simply did not recognize.

Fighting for breath, he drew back a little.

"May I—" His voice was ragged. He wanted her— now—but just as earlier, what mattered more to him was that she agreed, with no coercion, no doubt and no reluctance. Only yesterday he had thought he could override her feelings. Now he realized that he had been a blatant fool.

This time her response was not immediate. Silence fell for one seçond, two. Jack was just starting to wish he had not asked and risked rejection when she spoke.

"Yes," she said. "Please."

It was the *please* that undid him.

JACK PICKED HER up and dropped her in the center of the bed. Mairi was quite unprepared for the suddenness of it. The mattress springs protested as she landed and the eiderdown almost engulfed her. She lay on her back, arms and legs spread like a starfish, the red velvet cloak flying wide, her nightgown riding up about her thighs.

She saw the laughter in Jack's eyes vanish and her throat dried as his gaze narrowed, sliding over her from the hair that tumbled about her shoulders, over the low, lacy embroidered neckline of the nightgown and down to where her nipples pressed against the silk, and then lower still. Her heart had already been thumping so hard she had been afraid that she would faint. Now heat exploded through her body and with it a sort of shyness that she lay so open to his gaze. She started to move her arms down, but Jack was too quick for her, pinning her wrists above her head and holding them there in one hand while his knee came down between her legs, forcing them apart.

For a long moment she stared up into his face. He was so close now that she could see the stubble on his lean cheek and the thick gold of his lashes. She could see too the way his eyes had darkened with concentrated desire. It made her stomach tumble over and over.

It was too late for regrets and she was not sure she

felt them anyway. Instead of discipline and restraint she felt wanton longing as heady as wine. She wanted another taste of wicked delight in a barren existence.

Jack leaned closer. His lips touched hers gently this time with none of the fierce need that had swept them up earlier. He took his time with sweet teasing kisses that promised so much yet always seemed to hold a little back. Before long she was panting and eager. She wanted to reach for him, but still he held her in that inexorable grip, her wrists above her head, as he drove her step by slow step toward the most delicious bliss.

A part of her that Mairi had thought she had buried sprang to life. She could neither understand nor control the feelings she had for Jack Rutherford. They stormed through her and swept aside everything but desire.

She had lost her shyness now. It had been destroyed by the need to satisfy the excruciating ache that frustrated her. She no longer felt mortified that she was lying prone beneath Jack with little but a flimsy layer of near-transparent silk between them. She wished the silk to perdition, wished that Jack would release her hands so that she could touch him, wished that he would move his leg just an inch upward to the junction of her thighs so that she could press shamelessly against him and relieve that hot carnal pulse that beat inside her. And he must have known, damn him, because he deliberately moved back a little when she arched upward and he kept kissing her, deeper now so that she was hot and restless and squirming on the bed. Her skin felt too heated and too sensitive. She was acutely responsive to the touch of his mouth on hers, wanting to feel him everywhere.

He drew back a little. The world spun. The morning

light seemed too bright against Mairi's closed lids, her body aching, trembling.

"Open your eyes," Jack said. His voice was harsh though the kiss that punctuated the words was tender. "I want you to know it's me this time."

Mairi opened her eyes. The look in his eyes was harsh, as well; there was anger there and she knew in an instant that he had not forgiven her for the previous time when she had sought oblivion with any man, any lover. He still blamed her for that, as though she should belong to him alone. Yet there was gentleness in him too. He softened his grip on her wrists at last and then swept his hands down over her shoulders in a soft caress, pushing the silk nightgown aside, leaning down to kiss the hollow of her collarbone, the hot skin of her neck, the dip at the base of her throat. Mairi wriggled, feeling the sensual slip of the silk against her breasts almost, but not quite, as tantalizing as a lover's touch.

"Please…" She arched again.

Jack's hands stilled on her shoulders, warm and sure. Then he took hold of the front of the nightgown and tore it straight down to her navel, so fast and so violent that she cried out. Cold morning air flowed over her skin, hardening her nipples to tighter buds. Jack pushed the scraps of silk aside and took one tip in his mouth, tugging, licking and sucking on her. His stubble rubbed against her. Mairi's mind splintered.

"Open your eyes." His words were a whisper across her skin, enforced with a soft bite to the underside of her breast that was just short of pain. Her body jolted. The sting came again, to her nipple this time. Her whole body twitched. Her lashes flickered.

"I said open your eyes."

Nip. Harder. She almost came that time, but she did as she was told and opened her eyes. Her gaze was hazy with desire. She saw Jack's cheek resting against her breast, his tawny hair brushing her skin, dark golden against her paleness. He held her gaze; he raised a hand and cupped her breast, holding it in his palm, and she knew he was claiming her body as his. His fingers toyed with her nipples as though she were his plaything, his possession. Pleasure tightened within her and shimmered. The tension inside her ratcheted tighter like a chain pulled unbearably taut.

"Don't close your eyes." He licked her nipple, tasting her like ice cream this time, a deliberate caress. She gasped, arched. He smiled and licked her again.

He took hold of the ragged shreds of the silk and tore it the rest of the way down, then pressed his lips to the curve of her belly and the hollow above her mound. His fingers were at her core and then they were inside her. Mairi could not think, could not hold back. One glorious stroke of his thumb over her nub, and a second, and she shattered into a thousand tiny pieces, so sweet and violent that she would have screamed had Jack not covered her mouth with his again.

She felt him shift above her, fumbling to release his shaft. He was shaking. She noticed it even through the tremors that still convulsed her body, even through the cascade of pleasure.

"Look at me." Again the command came. He sounded less in control, though, closer to the edge. She felt a surge of power that made her smile. She kept her eyes closed.

His hands swept the length of her, from her shoulders, down over her breasts, her belly, claiming her again with his touch. The soft floating feeling of satiation within her faded. Sharp need snapped back. She could feel the tip of his shaft at her core and tried not to rise to meet him, tried not to beg for more. It was impossible. Instead she reached for him, spreading her legs wider to accommodate him between them, digging her fingers into his buttocks as she pulled him inside her. She heard his sharp catch of breath as her body clasped his.

"So hot. So tight." His breath stirred the tendrils of hair that clung damply to her neck. His lips brushed her neck. "I've dreamed of this, dreamed of you."

She thought he would take her hard and fast, showing that this time she was his to use. She would not have cared. Her excitement was already burning again, her body greedy for more. But he did not plunge into her. Instead he moved in long, slow strokes that took her earlier pleasure and stirred it up again, drawing it out, strengthening it by unhurried degrees until her body felt unbearably tight and wanting all over again. She opened her eyes and watched him; watched him as he made love to her, watched him as he bent his head again to tease her breasts, watched him as he slid his hands possessively over her hips, raising her to meet those long, deep thrusts. She was still watching when her body finally tipped over again into slow and blissful release and she tilted her head back and arched upward, taking Jack with her.

Gradually she became aware of her surroundings again, of the strengthening light streaming into the room and the birdsong beyond the window and the stir of the inn awakening around them. Her heart was still racing. She felt stunned by the discovery of a pleasure she had simply not known. It had felt different from the previous time. She struggled to try to understand why and realized that before she had craved only oblivion.

She felt a sliding sensation of fear. This time she had wanted Jack. She had thought of nothing but him. Her need for him had been overwhelming, and the difference it had made to her response had been overwhelming too.

Emotions swamped her, feelings she did not recognize.

"Jack," she said. It was the first time that she had used his name, and even as she did so she realized that something of how she felt must have colored her voice because she felt him shift, drawing away from her. Cold air lapped about her and she realized that she was naked, lying tumbled on the bed, legs still spread apart, abandoned and satiated, while Jack still had all his clothes on.

"You need to return to your own chamber before your maid comes looking for you." Jack's voice was cool, emotionless. "We don't want to cause further scandal." He sat up and fastened his breeches. He did not look at her.

Mairi flinched. Her entire body flushed with embarrassment.

She felt like a whore. Except that a whore would expect nothing more than a fat purse of gold, whereas she had expected at the very least a modicum of respect. In a flash she saw her mistake. She had allowed herself to be seduced. She had forgotten that Jack had blackmailed her into becoming his mistress, that their relationship did nothing but demean her, that he had no respect for her at all.

In that moment she hated herself; she hated what she had done and how she had felt and she wanted to hate Jack as well, but she could not and that made her all the more upset. Jack had never made any secret of the fact that he had no use for intimacy. He wanted no emotional commitment to anyone. She had known and understood that, but in the heat of desire she had forgotten it. Jack had not lied to her or made false promises. He had made love to her because he desired her, and now that his lust was satisfied he wanted her gone.

For a moment the humiliation held her quite still, and then she jumped from the bed, wincing at the cold of the bare boards against her feet, and grabbed her cloak as quickly as she could, wrapping it about her with hands that shook. Once it was tied and she felt vaguely decent again, she could look him in the eye. He, damn him, had already adjusted his clothes and was sitting waiting with ill-concealed impatience for her to be gone.

"Our betrothal is over," she said.

"I beg your pardon?" Jack raised one brow. She tried not to appreciate how handsome he looked, casually disheveled, so masculine. That was absolutely nothing to the purpose.

Mairi swallowed hard, gripping the cloak tightly, trying to find a dignity that was all too difficult when she was stark naked and could still feel the echo of Jack's touch through her body.

"Our betrothal is over," she repeated sharply. "It was a mistake. So was sleeping with you. I don't require your help. I don't want anything else from you and I will not be your mistress."

She broke off. Jack had come to his feet and he was looking dangerously angry. He took a step toward her and took hold of her by the shoulders. Despite the anger in his eyes, his grip was gentle and warm, and it made the heat seep once again through her perfidious body. Mairi shivered and clutched the cloak even tighter to her.

"There is a limit to how many times you can make love with me," Jack said softly, "and pretend that you don't want to." The gentle stroke of his hands over the velvet rubbed against her skin and made Mairi shiver all the more. He slipped one hand inside the cloak and found her breast, cupped it, rubbing his thumb over the nipple, which was already hard from the abrasion of the velvet. He leaned closer so that his lips were an inch from hers.

"You do want me, don't you, sweetheart?" he said, and it was not a question. He already knew the answer.

Mairi fought the hot, sweet heaviness that filled her blood. "That is not in dispute." She gasped as his stroking fingers tweaked and pulled on her nipple, drawing more of a response from her, making her knees weaken. In another second she would be back on the bed, flat on her back with him inside her again. She raised her chin, forced her mind to focus.

"I won't be treated like a whore. I won't be used and dismissed."

She felt Jack stiffen. His hand fell.

"So now you know how I felt when I woke that morning after you left me," he said. There was the glitter of anger in his eyes.

"Fine," Mairi snapped. "Now that you have had your revenge, had me, perhaps you could forget it." She pulled the cloak together again, ignoring the ache of lust in her belly, ignoring the deeper sting of hurt in her mind—the hurt that said it should not have been like this.

"I do not want your protection," she said, "and I certainly do not want your company and when we reach Methven you will oblige me by keeping out of my way as much as possible."

She fumbled with the door handle. She wanted nothing more than the privacy of her room, hot water and clean clothes. She could wash and refresh herself but she had a suspicion that it would not be so easy to dismiss the memory of Jack's touch on her body. He was right. She still wanted him, wanted the pleasure he could give her, but there was no way she would give herself to him without respect.

She closed the door softly behind her.

He said not one word to call her back.

DAMN AND DAMN and damn. Jack could not remember the last time he had been in such a filthy mood. He stood by the window watching as Mairi's servants loaded the traveling carriage. She stood waiting, impatience vivid in every tense line of her body. Frazer had a face like thunder. The grooms were scurrying around as though their shirttails were on fire. Evidently she had vented her fury with him on her staff, which was very out of character. But then, she had been very upset.

Jack knew he only had himself to blame. He had kicked Lady Mairi MacLeod out of his bed. He was a fool, and an ill-mannered one at that. Mairi was not a woman to accept that treatment from anyone. His only excuse—and it was no excuse at all—was that he had been so shaken and disturbed by what had happened between them that he had acted on instinct to distance himself from her.

He swallowed a curse. He had had no intention of treating Mairi like a whore out of revenge. Once he had started to make love to her, the thought had not even crossed his mind. He had forgotten that she had used him in the past. He had forgotten that he had wanted to exert his own mastery, make his own demands. He had been pushed beyond anything in his experience, dazed and bewildered by his response to her and the terrifying way that he had been at the mercy of his own emotions. He had meant to withdraw at the moment of climax too, but he had been so overwhelmed that he had not done so, which had been beyond irresponsible.

Scowling, he ran a hand through his hair. Good sex was nothing new to him. He had more than a passing acquaintance with great sex. But this had been different. This had been exceptional. He had felt a sense of connection with Mairi, a need that went beyond and beneath the physical. It had felt soul-deep. And since he had thought he did not have a soul or indeed a better nature of any sort, that was more than a little disturbing.

He pushed himself away from the windowsill and turned his back on the departing carriage. He was making far too much of it. He should forget it if only because he was never going to have the opportunity to make love to Lady Mairi MacLeod again and he was damned if he was going to torture himself by dwelling on everything he could not have. He would have to forget the satin-smoothness of her skin and the tight, hot clasp of her body about his. He would have to forget the sounds she had made as he had driven her toward her climax and the deep slumberous blue of her eyes as she had held his gaze and slipped over the edge into pleasure.

He was rock-hard again. If this was forgetting, he had better not try to remember. Mairi had severed all connection to him. He was fortunate she had not severed anything else in the process given her skill with a dirk. And he should be glad, because it meant no tedious pretence of being her fiancé and no tiresome obligation to take Lord MacLeod's commission to protect her. It meant no ties, no responsibilities and no commitment, which was exactly what he had always wanted.

He expected to feel relieved. He waited to feel relieved.

Nothing happened.

CHAPTER ELEVEN

THE ROAD TO Torridon was notoriously bad, a long, steep and stony track that skirted the great gray flank of Beinn Eighe—a forbidding mountain that looked like a huge fortress. There were few trees to break the barrenness of the bare rock. Waterfalls tumbled over the scree and splashed down into little lochans that reflected the blue of the sky. It was a majestic landscape but a lonely one, and Mairi far preferred the softer green rolling hills of the south.

With a sigh she turned away from the view out of the window. She wanted to sleep but she could not. Her mind was too active. Every time she closed her eyes she saw images of Jack, his body, strong and golden brown, poised over hers, their limbs entangled. She felt the brush of his skin against hers, heard his breathing, felt his warmth. It was as though she could feel the echo of his touch on her body, beneath the skin. She felt it in the beat of her heart and could not escape it.

She could not dismiss this time as a mistake. Jack had given her a choice right from the start. When he had proposed his devil's bargain, she had agreed despite all her reservations because she had wanted to taste passion again. She had been taken, seduced. And then she had been turned out, callously, with calculated coldness.

There were many reasons why she should not have

an affair with Jack Rutherford, of which that was the best one. She valued herself too highly to give herself to a man who could not wait for the sheets to cool before he evicted her from his bed.

Besides, it was too dangerous. She was fortunate that her courses were very regular and that it was a safe time for her, or so she understood it. She had not even thought of that when she had been in Jack's bed, and that was downright foolish.

She shivered, though there was a hot brick at her feet and a warm rug over her lap. The cold was inside her, not without. She had longed for a child for many barren years, and seeing Lucy's growing family was so hard for her. She wanted a baby but not like this.

One thought nagged at her mind and it was a persistent one. She had no idea now how she might counteract Michael Innes's threats. In rejecting Jack's help she had made herself vulnerable again, but she told herself that she would manage to find a way. She always managed alone. The price of Jack's protection had been her self-respect, and that was a price that was too high.

She must have dozed off because the next thing she noticed was the carriage slowing, jolting her awake as it rattled over a particularly deep pothole in the road. It jolted again, violently, throwing her from her seat. There was the sound of a shot, then another closer at hand. Mairi made a grab for the carriage pistol, reaching for the pouch that held it, but the coach slewed, throwing her off balance again. There was shouting and more shots, and the coach creaked to an abrupt halt, throwing her to the floor in a tumbled heap.

With a sick lurch of the heart Mairi realized that she had been so wrapped up in what had happened with Jack that she had forgotten entirely to warn Frazer and his sons about the potential danger from Wilfred Cardross. She had not really believed that Wilfred would attack them. He had no real quarrel with her and it seemed a foolhardy thing to do so close to Methven.

The door was wrenched open and a figure blotted out the light. It was Cardross, but not as Mairi had ever seen him before. Gone was the elegant beau of the Edinburgh ballrooms. His hair was unkempt and his jacket dirty and ragged. There was a pistol in his hand and a rather unpleasant sneer on his face. Behind him Mairi could see a melee in progress as fierce fighting erupted between her servants and the scruffy bunch of men Wilfred seemed to have brought with him.

"Surprised to see me, coz?" Wilfred drawled, motioning with the pistol that she should stay sprawled on her hands and knees on the floor. She knew he meant to humiliate her and it just made her fury burn all the stronger. The sick smile on his face churned her stomach. At the first chance she got she was going to kill him.

"Yes," Mairi said. "Shouldn't you be in jail?"

Wilfred grinned. It was neither a pretty nor a reassuring sight. "You can spring any trap with the right amount of bait," he said.

"A metaphor involving vermin," Mairi said coldly. "How appropriate. What do you want, Wilfred?"

"You," Wilfred said. "I have a friend who has an interest."

"Most people call on me rather than kidnap me," Mairi said. "I don't like your friend's methods. He doesn't stand a chance."

She tried to scramble up from the floor, making another grab for the pistol in its pocket to the side of the door, but Wilfred was too quick for her. He brought his fist crashing down, catching her a glancing blow on her temple and sending her toppling back into the seat. Her head spun in sickening waves and she lay there for a second, winded and nauseated.

"Let's see what my friend will be getting, eh?" she heard Wilfred say. He put out a hand and casually tore open her jacket, pulling down the neck of her gown, trying to expose her breasts.

"You're disgusting," Mairi snapped. She scrambled to cover herself but froze as the pistol touched her cheek in a murderous caress.

"Oh no, coz," Wilfred said. "Let's see the goods. I hear you've been a whore spreading yourself around, so you shouldn't mind, should you?"

A jerk of the pistol directed her to pull the jacket farther apart, but Mairi turned her head sharply away and refused to move. After a second Wilfred laughed and reached forward again to do it himself, only to be brought up sharp by a furious bellow from outside the carriage.

"Cardross!"

It was Jack, sword in hand. For a moment his eyes met Mairi's. They were dark with concentrated ferocity. Wilfred whipped around, raising the pistol, and Mairi took her chance, kicking out at his shins and making him swear long and virulently. He made another grab for her and she realized he intended to use her as a hostage. She bit his hand hard and he gave a howl of pain and the gun went spinning away.

Jack caught Wilfred by the scruff of the neck and pulled him back; he went down with another oath. Mairi dragged her gown and jacket together and crawled to the door.

There was mayhem outside the carriage. Wilfred's ragged outlaws were fighting like men possessed, but against the strength and training of Mairi's men they were hopelessly outmaneuvered. Three of them were engaging with Jack in an attempt to give Wilfred the chance to escape and grab her again, but their efforts were hopeless because Jack was simply too good for them. He had discarded his jacket, and the sweat-damp shirt clung to his shoulders and back. He was fast and he fought with formidable concentration, a natural swordsman. Mairi had never seen anyone with so much innate skill. He sent one man's sword sailing into the heather and dealt another a slice to the forearm that had him howling in pain. As he parried, swayed, crouched and sprang, Mairi found that she was feeling a little faint and not just from Wilfred's blow to her head.

Jack dispatched another man and turned on Wilfred now. Her cousin took one look and scrabbled up onto the back of a shabby pony. Abandoned, his men let out a collective roar of fury and fell back, running for the sparse tree cover on the upper slopes.

Mairi hauled herself to her feet, grabbing the pistol that Wilfred had dropped. He was already fifty yards away and hauling himself into the saddle, but she was sure she could bring him down from that distance. She spun around, and almost immediately was knocked to the floor again, all the breath squashed from her body as Jack landed on top of her. A split second later a shot whistled past her ear so close she felt the air ripple.

"Stay down!"

Mairi had little option. Jack's body held her pinned

to the floor of the carriage while beyond the door there was the sound of more shouts, muffled blows and then silence.

She was not sure how long they lay there with his body covering hers. It was no more than seconds, in all probability; seconds in which she was aware of nothing but the pounding of her heart, the sound of his breathing in her ear and the press of Jack's body on hers. She opened her eyes. His elegant shirt had a rip a foot long down the sleeve that had clearly been made by a sword. She could smell the sweat of exertion on him, an earthy smell that tugged at her senses. The strong brown column of his throat was only inches from her lips. He bent his head and his hair brushed her cheek. She could feel the elemental burn of the fight still coursing through his blood. It was in the touch of his hands on her and the strength of his arms, bands of steel holding her close.

He had rescued her. Suddenly she felt shaky, close to tears and far too vulnerable and she had no intention of allowing all that to show.

"You spoiled my line of sight," she said crossly, shoving ineffectually at his chest. "I could have brought Wilfred down."

"And been shot in the process," Jack said. He rolled off her. "I saved your life," he added. "A little gratitude would not go amiss."

"Thank you," Mairi said, "but I told you I didn't want your protection."

Jack looked deeply annoyed. "Well, you've bloody well got it," he said through gritted teeth, "so get used to it."

He extended a hand to help her up on to the seat. For some reason his solicitude irritated her, as though she were some maiden aunt who could not care for herself. His gaze went to her ripped jacket and she saw his scowl deepen.

"I saw what he did to you, the bastard." He bit the words out; they were a contrast to the gentleness of his hands as he drew the ragged panels of her jacket together and fastened the buttons with great care.

"It's all right—" Mairi started to say, only to be silenced by his glare.

"No," he said. His voice was thick, charged with anger. "It is *not*." Then: "I'll kill him for this."

His hand came up, turning her face to the light, again with such tenderness she could have cried. His fingers stirred her hair, a light touch, but still it hurt. They came away with blood on them and for the first time Mairi felt the hot stickiness of it and the sting of the cut. When Jack spoke his voice had changed again. It was gentle but there was something in it that made her terrified.

"Cardross did this to you too?"

The look on his face frightened her now. Her heart bumped her ribs. Suddenly there was such fury in his eyes, such tension in his touch, light as it was as he pressed a folded handkerchief to the graze.

"He was trying to abduct me," Mairi said, shaken by the anger she saw in him. "He didn't like it when I objected." She was shivering, her teeth chattering together. She heard Jack curse. He grabbed her cloak and slipped it about her shoulders. Mairi grasped the folds to her, realizing that she wanted to tell him that it was the comfort of his arms she needed to steady her. She craved his warmth and the scent of his skin. She shivered again. Wilfred's attack had made her too vulnerable. She did not want to need Jack Rutherford. She was still livid with him for the way he had treated her earlier. Just because he had saved her life did not mean she had forgotten it—though it felt odd simultaneously to want to slap him and kiss him.

Jack was scanning the carriage. "Do you carry brandy in here as well as a pistol?"

"Of course," Mairi said. "It is in the cupboard beneath the seat if you require it."

"It's for you," Jack said, "not for me."

"I hate brandy," Mairi said. She knew she sounded spoiled and petulant and hated herself for it.

Jack gave her a look that told her quite plainly to do as she was told and put the brandy flask in her hand. She was surprised to find she was trembling. After a moment he said:

"Drink it or I'll tip it down your throat myself."

"Your reputation for charm is overrated," Mairi said, but she raised the flask to her lips and took a long swallow. The brandy burned her throat, almost choking her and reminding her why she disliked it, but almost immediately it spun a warm lassitude through her blood and she felt calmer and more steady.

Frazer stuck his head around the door. "Madam?"

"She's fine," Jack said tersely. "Shaken but largely unhurt."

Mairi saw Frazer's gaze go to the bloodstained handkerchief in her hand. His lips tightened. "Damn his soul...."

"I could have shot him," Mairi said, "had Mr. Rutherford not chosen that moment to save my life."

Frazer laughed. "You're a bonny fighter, sir," he said to Jack. "We're glad to have you on our side. The boys would like some training when you can spare a moment."

"The boys did a good enough job on their own," Jack said, grinning, "but I'd be glad to."

"Are any of them hurt?" Mairi said.

"Against that rabble?" Frazer sounded as though he would take it as a personal insult if a single one of his sons had come to harm. "No, ma'am, barely a scratch."

"And Jessie?" Mairi said. Her maid had been traveling in the second carriage with the portmanteaux. Mairi felt guilty now for banishing her. She had not wanted Jessie's chatter that morning.

"Jessie kicked one of them in the balls," Frazer said with evident satisfaction. "You could hear his howling in the next glen." He nodded to Jack. "If you'll excuse me, sir, ma'am. I'll get us sorted out to head to Methven."

"Send a couple of the boys ahead to tell my cousin what's happened," Jack said. "He'll send men out to escort the carriages."

Mairi looked from one to the other. "I give the orders here," she said. "One blow to the head does not render me incapable of decision-making."

Jack raised an eyebrow; Frazer smothered a grin. "Yes, ma'am," he said.

"Do as Mr. Rutherford suggests," Mairi said.

"Yes, ma'am." Frazer saluted and stood down.

Jack gave her a smile. "Thank you for that," he said.

"You're welcome," Mairi said. "It would be foolish to gainsay you. Frazer and his sons already think you walk on water."

"You don't do so badly yourself," Jack said. He sat back on the seat, surveying her lazily. The turbulent anger she had seen in him earlier appeared to have gone, and yet Mairi was not so sure. She would not want to be in Wilfred Cardross's boots when Jack caught up with him.

Jack looked at her, his eyes narrowing thoughtfully. "Would you really have killed him?" he asked. "Your own cousin?"

"Without a single qualm," Mairi said. "And anyway, he's not my cousin. We're only distant kin and it's a courtesy title. Wilfred doesn't deserve the courtesy," she added. "The king should have hanged him when he had the chance. I would have been happy to oblige. He's the scum of the earth."

"Robert says your sister is as fierce as you are," Jack said. "I must admit you'd never know it to look at the two of you."

"We're descended from Malcolm MacMorlan, the Red Fox of Forres," Mairi said. "What do you expect? Smelling salts and swooning? We leave that sort of thing to Dulcibella."

Jack laughed. "You do know that your clan and mine were traditionally old enemies? We shouldn't be fighting on the same side."

A ripple of emotion ran though Mairi. She repressed a shiver of a different sort. There was a warmth and intimacy building again between them. She could feel her awareness of him spark into life, and she did not want that. She was determined to fight it. She was not going to make all the same mistakes again.

His gaze was still on her, and heat flickered in the depths of his eyes. It seared her.

"That would explain the antagonism between us," she said lightly.

Jack's eyes darkened. He leaned forward. "Is that what you feel for me, Mairi MacLeod?" he said. He brushed his lips to hers.

"Among other things," Mairi said. She held herself stiffly, refusing to respond to the seduction of his kiss, willing herself to resist. Even so her heart fluttered and it felt as though honey were flowing through her veins.

"Don't break the betrothal yet, Mairi," Jack said softly. "I cannot protect you if you are not mine." He touched her cheek gently, then jumped down from the carriage and strode away.

"Arrogant bastard," Mairi whispered, but she realized that her fingers were pressed to her mouth as though she could still feel the touch of his lips on hers.

IT WAS THREE hours before they arrived at Methven. The journey was entirely without incident, but Mairi was never more relieved than when she saw the solid gray of the walls piercing the sky.

Jessie had traveled in the coach with her this time. "Mercy me," the maid kept saying. "That Earl of Cardross is a very bad man, madam. First he tried to abduct your sister and now he wants to kidnap you! He does not seem very choosy which sister he takes."

"Thank you, Jessie," Mairi said. "I don't believe Wilfred wanted me for himself. He said something about a friend who had an interest."

"Oh, aye," Jessie said. "He wouldnae be the first man to have an interest in you, madam, but Mr. Rutherford will see him straight now that you're betrothed." She looked at Mairi out of the corner of her eye. "He's a good man to have on your side in a mill. And you've been on your own too long, madam, after Mr. Archie went, and before for that matter. Now, Mr. Rutherford isn't like Mr. Archie."

"He certainly isn't," Mairi said. There were no similarities that she could see between Jack and Archie. If anyone had attacked Archie's carriage he would probably have handed over the strongbox and his wife besides.

Jessie smiled. "Mr. Rutherford's a wee bit dictatorial, maybe…"

"More than a little," Mairi said with feeling.

"But you like it," the maid said slyly.

"My head aches too much to argue," Mairi said. It was a half-truth. She was surprised to find that it was actually a refreshing change to allow someone else to take charge sometimes. Not that she would ever admit that to Jack. She glanced out of the window at the Methven men riding beside the coach. As soon as he had received Jack's message, Robert had sent armed clansmen to escort them safely, with the result that their arrival resembled something like a medieval progress. She was impressed by Jack's show of authority, but she was even more impressed by the way he had consulted Frazer on all his decisions. She had even heard him address Frazer's sons by name; clearly he had taken the trouble to get to know them all. She was reminded of the camaraderie she had seen between him and the men at the Inverbeg Inn. He had a gift of relating easily to people and yet at the same time he was a very private man. In some ways his openness was as much pretense as hers. Neither of them gave away what really lay beneath.

They drove through the gateways with their towering pillars surmounted by griffins and drew up on the graveled sweep in front of the castle. Jack opened the carriage door and before Mairi could protest he had lifted her down and was carrying her to the main door, where she could see Robert, Lucy and the Dowager Marchioness of Methven waiting to greet them.

Mairi was mortified. Jack taking charge was one thing; carrying her as though she were an infant was quite another.

"Put me down," she hissed. "I am perfectly capable of walking." She wriggled. Jack responded by tightening his grip on her. She could tell he was enjoying himself.

"Just for once," he said softly, bending his head so that only she could hear, "stop fighting me and allow yourself to be looked after."

His hazel eyes blazed down into hers. Mairi felt her insides tumble. There was possession in his grip and in his eyes, deep and primitive. She remembered the way he had kissed her in front of everyone at the inn. He was making no bones about the fact that she was his now.

She wondered suddenly if Lord MacLeod had told anyone about the betrothal. She hoped he had not yet had time and particularly that word had not yet reached Methven. She wanted to do this in her own way, although she had barely had time to think how that might be.

"Mairi!" As they came up the steps, Lucy rushed forward. "If you could carry her up to the Blue Chamber—" she started to say to Jack.

"I am perfectly well," Mairi said crisply. She had had enough now. "Mr. Rutherford, please let me stand on my own two feet."

She felt flushed, ruffled and utterly at a disadvantage. She could see that Robert Methven could barely contain his amusement as he looked from her face to that of his cousin.

"As my lady orders," Jack drawled, and for a moment Mairi had the horrid feeling that he was simply going to drop her where they stood, but then he placed her on her feet as gently as if she were made of spun glass, steadying her with a hand beneath her elbow.

"Very pretty, Jack." The Dowager Marchioness of Methven had come forward to greet them now. She was a small, upright figure who crackled with energy. Mairi had met her only a couple of times previously in Edinburgh and was frankly terrified of her sharp gaze and equally sharp tongue. Lucy had told her that the dowager was as soft as butter beneath her fierce exterior; Mairi was certain she would never see beneath that exterior, least of all win the dowager's approval, particularly when she jilted her grandson.

She dropped a respectful curtsey and was surprised when the old lady put out both hands to grasp hers and drew her down to kiss her cheek.

"I am so pleased to meet you again, my dear," the dowager said, smiling warmly. "I was very happy when I heard that you are to be my grandson's future bride."

Mairi's heart plummeted. Lord MacLeod had been very quick off the mark with the good news. And there was such bright pleasure in the dowager's eyes. It made Mairi feel inadequate and a total fraud.

"Thank you, ma'am," she said. "I had not realized that word would have reached you so swiftly."

"Oh, Jack sent word last night from Kinlochewe," Lady Methven said serenely. "I expect he was so pleased to share the exciting news that he simply could not wait."

"Absolutely," Jack said smoothly. "I saw no need to wait."

"Of course you did not," Mairi said. He must have seen the anger in her eyes because he arched one dark brow at her. She resisted the urge to drill her heel into his foot. It would achieve nothing other than bruising her. But it certainly took some audacity, she thought, for Jack to send word to his family of a respectable betrothal at the same time as he was seducing her into his bed.

"You have quite upset my plans of course, Jack," Lady Methven said, her shrewd blue eyes searching Jack's face. "I had invited a number of ladies to Methven in the hope that one of them might take your fancy as a future bride, but as they are now quite *de trop* they made their apologies and left this morning."

"I can hear the sound of hearts breaking all over Scotland," Mairi murmured. Now she understood Jack's haste in sending word of their engagement. He had spiked his grandmother's plans for him very neatly.

"I am very sorry, Grandmama," Jack said, smiling so smugly that Mairi again had to resist the urge to slap him.

"I doubt that very much, Jack," Lady Methven said dryly. "Nor—" her glance warmed as it rested on Mairi again "—do you have anything to regret. You have a fiancée who is as accomplished, brave and beautiful as any you could find. Be sure to live up to that."

Mairi blushed. She felt humbled. She also felt guilty. It was impossible not to in the face of Lady Methven's sincere pleasure at the betrothal. The very genuineness of Her Ladyship's happiness made the pretense feel cheap and unworthy, and with each minute that passed it felt more and more difficult.

Robert stepped forward to shake Jack's hand. His eyes were alight with amusement as he looked from Mairi's embarrassed face to Jack's bland one. "I have to hand it to you, Jack," he said. "I've known you a long time and yet you still have the power to surprise me." He too kissed Mairi's cheek. "Congratulations, Lady Mairi," he said. "I am very happy for you both."

"As am I," Lucy said. "Of course." She gave her sister a meaningful stare. "But you and Jack! I can scarce believe it! I am most curious as to how your change of heart came about when you disliked him so intensely. Why, I remember you saying at our wedding that Jack was an arrogant pig and you loathed him—" She fell silent as Robert cleared his throat very loudly.

Mairi blushed. Since Jack had been well aware of her dislike for him and had felt exactly the same way about her, she was at a loss as to why Lucy's tactless remarks should embarrass her, but they did.

"I became aware of all Mr. Rutherford's fine qualities," she said, and saw brilliant amusement flare in Jack's eyes.

"I daresay," Lucy said on a note of wonder. "But— you and Jack together?"

"Jack and I," Mairi confirmed, privately resolving that if Lucy said that one more time she would throttle her sister.

A scream rent the air so sharply that they all jumped. It seemed to echo off the surrounding mountains and fade away down the glen.

"Good God," Mairi said. "Has Wilfred launched another assault?"

"I'm afraid that is Dulcibella," Lucy said, as more screams followed. "She has been having the hysterics ever since last night when we learned that Wilfred had escaped from Edinburgh Jail. She is convinced that he is going to break in to the castle and murder her in her bed."

"I might beat Cardross to it if she does not stop soon," Robert murmured, as Dulcibella's screams rose to chandelier-shattering pitch. "A more self-absorbed creature would be hard to find. I almost feel sorry for your brother that he eloped with such a wife, and that is not a phrase I ever thought to utter."

"Robert," Lucy said reproachfully. Her lips twitched into a smile she could not repress. "Poor Lachlan. He has a lot to bear."

"Never was there a clearer case of a man getting what he deserves," Lady Methven said with rich satisfaction. "Just think, Robert. That could have been you."

"I give thanks every day that it is not," Robert said, smiling at Lucy with such warmth in his eyes that Mairi felt a pang of envy.

"We mustn't keep you standing out here in the cold after your ordeal," Lucy said quickly, sensing her sister's discomfort. She took Mairi's elbow, drawing her inside. The pitch of Dulcibella's shrieks had dropped slightly, though there was still the sound of both male and female voices raised in anger and the thud of various heavy objects making contact with one of Methven's walls. Something smashed.

"I thought I had removed all the fragile china and other breakables from Dulcibella's chamber," Lucy said, frowning. "She is a shockingly expensive houseguest."

The crashing reverberated through Mairi's head, waking the ache that was dormant there.

"I think I will delay greeting Lachlan until later," she said. "The rest of the family, as well. Is Papa here?"

Lucy shook her head. "Papa is not well," she said. "Nothing more serious than the gout, but in the end he preferred not to travel. Though I wonder…" She paused as the sound of Dulcibella and Lachlan's quarrel rose once again in pitch. "Whether he simply could not face the thought of so much domestic strife."

Mairi noticed that the footmen standing on either side of the entrance door had turned pink and were trying to look as though they were not listening, but it was impossible to be deaf to the insults that were tumbling through the air.

"Restrain yourself, wife!" Lachlan was bellowing while Dulcibella shrieked: "It's all very well for you, you insensate oaf! He doesn't want to kill *you!*"

"It is frightful bad manners to inflict one's hysterics on everyone else," Lady Methven said. "If she is going to indulge, the wretched girl should indulge in private."

"Rather like a love affair," Jack whispered in Mairi's ear.

Murdo and Hamish were bringing in her luggage. "I've put you in the blue room," Lucy said, as she ushered her toward the elegant sweep of the main stair. "I know that you asked to be as far away from Jack as possible originally—"

"Did you, my sweet?" Jack said, with a wicked smile.

"But given your betrothal, I thought…" Lucy stopped, as though becoming aware that she might be leading the conversation in an indecorous direction. "Anyway—" She flapped her hands in a flustered manner. "Jack is in the adjacent suite of rooms should you need...I mean require..."

"I would stop now," Robert said, "before you make matters any worse."

"As long as I am in a different wing from Dulcibella," Mairi said. Her head was aching monstrously now.

"Never was a female more inaptly named," Lady Methven said, as Dulcibella screamed something at Lachlan and ran off along the gallery, slamming the door behind her. She turned back to Mairi. "News of your betrothal only made matters worse, I'm afraid, my dear," she said. "Lady Dulcibella does so hate not to be the center of attention, and when I mentioned that we would be holding a celebration ball for you and for Jack, she became even more shrill."

"Oh, please," Mairi said involuntarily, "this house party is supposed to be a celebration of Ewan's christening, not of our engagement. I beg you not to make a fuss."

"Nonsense, my dear." The dowager patted her arm. "It is a double celebration. But I realize you need to rest now. Such a nasty experience with that ghastly Cardross fellow. When you are stronger we must plan something."

Mairi felt a sinking feeling. Lady Methven was a force of nature and as cunning as she was charming. At this rate Her Ladyship would have booked the church and spoken to the minister. Mairi would not lay a wager against being married off before she had the chance to jilt Jack. When Lady Methven wanted something she got it, and Mairi could see quite clearly that the dowager was determined that Jack should wed.

A group of men on horseback clattered into the

courtyard. "We need to discuss Cardross's attack," Robert said. "Perhaps after dinner? You look done up for now, Mairi." He turned to Jack. "I'm sending out patrols to hunt the man down. Do you want to join me on the next?"

Mairi could see how much Jack wanted to go. She could sense the impatience in him, the desire to be outside doing something active. It struck her that in all the time she had known Jack Rutherford, there had always been that restiveness within him. He was always on the move, never settled. It was as though he did not know how to stay still.

Jack grinned. "You read me like a book, Rob," he said. He glanced at Mairi. "I will not be away long, sweetheart," he said. "You need to rest anyway. We will talk later."

"Yes," Mairi said. "We will." She was starting to feel seriously annoyed by the casual endearments Jack used with such ease. Perhaps he addressed all his mistresses as "sweetheart" so that he did not need to remember their names. The thought did nothing to improve her temper.

"Don't let me keep you," she added. "I have no need of you here."

"Always so gracious," Jack said ruefully. He came across to her and without warning took her in his arms.

"Do I get no thanks at all for my services today?" he murmured, for her ears alone. Suddenly he was so close and his masculinity was so overpowering that Mairi's throat was bone-dry. She had been naive, she realized, in thinking that he was using her to evade Lady Methven's matchmaking. His grandmother might wheel out fifty eligible debutantes and he would not give a damn.

What Jack wanted was to continue to use their false engagement as an excuse to carry on exactly where they had left off, in bed, in a passionate affair with no real promises given on either side. He thought he could ignore her objections and her demand for his respect and simply take her body in some sort of payment for services rendered.

Well, if he thought that he was going to be sorely disappointed. It was not that she was not tempted. She was. Very tempted. She could not pretend otherwise. Considerations of propriety held no sway with her when she was in Jack's arms. She wanted the sex as much as he did even if it was not particularly ladylike of her to admit it. But she was also damned if Jack was going to get everything his own way. "You have had everything from me that you will be getting," she murmured.

She saw the ready amusement spring into his eyes. He raised her hand to his lips, turned it over and pressed a kiss to the palm. She felt the touch of his lips on her skin and shivered. Before she realized what she was doing, she had closed her fingers, trapping the kiss.

"Be careful," she said lightly. "It would spoil the festivities if you got yourself killed."

Jack laughed. "Cardross isn't going to be able to kill me."

A shiver touched Mairi's spine like a shadow. She caught his sleeve between her fingers, her grip suddenly urgent. "Promise me you *will* take care."

She knew at once that she had said quite the wrong thing. The laughter faded from Jack's eyes. Their expression changed completely and went blank, like a door slamming shut. He drew back slowly.

Mairi's stomach lurched. She had no idea why she

had said the words, why she had even felt them. In that moment she had feared for him. She had been terrified he might be hurt. The sensation had been so intense that she had blurted out the words without thinking. Now she was mortified, her whole body burning with embarrassment for the way in which she had betrayed herself.

But everyone was looking at her approvingly. She realized that they had overheard and that her display of wifely concern was just what was needed to reinforce the idea of a love match. Jack realized it too. After a moment she saw the expression in his eyes ease and he drew her back into his arms.

"What an accomplished actress you are," he said softly. "Bravo." His gaze was cool now, remote. He gave her a brief, hard kiss and released her, caressing her cheek as he let her go. It was a sweet added touch; Mairi heard the dowager sigh in a most sentimental fashion. Soon, she thought, she and Jack would be outdoing each other in their pretense of affection.

Except for her in that moment there had been no pretense. And that was what scared her.

CHAPTER TWELVE

THEY FOUND NO trace of Wilfred Cardross on Jack's patrol. Later in the day he went out with the Methven men again, quartering the hillsides above the castle, searching the glens as far eastward as Kinlochewe and to Sheildaig in the west. They found nothing but a confusion of hoofprints and a burned-out fire within the shelter of an old shieling, no doubt from the previous night when the outlaws had lain in wait. Jack suspected that they had weakened Wilfred's attack sufficiently that he would lie low for a while, but men could melt into these wild mountains as easily as ghosts. Robert had sent word to Edinburgh and soon there would be soldiers combing the countryside for their fugitive. But Cardross was wily and he had a grievance. Jack knew that they had not seen the last of him yet.

He felt frustrated as he rode back into Methven Keep. Anger with Cardross still burned fiercely in him. He wanted to string the bastard up for the way that he had treated Mairi. And one day he would hunt Cardross down and do precisely that. Mairi was under his protection now and it was a point of honor for him that he should keep her safe. He was the only one who could.

Dinner was a subdued affair that night, the grandeur of the great hall at Methven adding a somber cast to the proceedings. Dulcibella MacMorlan did not attend, much to everyone's relief, and Mairi had pleaded tiredness to take a tray in her room. Lady Methven was also absent. Robert had told Jack that she was still weak after a recent bout of fever but that news of his engagement had lifted her spirits enormously. Jack tried not to feel too guilty. He doubted his grandmother would be as happy when she discovered that once the false betrothal had served its purpose Mairi would jilt him, thoroughly, so she had said, and with considerable satisfaction.

His mouth curved into a reminiscent smile. He was enjoying crossing swords with Mairi. She was quite a woman, brave, fierce at times, sharp-witted and with a sense of humor after all. That had surprised him. But he liked it. He liked the challenge she represented. He knew he was going to have to work hard if he wanted to persuade her back to his bed. He had respect for her now and he was going to have to show it. This betrothal was proving a great deal more interesting than he had ever anticipated.

A question from Robert on the latest consignment of Baltic timber he had imported through Leith drew him back into the conversation. Angus MacMorlan, Mairi's elder brother and heir to the dukedom of Forres, was interested in investing and waffled on about government policy and profit and loss ratios through the removal of the roast beef and the arrival of the pudding. Eventually Lucy withdrew with her sister Christina and sister-in-law Gertrude to the drawing room while the gentlemen took port and a little while later they all took a dish of tea together. It was all perfectly exemplary and tediously boring and Jack found himself yawning the whole way through.

He had thought to have time alone with Robert later

in the evening, but Lachlan MacMorlan wanted to talk to them both about Wilfred Cardross's attack and the steps they were taking to hunt him down. Jack did not have much time for MacMorlan. He thought him weak and shallow. It had not escaped his notice that while he and Robert had ridden out with the patrols, both Mac-Morlan brothers had stayed behind, Angus because he thought himself too important as heir to a dukedom to risk his skin and Lachlan ostensibly to calm his wife. It seemed that the fierce blood of Malcolm MacMorlan, the Red Fox of Forres, had bypassed the male side of the family and now resided solely in the women. Jack wondered idly whether Christina MacMorlan, who was so quiet as to be almost invisible, was secretly as forceful as her sisters.

Jack sat quietly while Robert dealt with MacMorlan's concerns. The man was plainly terrified that as Dulcibella had taken all the Cardross estates when the earl had been tried for treason, Cardross was out to murder them both. Jack did not believe a word of it, but he admired his cousin's patience in dealing with MacMorlan's fears.

"You are an exemplary host," he said to Robert with a grin as the library door finally shut behind Robert's agitated brother-in-law. "I would have told him that if he was so worried he should go after Cardross himself instead of leaving the dirty work up to other people."

Robert laughed and went across to the side table. "MacMorlan is a lover, not a warrior," he said. "Besides, swordplay would mean he had to adjust the set of his coat." He picked up two glasses and the bottle of brandy, then turned to Jack and hesitated.

Jack shook his head. He wanted the drink, wanted to feel it burn, but he knew he could not risk it.

"I'll take a glass of capilliaire," he said. No one at Methven questioned his odd drinking habits. Elsewhere his preference for coffee and fruit juices raised eyebrows but he never explained himself. He did not give a damn what people thought.

He felt unsettled tonight, on edge. It was something to do with Mairi. He knew that she was safe within the walls of Methven Castle, so he was not sure why he still felt disturbed. He had been disappointed when she had failed to come to dinner. He wanted to see her, talk to her. Again he was not sure why; he was not even sure what he wanted to say to her. He frowned, taking the glass from Robert and swallowing half the contents without even really noticing.

"I think MacMorlan's concerns are groundless," he said abruptly. "I think Mairi was Cardross's target all along."

Robert took the wing chair opposite and set his own glass down gently. "Why would Cardross seek to kill Lady Mairi?" he said.

"He didn't want to kill her," Jack said. "He was trying to abduct her." He raised his gaze from the contemplation of the cordial to meet his cousin's dark eyes. "I heard him telling her that he had a friend who had an interest in her."

Robert's brows snapped down. "What did he mean by that?"

"I don't know," Jack said. "But Mairi once told me that the reason she travels with half an army is that plenty of men fancy wedding her for her money."

Robert sat back in his chair. "I suppose someone

who did not want to be identified might pay Cardross to abduct her," he said. "You're right—it would not be the first time a man has tried to force Mairi into marriage to get his hands on the MacLeod millions, but…" He frowned.

"What is it?" Jack said urgently.

Robert shook his head. "I'm not sure. I have a bad feeling about this business."

"It's not like you to be superstitious," Jack said.

"I know," Robert said gravely. "That's why I have a bad feeling about it."

Jack laughed, but sobered quickly. "Well, Cardross will have to get past me first," he said. "I don't give much for his chances."

He could feel Robert looking at him with interest and wondered what his cousin had read into his words. It was true that he felt inordinately protective of Mairi. It was the main reason why he was not prepared to allow her to break their fictitious betrothal. He was committed now, she was his responsibility and he was not going to be the one to tell Lord MacLeod that he had failed in his bid to defend her. It was nothing to do with emotion and all to do with his reputation. Or so he told himself. Having undertaken to give Mairi his protection, he would not break his word.

"Jack," Robert said. "Please don't feel you have any obligation to tell me anything at all, but Lucy is worried about your relationship with Lady Mairi, and I…" He paused. "Well, I admit to a certain curiosity. The last time I saw you, you were reluctant even to escort her here to Methven. As I recall, you said that you disliked her extremely."

"It's complicated," Jack said evasively.

"You astound me," Robert said dryly. "Your relationships with women are never complicated."

"And I am not sure that I said I disliked Mairi," Jack added. "You might have inferred it. I never said it." It gave him a shock to realize just how much his feelings for Mairi had changed. In Edinburgh he had considered her a spoiled and disdainful creature. Now he realized how complex she was. There was so much warmth and passion and sweetness in her as well as that strength and confounded stubbornness. He felt it every time they made love. His body tightened at the thought.

Robert raised his brows. "There was a certain degree of antagonism between you," he murmured.

"I'll grant you that," Jack agreed.

"Furthermore," Robert said, "you were completely besotted with a mysterious lady you had met at an Edinburgh masquerade—" He stopped dead, an arrested expression entering his eyes. "Hell and the devil, Jack," he said. "Surely it wasn't Lady Mairi—"

"I wish I'd never told you about that," Jack said fiercely. He felt another surge of protectiveness toward Mairi. He did not want Robert thinking any the less of her because she was his mistress. And even he could see how contrary that attitude was. Cursing vehemently, he ran his hands through his hair. He was starting to resent the way that Mairi seemed to be able to engender all sorts of emotions in him that he did not care for. He was determined to get back to desire, impure but simple. That was all he understood. That was all he wanted.

"It's forgotten," Robert said. There was a glint of amusement in his eyes.

Jack's tight muscles eased a little. "Thank you."

"Tell me to mind my own business if you wish,"

Robert said, after a pause, "but this betrothal between you—"

"It's temporary," Jack interrupted. The tightness was back; he could feel it in the muscles of the back of his neck and in the tension in his shoulders. "Neither Lady Mairi nor I have any desire to wed."

Robert was studying his brandy with sudden fascination. "I won't interfere," he said, after a moment, "but among other things you are misleading our grandmother."

"I know," Jack said. He clenched his jaw. "But I cannot marry to oblige our grandmother just because she is ill and wishes to see me settled before she dies."

Robert sighed. "As long as you do not wilfully hurt her," he said. "Nor Lady Mairi for that matter," he added. "She may act like a fast widow, but she is not."

"I know," Jack said again. Conscience stirred in him again. "Damn you, I know that."

"Well, then," Robert said, "be careful." He smiled a little. Glass clinked as he refilled his brandy. He gestured to Jack's glass. "Another?"

"No, thank you." Jack said. There was only so much fruit juice a man could take.

"So if it's temporary," Robert said, after a moment, "what is the point of it?" He cocked an eyebrow. "I take it you are offering Mairi your protection? In both senses of the word?"

"Bloody hell, you're asking for it tonight," Jack said abruptly. It was interesting how his cousin's words seemed to catch him entirely on the raw at the moment. Interesting and troubling and yet another thing to lay at the door of Lady Mairi MacLeod.

"Since when is my sex life your business, Robert?" he asked.

"Since it involves my sister-in-law," Robert said. "I'd hate to have to call you out for ruining Mairi's reputation." His words were mild, but the look in his eyes was harder than granite. Jack had seen that rigidity in Robert before. His cousin had a stern sense of morality and an equally strong sense of family, neither of which he shared. It seemed, however, that Robert was intent on imposing his own principles on him in this case. Jack was sure they would be a very bad fit. Principled he was not. Nor did he have any intention of being dragooned to the altar.

"I suspect you would have to stand in line behind the Laird of MacLeod," he said. "He may be elderly, but I'll warrant he still knows how to shoot straight."

Robert smiled reluctantly but refused to be deflected. "Is MacLeod involved in this? Did he broker the betrothal?"

Jack sighed. He wished fiercely for brandy. He had had no notion this interview was going to be so tough. Sometimes it almost killed him to be so abstemious.

"MacLeod asked me for my help," he said. "Lady Mairi is being threatened by his heir. There is a whispering campaign against her, unpleasant gossip. Worse, MacLeod believes the heir, Michael Innes, will try to dig up old scandal to get his hands on Lady Mairi's fortune. I said I would offer her the protection of my name until the situation is resolved."

"How gallant of you," Robert said dryly. "And how out of character."

"What are you saying?" Jack said. "That I'm some lazy bastard who doesn't give a damn about others?"

Robert's lips twitched. "Don't you define yourself in precisely that manner?" he asked. "You're not lazy," he added. "You just don't get involved."

"I had an incentive," Jack said pleasantly.

The smile died from Robert's eyes. His mouth tightened to a thin line. "Lady Mairi. Yes, I understand. Sometimes you *can* be a complete bastard, Jack. And yet—" His hand checked as he reached for the brandy bottle and he cast his cousin a thoughtful look. "The more you protest, the less convinced I am." He smiled suddenly. "Shall we change the subject before we come to blows? Do you think there is any connection between Wilfred Cardross and Lord MacLeod's heir? Two men with a grudge who might join forces to exploit the situation?"

"I don't see where Cardross fits in," Jack said, frowning. He felt as though he was missing something. There was a pattern, but he could not see it. And if he could not see it, he could not keep Mairi safe.

"We'll have to find him and ask him," Robert said, his tone giving no doubt that the nature of the questioning would not be friendly. "We'll keep up the patrols and no doubt they will send a troop from Edinburgh, but it will take several days to arrive and out here in the wild glens…" He shrugged expressively. "Well, it's going to be a challenge to capture him."

"I intend to call on Michael Innes when I return south," Jack said. "MacLeod told me that he is out of Edinburgh at present on business, but when he returns I will get a measure of his involvement. Perhaps he can shed some light on where Cardross fits in."

Robert grinned. "I imagine that is one interview you

will enjoy." He looked up, meeting Jack's gaze. "I almost feel sorry for the man."

"Don't," Jack said. "He doesn't deserve it." He thought of the danger to Mairi. Until they could get to the bottom of this business, she would be forever under threat. He thought of her gallantry and felt another pang of protectiveness. He would kill for her, he realized.

He finished the last of his cordial. The brandy beckoned to him like a temptress, offering refuge from feelings he did not want to acknowledge. He stared hard at the bottle for several seconds. Then he pushed his glass away.

"There's just one more thing," he said slowly. "MacLeod spoke of an old scandal that involved Lady Mairi's husband. He implied that it would be damaging even now were it to come out. Do you know what that might be?"

Robert did not answer immediately. "I never knew Archie MacLeod," he said after a moment. "He was already dead when I met Lucy. I've never heard any scandal about him. By all accounts he was a thoroughly decent fellow."

"I heard that too," Jack said, through his teeth.

Robert laughed. "I believe they were childhood friends."

"I believe so." Jack was beginning to wish he had not asked. He disliked the idea of Mairi and Archie knowing each other forever, with the bonds of deep intimacy that a childhood friendship implied.

"Mairi married him in opposition to her father's plans," Robert said. "That I do know. The Duke of Forres had planned quite a different match for her. Lucy says he was not happy to be thwarted."

"Mairi must have wanted to marry MacLeod very much if she was prepared to defy her father," Jack said.

"Or," Robert said gently, "she wanted to avoid her other suitor very much." He let that sink in. "I do know one other thing," he added. "Probably I should not tell you." His eyes met Jack's briefly. "Lucy said that Mairi once told her that she and her husband were not intimate. They did not share a bed. I don't know why. I don't know if it was always the case, but they were estranged, at least as husband and wife. And I've already said too much."

Jack felt the hairs on his neck lift. He thought of the night that Mairi had seduced him. She had said she had been seeking oblivion. He had assumed that she was mourning her husband's death, but perhaps she had been mourning something quite different, the loss of a friend or the loss of trust in a relationship that had gone awry.

"Jack." Robert's voice recalled him to the room. In the lamplight his cousin's dark gaze was very grave.

"Allow me to give you some advice," Robert said. "If you want to know the truth, ask Mairi. If she trusts you she will tell you. But—" there was a hint of laughter in his voice "—you may have to work on that given your record."

Jack grimaced. He had given Mairi no reason to trust him and every reason to be wary of him. She might have granted him her body, but she had no intention of revealing her secrets. If he wanted to change that he would have to gain her confidence. No attempts at seduction behind the topiary. No stealing into her bedchamber after the household had retired. He was not sure how long he could keep that up.

He groaned. He wanted Mairi very much and he was

not accustomed to denial. Usually if he wanted something he got it. If it was a commodity he bought it. If it was a woman she was generally as eager as he to explore their mutual desire. Mairi, in contrast, had told him he was a cad, a set-down he had richly deserved. She had said she was too good for him.

She was correct.

He felt the old bitterness twist inside him, rolling in like a dark tide. Memories returned, memories of failure and regret. For a moment he had been in danger of forgetting that he was no one's savior. He had seen himself as her knight protector.

Don't get close.

Don't take that risk.

"I don't need to know Mairi's secrets in order to deal with either Cardross or Innes," he said lightly. "Good night, Rob." And he turned and left, before he could see the disappointment he knew would be showing in his cousin's eyes.

"WELL?" AS HER HUSBAND came into the bedroom, Lucy put down the novel she had been reading and fixed him with her very bright blue eyes. "You have been gone an age! I had almost despaired of you." She waited and then when Robert did not immediately reply she gave a little impatient wriggle. "Robert! What did he say? I have been positively expiring with curiosity here! Did he blackmail her into the betrothal? Did she blackmail him? Is he in love with her?"

Robert laughed. "One question at a time, my love." He discarded his dressing robe and slid into bed beside her, drawing her into the crook of his arm, her head resting against his shoulder. For a long moment there was silence between them, peaceful silence, comfortable silence full of unspoken thoughts and warmth and love. Lucy smiled and nestled closer, placing a hand on his bare chest.

"It might be better not to do that if you wish me to concentrate on your question," Robert said mildly, his hand coming up to cover hers and hold it still against his heart. "Jack agreed to the betrothal as a favor to Lord MacLeod."

"How unlikely," Lucy said. She frowned. She did not know Jack well. He let no one close and gave the impression that he wanted little truck with his family. Yet she suspected that he did care for them. He and Robert had worked together for years and had strong mutual respect and loyalty. She was sure he loved his grandmother too, although he would probably die rather than admit it. But Jack's skill lay in being incredibly charming while giving nothing of his true feelings away.

"It is not like Jack to offer his help if he gets no return," she said, a little tartly. "There must be something in it for him."

"I am sure that there is," Robert said, his tone very dry. "I am sure he has exacted a price for his help from your sister."

"And I am not sure that she objected," Lucy said as dryly as he. "When I asked Mairi about the betrothal, all she would say was that Jack was the best lover in Scotland. I know she meant to shock me into leaving her alone." She sighed. "It is ridiculously romantic of me," she said, "but I *did* hope that they were in love."

"Jack loves no one," Robert said.

"Except himself," Lucy said.

Robert gave a slight shake of the head. "Least of all

himself. He blames himself for the death of his mother and sister. He will never let himself love anyone else for fear of losing them too." He turned his head slightly to look at her, his dark eyes warming as they dwelt on her face. "You want Mairi to be happy. That is sweet of you. Did she say anything else?"

"Nothing," Lucy said. She felt a familiar sense of frustration. She and Mairi had never been close enough to confide, and that fact grieved her. "She told me she had the headache and sent me away with the supper tray as though I were a servant."

Robert dropped a consoling kiss on her hair. "I'm sorry," he said. "Sorry that she did not want to talk to you."

"I'm accustomed to it," Lucy said. She drooped a little. "But it does hurt." She cuddled closer to him. "Mairi and I don't really talk. I suppose that Alice and I, being twins, excluded everyone else when we were children. We didn't do it on purpose but we needed no one else. And when Alice died Mairi was already wed. Then she was widowed and acting the role she plays now of the fashionable widow. But it is all an act. I know it is." She rolled over and stared up at the blue velvet drapes of the bed. "What makes it worse is that I am sure Mairi is hurting too, Robert," she said. "She pushes people away because she is afraid to love them. It is Archie's fault." Her voice sharpened. "I am sure of it. She trusted him and he did something bad, betrayed her in some way."

It was clear to her that Robert was losing interest in the topic. He was playing with her hair now in the way she loved. There was concentrated warmth in his eyes as he threaded the auburn strands through his fingers.

"So your sister thinks Jack is the best lover in Scotland," he said. He moved suddenly, turning to face her. His hand dropped to the ribbon tying her nightgown. "What do you think?"

"I admit," Lucy said demurely, but with a very naughty twinkle in her eyes, "that I have sometimes wondered whether it was true. Jack is so very wicked and of course he has a great deal of experience."

Robert's fingers paused on the satin ribbon. He looked at her, incredulity in his eyes. "You have been wondering what my *cousin* would be like in bed?"

Lucy blushed. She could not quite banish the little smile that played about her lips. "Only in a purely academic sense," she murmured. "Out of intellectual curiosity. You know how *very* curious I can be, Robert."

Robert rolled her beneath him. "I do indeed, madam," he growled. He kissed her, driving his hands into her hair, parting her lips with such hungry possession Lucy was lost in the overpowering intimacy of it. Robert tugged hard on the ribbon. It unraveled and he slid a hand inside the bodice of her nightgown, cupping her breast. Lucy gasped.

"Still curious about Jack?" Robert demanded. He kissed her again, slow, deep and hot, until she moved feverishly to draw him closer still.

"Who?" she said.

CHAPTER THIRTEEN

By the end of the first week at Methven Castle, Mairi had remembered all the reasons she disliked house parties. She was cooped up with a disparate group of relatives and acquaintances, most of whom she would not have chosen to spend time with under other circumstances. Her elder brother, Angus, had never been a favorite of hers. He was pompous and self-important, had bullied her as a child and was still trying to tell her what to do. His wife, Gertrude, was a ghastly overbearing matron who was busy dragooning Mairi's elder sister, Christina, into acting as chaperone for her daughter the following season. Lachlan had always been a wastrel and now seemed miserable and fretful as a small child and Dulcibella was frankly poisonous, her china-doll prettiness belying a tongue as sharp as a needle. Lachlan was most often the brunt of his wife's bad humor, but when Dulcibella had seen Mairi at breakfast on the first day, her gaze had sharpened and she had positively glowed with the pleasure of having a new quarry.

"I am so glad you were able to find the time for us in your vigorous social life, Lady Mairi," she had purred. "I know the gentlemen are all wild for your... company...and you so hate to disappoint them."

"I restrict all my affections to one particular man, Lady Dulcibella," Mairi said, smiling across the table at Jack with the most starry-eyed look she could summon up. "I always feel it is an advantage actually to *like* the person one is betrothed or married to, don't you agree?" She cast a meaningful glance at Lachlan, who had taken his plate of rolls and butter to the end of the table the farthest from his wife and was perusing the newspaper with morose concentration.

She envied Jack in those first few days. He at least was able to escape the confines of the house party by riding out with the regular patrols that scoured the hills for Wilfred Cardross. Mairi felt hemmed in and restricted. In part that was because she was limited to the physical boundaries of the Methven estate for safety, but it was also because she felt so on edge and aware of Jack that she could not relax. It disconcerted her that he was acting the role of the perfect attentive fiancé. He brought her cups of tea and glasses of lemonade on the hot afternoons. He sat beside her and talked to her, he turned the music for her when she played the piano after dinner and he walked with her in the gardens. He did it all with the utmost propriety and with a wicked hint of amusement in his eyes.

He never kissed her.

She assumed that like her he was aware that public decorum had to be observed, and yet it was contrary to everything she knew of his character. The Jack Rutherford she knew should have been trying to debauch her in the long gallery or whisk her into the maze for a quick dalliance. The fact that he did none of these things wrong-footed her. It disappointed her too and then she was exasperated with herself as well as him. On more than one occasion she lay in bed staring at the door that connected her room to the little dressing room next to

Jack's chamber. But she was damned if she would break her word and open that door. Jack might be attractive, but he was not irresistible. Or so she told herself.

She had taken to visiting the library each night to select a book to help while away the long hours when she could not sleep. She chose works of philosophy and economic theory, the biographies of great generals and dry historical tomes in the hope that they might bore her to sleep. She thought that such dispassionate works of literature would be just what she needed to quell any lustful urges. Unfortunately the opposite seemed to be the case; the dryer the book the more frustrated she felt.

Although the prime purpose of the family gathering was to celebrate Robert and Lucy's second son's baptism, Mairi's betrothal also seemed to generate a great deal of attention. She cursed herself that she had not foreseen this. Day after day, visitors came to call, ostensibly to bring gifts and congratulate Lucy and Robert on Ewan's forthcoming christening but also to glean the latest gossip on Mairi's engagement. It was the talk of Edinburgh; Lord MacLeod had seen to that with announcements in every newspaper. It was fast becoming the talk of Scotland. The dowager marchioness in particular seemed overly excited with talk of trousseaux and family jewels until Mairi felt so guilty that when she saw Lady Methven coming she wanted to run for cover.

One evening after dinner as Mairi was standing on the terrace, listening to Dulcibella's fluting tones rise and fall like a peal of bells as she upbraided Lachlan on spending too much time in the billiards room, Jack strolled over to her side, turning half to face her, propping his back against the balustrade. He was in immaculate evening clothes, austere black and stark white.

He looked shockingly handsome and rather dangerous. Her pulse fluttered in response to the thought before she composed herself. She was not going to swoon at his feet.

"I have been waiting on tenterhooks for you publicly to dismiss my services," Jack said. "Can it be that you have discovered you enjoy having someone to fetch your wrap or fill your champagne glass?"

Mairi smiled reluctantly. "I have plenty of servants who could do that," she said.

"In which case you must have decided that you want me for another purpose," Jack said.

"Not a very admirable purpose," Mairi admitted. "I am afraid that I am using you to thwart Dulcibella. I did think about breaking off our association, but I could not bear to give her any more ammunition. Besides, I am relishing the novelty of being lauded for my respectability."

Jack laughed. "It is oddly enjoyable," he agreed. He leaned closer. The back of his fingers brushed her cheek as he gently touched a strand of her hair. "Though I would enjoy being thoroughly disreputable a great deal more."

"I daresay you would," Mairi said. "However, our relationship is taking a reverse route to that which is considered the norm. It started with a consummation and ends with us going our separate ways. At present we are in the middle phase where you dance attendance upon me and I refuse to sleep with you."

Jack caressed the nape of her neck. "May we not reverse the process?" he said softly.

Mairi was momentarily confused by his touch. It was so warm and so seductive. His fingers tangled in her hair, stroking with the most beguiling gentleness. It made her tremble helplessly. In a flash she remembered the procession of sleepless nights lying staring at the connecting door and defying herself from going to him.

"No," she heard herself say, and even she could hear the regret in her tone.

Jack laughed. She knew he had heard it too. "A pity." He exerted the slightest pressure to bring her closer to him, so close that the skirts of her gown brushed his leg. "Can I not persuade you to change your mind?"

His lips grazed hers. He nipped at her jaw. Mairi shivered. It was impossible to deny the heat that flared between them. Her body hummed with it. He had not touched her for four days. She had been waiting for this.

"There you are!" Neither of them had noticed Lady Methven bustling out to join them. Or so Mairi assumed. Hot on the heels of that thought came another: had Jack seen his grandmother approaching and flirted with her to add another layer of verisimilitude to their false engagement? A cold shard wedged in her heart. Just for a moment she had been seduced into believing he was sincere.

"I cannot blame you for taking refuge out here," Lady Methven said. "I have just heard Lady Dulcibella telling poor Lucy that she spoils little James shamefully. Since she has no children of her own, how can she possibly be an arbiter of such matters?" Without waiting for a reply she patted Jack on the arm with her fan. "Anyway, there is something I wished to discuss with you both. Your wedding."

Mairi stiffened. She shot a glance at Jack.

"Grandmama—" he started to say.

"I think you should set a date." Lady Methven was

like a ship in full sail. "The autumn would be nice, before the weather turns too bad to travel. Shall we say six weeks? That is long enough to put together a modest trousseau, and as Lady Mairi is a widow and you are no green youth, Jack, there can be no need for a grand event."

Mairi felt Jack look at her. "Lady Mairi and I have been betrothed for barely a week—" he said.

"Well, that is no reason to delay," Lady Methven said robustly. "Neither of you is young. You should know your own minds."

"Lady Methven." Mairi thought that she would give it a try, but Jack caught her hand in his.

"Please excuse us, Grandmama," he said. "I think that Lady Mairi and I need to discuss this in private."

"Of course," Lady Methven said. She looked triumphant. "I knew you would see my point of view."

"I'm sorry for that," Jack said. He had ushered Mairi back inside and appropriated the small study off the library, shutting the door against the rest of the party. He did not sit and she could see tension across his shoulders. "I suppose we might have anticipated that this would happen," he said. "Grandmama has been trying to marry me off for years, and now that she thinks the moment is finally here she sees no reason to put it off. Are you cold?" he added, seeing Mairi shiver and draw her gauzy silver wrap closer about her.

"Just a little," Mairi said, seizing any excuse for the misery that suddenly racked her. She could not explain it, nor did she know why her spirits had dropped so hard. All she knew was that she had had enough of pretense.

"Jack," she said. "I think we should put an end to this.

It will suit neither of us to be dragooned into marriage. I will explain to Lord MacLeod—"

"And will you also shoot Wilfred Cardross and deal with Michael Innes?" Jack demanded. There was a hard edge to his voice now. He strode across the room, repressed anger in every line of his body, and turned abruptly to face her.

"If I have to," Mairi said. "I have always managed to deal with problems on my own."

"So you keep saying." Now Jack seemed even angrier and Mairi was at a loss to understand why. "It does not suit my purposes to end this engagement now," he snapped.

"Oh." Mairi hesitated. "Well, if you can stall your grandmother for a little, then I will be very happy to break our engagement as soon as it is convenient to you," she said stiffly. "I have no intention of trapping you into marriage. I don't wish to wed."

Jack's lips lifted into a slight smile. "I am aware," he said coolly. "You have made your feelings on that matter quite clear."

The silence between them buzzed with frustration.

"I don't understand!" Mairi burst out. "You have no more desire to be married than I do, so why are you being so difficult? You did not want to help me in the first place—"

"I changed my mind," Jack said. He drove his hands into the pockets of his jacket, turning away from her. All she could see was his broad, uncommunicative back. She felt violently irritated.

"You changed your mind because you wanted to sleep with me," she said.

He spun around so quickly she almost flinched. "I

am trying to defend you from varying degrees of danger," he said. His tone was pleasant, but there was a dangerous glint in his eyes. "The least that you can do is accept my protection."

"But I did not ask—"

He grabbed her, jerking her hard against his body. "It is less than a week since Cardross's men almost killed you." His tone was harsh. "Until that danger is past and the threat from Michael Innes too, you are my responsibility."

Mairi's mouth fell open. "I beg your pardon?"

"You are betrothed to me," Jack said with deadly softness, "and therefore I have responsibility for you. Until we sever our agreement, that will be the case and I am not prepared for it to end until I say so." He released her as though the matter were quite settled.

"Now you are being absurd," Mairi said furiously. "I am an independent woman. I will not be told what to do."

Jack shrugged. It maddened her that he seemed so unconcerned. "I do not seek to limit your independence," he said. "Unlike many of my sex, I don't feel threatened by a strong woman. But the truth is that you need this engagement, Mairi, and therefore you must be prepared to compromise a little to society's demands."

"And to yours!" Mairi said. She marched out of the study, infuriated that Lady Methven and Lucy were in the library taking tea and that they smiled indulgently at her as she passed, as though she had been thoroughly kissed rather than thoroughly annoyed. She stalked out into the hall and started up the stairs, uncertain where she was going or what she was going to do next. It was one thing to walk out in high dudgeon but she had given no thought as to what happened afterwards. It was too early to retire for the evening and she felt too agitated to settle calmly with a book and a cup of tea. She cursed Jack vehemently under her breath. It was a show of pure male bravado to posture around insisting that she accept his protection until he had dealt with the threats to her.

There was a step behind her and she spun around to see that Jack had caught her up on the top step. Their eyes met and she caught her breath. He looked absolutely furious.

He waited while a housemaid slipped past them, eyes averted, her arms full of clean linen; then when she had disappeared from sight down the curve of the stair, he caught Mairi's hand and almost dragged her behind an enormous marble statue that stood in the doorway of the portrait gallery. He spun her around to face him.

"You will not walk out on me like that again." His tone was clipped.

"Then do not treat me like a possession!" Mairi snapped. She was shaking.

There was a tight, tense silence and then Jack smiled ruefully and raised a hand to touch her cheek. "Why are we quarreling," he said, "when what we really want to do is make love?"

Mairi's heart was thudding hard against her ribs. Longing fizzed in her blood like moonlight. His words crystalized the need in her. She did want him and she did not want to have to deny that desire.

"I do want to make love with you," she whispered, lifting her gaze to meet his. "But I won't be tumbled and dismissed like a lightskirt."

She saw him smile again briefly. "That was a mistake," he agreed gravely.

"Yes," Mairi said. "It was."

His smile faded and his gaze was very direct, intent, unsmiling now. "I cannot offer more than an affair," he said. "Just so that we are clear."

Mairi did not reply immediately. Her throat felt drier than sand. Her heart still beat an urgent tattoo. She knew she had to be certain because Jack was being brutally honest and she had to be honest in return. She did not know if she was able to separate out physical love and emotion, did not know if it could be so simple for her. She had no desire ever to remarry, but that did not mean that she could not explore the world of her senses, a world that had been closed to her before she met Jack. It did not mean she should turn her back on that lovely seductive passion.

The voice of reason whispered to her that she should not do this again, but hearing it did not change anything. Not when her stomach was already knotted tight with the lovely pain of arousal and when she wanted him more than anything she could remember wanting in her life.

She swallowed hard. "I understand," she said.

AT LAST.

It felt as if it had been an eternity. Jack knew he was not cut out for celibacy, least of all where Lady Mairi MacLeod was concerned. He had been on the edge of arousal for the entire day, for the entire week, if truth be told. Even as he had schooled himself to play the part of the perfect fiancé, he had been almost consumed with lust. And he had known that sooner or later he would fall.

He drew Mairi into his arms and she came willingly, eager for his embrace, and his heart leaped.

"I've waited all week for this," she whispered as his lips left hers. "I wanted it. Wanted you." She put a hand on the nape of his neck and pulled his head back down to hers.

Right from the start Jack felt desperate, almost out of control. His hand cupped the back of her head as he kissed her, his fingers delving into the satin-softness of her hair. He felt driven, wilder for her than he had ever been for a woman, and yet almost afraid that in touching her he would unlock some emotion within himself that once free could never be controlled. For a second he almost drew away, but the need he had for her was too great. He kissed her again, pulling her deeper into the shadows of the portrait gallery, giving himself up to pleasure and undeniable lust.

The neckline of her gown was low. That fact had been tormenting Jack throughout dinner. He was almost certain she had chosen the daring décolletage and the tight silk to tease him. So now it was time to pay her back for the provocation. He tugged; one of her breasts popped out very pleasingly from beneath the shimmering silver gauze, the nipple begging for the nip of his teeth. He bent his head to suckle. Mairi gasped, her head going back, her hair rippling down like a dark river over her naked skin. Briefly Jack considered pulling the bodice of the gown down to expose her breasts completely, but he thought she looked more wanton as she was, totally, deliciously rumpled, with one breast demurely covered and the other shamelessly bare.

He lifted her. Her legs wrapped instinctively about his waist, her back came up against the paneling. The gauze of her skirts was slippery and he struggled to burrow beneath it, his elbow catching the nearby bust of Julius Caesar, which rocked ominously on its pedestal. Then his questing fingers found the slit in her drawers and the warmth and wetness beneath, and his shaft hardened to epic proportions.

Mairi had realized he intended to have her right here, right now. Her body stiffened with shock and she pulled her mouth away from his.

"Here?" Her shaken whisper sounded horrified, like a maiden aunt confronted by debauchery. "Jack!"

Jack smiled, pressing his lips to the pulse that beat frantically in the hollow of her throat. Fumbling with the fastening of his breeches, he freed himself and thrust up into her, covering her mouth with his to smother her cry. "Right here," he confirmed, against her lips.

He broke the kiss and turned his face against the hot damp skin of her neck. He ran his tongue along it, tasted her, bit down gently, all the time driving up into her in long, hard strokes. He dipped his head to her breast again, pulling on the nipple, hearing her stifled cries and feeling her body flutter and close around his. There was no doubt that she was shocked that he had chosen to ravish her in a public place. This was taking their intimacy to an entirely new level of wickedness. Yet he could sense she was also wildly excited by the sheer wantonness of it. She never normally took risks and he had taken control and she was helpless.

Almost on cue, a door opened at the far end of the gallery. Light flared. Voices. Had Robert and Lucy chosen this frightfully inconvenient moment to show their guests the ancestral portrait collection? The thought made Jack smile.

He felt Mairi go rigid as she heard the voices too. She tried to pull away from him, but she could not move and he held her more firmly and simply allowed her to slide down deeper on his shaft. She gasped as he filled her to the hilt.

"You must stop." She sounded breathless, her words a whisper in his ear. "Please. They might—"

Jack smiled against the hot bare skin of her shoulder. "They might see us?" He nipped her throat hard enough to make her gasp, then drove up into her again. She bit back a little keening cry. He bent his head to her breast and repeated the caress there, a nip of his teeth and a salve of the tongue. Her breath fractured.

There were footsteps on the gallery's wooden floor.

"Jack!" She sounded frantic. She squirmed. He held her still, impaled.

"Hush." He continued to thrust upward into her, smooth and unhurried in his strokes. "You don't want them to hear you. Think how shocked Angus would be. Think how jealous Dulcibella would be."

Mairi gave a little whimper. Her body clasped his; she arched upward, he rocked higher. Light bloomed closer. The voices were louder, Robert, Lucy, Lachlan, Dulcibella, the entire house party.

"This is my great-grandfather," Robert was saying. "He fought in the Jacobite uprising in seventeen nineteen, and along here…"

Mairi gave a little moan. Her sweat-slicked skin clung to Jack's.

"They'll all see you in a moment," Jack whispered, "naked to the waist with me inside you."

The wicked words were sufficient to push her over the edge. She came hard, the violent pulse of her body taking him with her in so intense a climax that he staggered. They crashed back against the paneling, her body still gripping his whilst wave after wave of pleasure beat over him.

"Who's there?" It was Dulcibella's voice, cutting through the bliss, sharp as needles.

Jack straightened, lowering Mairi gently to the floor. He saw that he had knocked the portrait of the fifth Lord Methven awry and that it was hanging lopsided. Julius Caesar had tumbled to the floor, chipping his nose.

"It's only one of the servants," Robert was saying. "Now, over here is a portrait of Clementina, Lady Methven..."

"Quick." Jack opened the nearest door, bundling Mairi through. One of the benefits of being the previous marquis's grandson was that he at least knew his way around the castle. He steered Mairi through a couple of antechambers, pausing only to kiss her on the way. She was panting and beautifully disheveled, laughing, with a hectic light of excitement in her eyes.

"You are shocking," she said. She kissed him, her lips clinging to his, her tongue sliding deep to tangle with his in a welter of heat and demand. Jack felt his body harden into arousal again. She was astonishingly responsive and it made him feel like a youth, impatient to have her all over again.

"And you like to be outrageous," he said, pushing her against the wall to kiss her again. "Who would have guessed?"

It took them another thirty minutes finally to make it back to the landing, by which time he had taken her again on the table in the upstairs billiards room and he knew that the rest of the company would be assembling for supper and wondering where they were.

"I've lost one of my slippers," Mairi complained as they came out of the warren of antechambers. Jack adjusted the bodice of her dress, tweaking it back into place. She spun around to view her image in one of the long pier glasses at the top of the stairs, and her hands went to her hot cheeks.

"Oh!" she said. "I cannot possibly go back down to the drawing room looking like this!"

"No," Jack agreed. "You look completely ravished."

She touched his cheek in a light caress. "I must go and make some repairs." She stood on tiptoe and kissed him, very sweetly.

"Thank you," she whispered. "Come to my room later." She disappeared down the corridor toward her bedchamber.

Jack checked the impulse to follow her. He felt supremely physically satiated but at the same time dissatisfied in a way he could not explain. He had told Mairi that he wanted no more than an affair with no emotional commitment on either side, and then when she had treated the sex as a meaningless if pleasurable physical transaction, he had wanted to smash his fist down on the newel post in frustration. He had exactly what he thought he wanted, yet it seemed he did not want it anymore.

There was an irony in there somewhere, but he was damned if he could appreciate it.

CHAPTER FOURTEEN

IT WAS THE morning of Ewan's baptism. Jack woke abruptly, drenched in sweat and shaking. The room was dark and for a moment he had no notion where he was for the shreds of the nightmare still clung so tightly to his mind. With a groan he rolled over onto his back, shading his eyes with his forearm. There was a bitter taste in his mouth. Images still danced before his closed eyes; he was a small boy, standing in church, a huge church where the pillars soared upward so far that he could barely see the tops, as though they reached to heaven itself. His father was there, beaming, and his mother was smiling too with a tiny baby in her arms dressed in the most exquisite lace and satin christening robe. He was in his Sunday best; his collar was too tight and his jacket too small and he had been washed and polished, spick-and-span. No one took much notice of him. They were too busy cooing over the baby and his parents were too busy cooing over each other.

"You are Averil's brother." His grandmother had enfolded him in her scented embrace. She smelled of violets and her silk gown was slippery. He struggled because he had to pretend he disliked being hugged, but actually he adored her. "That is a very important thing to be, Jack. You are the elder. You must look after her."

You must look after her....

The sour taste in Jack's mouth deepened. A vast desolation filled his heart. He rolled over and grabbed the tinderbox, but in his clumsiness he knocked it to the floor. Cursing, he got up and walked to the window instead, pulling back the curtains.

Night still lay over the glens. There was no moon tonight. The clouds pressed low on the mountains. Jack let the curtain fall and reached again for a taper, managing this time to light the candle. It cast a golden glow into the room, the warm light only serving to make him feel cold and isolated.

He seldom had the nightmares these days. When he had first left Scotland to join Robert in Canada, he had been haunted by bad dreams, but the passage of the years had softened the edges of them and had almost smoothed them away. Which made the palpable sense of dread that hung over this one all the more disturbing. He suspected that it was coming back to Methven that had prompted it. A christening was a joyful occasion for most people, but for him it awoke bad memories.

He decided to take a walk; dawn would be coming soon and he could let the fresh air blow away the last of the dreams.

He dressed carelessly, not bothering to call for the valet Robert had lent him for the duration of the stay. A faint haze of rain was falling over the terrace as he went out of the conservatory door. Robert had a guard on duty at all the doors in case Wilfred Cardross decided to attack the castle itself. The man was yawning at his post and he nodded to Jack and let him through. In the gray morning light, Methven's gardens spread out before him in elegant splendor. It was very different from when he had first come here as a child, in his grandfather's time. The old laird had let Methven and all the rest of his estates fall into ruin, and while the tumbledown walls and neglected buildings had been an exciting playground for a child, the air of melancholy that had hung over the place had been dark and depressing. Robert had taken all of that and with Lucy transformed Methven into a family home alive and vibrant with life. He had brought love back to Methven. For a moment Jack thought of Glen Calder, his own estate, a few miles to the north. Glen Calder was equally as beautiful as Methven, an ancient stone castle with a view over the sea. The estate was efficient, it was prosperous, but it was not like Methven. It was not a home. It had no heart.

The castle was coming awake. He could hear voices, the clatter of pots and pans from the kitchen, the sound of a door opening. Jack straightened his shoulders. He needed a wash and a shave if he was to appear even remotely respectable in church.

He glanced up at Mairi's window. The heavy velvet drapes were drawn. None of the guests would be awake yet. An urgent need to see her caught him by surprise. He wanted to talk to her. Simply being with her would steady him in some way that he could not define.

Hell.

He needed no one. Reliance on others was a weakness. He remembered the nightmare. If you opened yourself to love, sooner or later you also opened yourself to grief.

He ran a hand over his jaw, feeling the stubble rough beneath his fingers. He would grit his teeth and endure the christening ceremony, witness Robert and Lucy's happiness, mingle with the guests, chat as though there was nothing wrong.

And then he would find a bottle of brandy and get roaring drunk. He knew he was going to do it. He knew it with a faint sense of despair and a complete sense of inevitability. There was nothing else that he could do.

"Do you know where Jack is?" Mairi asked Lucy. It was evening and Ewan had long been taken back to the nursery along with his elder brother while his parents and their guests had dinner and talked and enjoyed some fine Highland hospitality. Mairi was exhausted. She had stood in church as her nephew's godmother and had made her vows, promising to love and support Ewan and his family. The tears had stung her eyes and closed her throat then, tears of happiness with an edge of pain. She hoped she would be a good godmother to her nephew. But she had felt distinctly guilty when she had been standing in church since her association with Jack was so disreputable. However, it would soon be over, and then, she promised herself, she would revert to being the most proper of godmothers. Leaving aside all moral considerations, she suspected that Jack's lovemaking had probably spoiled her for any other lovers. She would make do with needlepoint and watercolor painting as her future entertainments.

Jack had been standing with his grandmother then. She remembered how handsome he had looked, but so unsmiling and severe, his demeanor so different from Lady Methven's joy to see another generation establishing itself in her ancestral home. When the service was over Jack had exchanged a quick word with his grandmother and then he had vanished. Mairi had seen him briefly, later, mingling with the guests, but now he had vanished again.

Lucy frowned slightly. "Jack is indisposed."

"Indisposed?" Mairi said. "What do you mean?" It seemed extraordinary and yet Jack had been distant all day, not just with her but almost as though his mind was elsewhere.

Lucy nibbled her lower lip. Mairi thought she looked cross, and furtive and exasperated all at the same time. "Robert says I should not be angry with him," Lucy said. "But I am. I can't help myself."

Mairi's concern increased. She took her sister's arm and led her away from the crowds milling in the hall and drawing room, finding refuge in the little book room off the library that was Robert's office.

"Now," she said, closing the door, "what is going on?"

Lucy subsided into a chair in a rustle of silk. "You know that Jack refused to stand as godfather to either James or Ewan?" she said. "I tried not to be too hurt because Robert explained that Jack had had a difficult time as a child. He lost both his parents young and then his sister died...." She frowned again. "And I *do* understand that...." Her tone implied that she did not understand it at all. "But I would have thought that someone without their own family would seize the chance to be part of ours. Yet instead Jack pushes us away at every turn."

Mairi was thinking of Jack's words to her at Mac-Leod, his claim that he cared for no one. "Sometimes," she said slowly, thinking of her own experience, "it's too painful to get close. The risk of hurt is too great. Perhaps that is how Jack feels."

Lucy was looking at her blankly. "Well, I don't see why he has to go off and get drunk!"

"Oh!" Mairi said. "That sort of indisposed!"

"Foxed," Lucy confirmed. "And in a foul temper. He threw a jug at poor Shawcross when he went to take him some more brandy. Robert says..." She fidgeted, then looked up and met Mairi's eyes half-shamefacedly. "Oh, I was not supposed to tell anyone this, but you have a right to know. Jack used to have a terrible problem with drink. After his sister died he ran mad for a while. He drank too much and ended up in a fight in which a man was killed. They locked him up in the tollbooth and Lady Methven had to go to buy him out."

Mairi felt chilled. She remembered that Jack had drunk not wine but water at the Inverbeg Inn. She had thought it odd at the time. Now she realized that she had never once seen him take wine let alone brandy.

She sank down into the chair opposite her sister. "When did this happen?" she whispered.

"I'm not sure." Lucy said. "Jack must have been about seventeen or so. He was very young anyway."

Seventeen. The horror of it made Mairi flinch. When she had been seventeen, her father had arranged a match for her with a man old enough to be her grandfather. Even now she could remember the sense of horror and powerlessness she had felt, the way she had rushed headlong from the misery of one intolerable situation only to find herself in another. She had felt very alone and very afraid. Had Jack felt the same, losing almost everyone he cared about? Jack had told her that he had run wild as a youth. She had assumed it was the typical carousing of a privileged young man, too much gambling, too much wine, too many women. She had had no idea.

"I must go to him," she said, starting up.

Lucy looked alarmed. She caught her hand. "I wouldn't. Really, Mairi, I think you should wait until he is sober."

"I've seen plenty of men in various stages of drunkenness," Mairi said. "Don't you remember what Lachlan was like when first he discovered brandy?"

"I don't mean that," Lucy said. "I mean that Jack will hurt you. He won't mean to but he'll do it all the same. This isn't like Lachlan getting drunk on a night out in Edinburgh." She made a helpless gesture. "Drink devastated Jack's life, Mairi. It made him dangerous. Please—"

"I have to try, Luce," Mairi said. She knew her sister was right. Jack would not welcome her interference, but that was not a good enough reason to leave him with nothing but his bitter memories and the brandy bottle for company. "I can't leave him to deal with this on his own," she said.

She stood up, smoothing her skirts, suddenly nervous although she was not quite sure why.

On the stairs she met Shawcross coming down. He confirmed that Jack was in his dressing room. He echoed Lucy's words.

"I wouldn't recommend disturbing him, my lady. Mr. Rutherford has an uncertain temper when he is foxed."

This was confirmed as soon as Mairi opened the dressing room door. It was a small room, cheerful with a fire in the grate and candles burning, but it stank of spirits. Jack was sprawled in an armchair, his neck cloth and jacket discarded, his long legs stretched out in front of him and a three-quarters-empty glass dangling from his hand. He looked dangerous in every way possible.

"I told you I didn't want to be disturbed, damn you," he said, without looking up. "But as you're here you can pour me another glass."

"You've had enough," Mairi said.

Jack's green gaze came up and fixed on her in a glittering, unblinking stare. Mairi felt the intensity of it down to her toes.

"You," he said. His voice was rough and his gaze was as hard and uncaring as though she was a stranger. "What do you want?"

It hurt. It hurt a lot but Mairi gritted her teeth. She knew that he was in pain and was trying to escape it; knew too that he could not and so he was tormented.

"I came to make sure that you were all right," she said.

That glittering gaze did not leave her face. "Well," Jack said, "as you can see I am absolutely fine." He reached for the brandy bottle himself, slopping some liquid into the glass, splashing it on the table. "You may leave me to go to hell on my own," he added, turning away from her.

"No," Mairi said.

She saw his hand check in raising the glass to his lips. He smiled mockingly at her. "No?" he echoed. "I am sorry—do you require more clarification? I said get out—if you please."

"No," Mairi said again. She was shaking. She went down on her knees beside his chair. "I'm sorry," she said. "I'm sorry today was so painful for you."

His eyes narrowed on her with anger and dislike. "I beg your pardon?"

"You're drinking to escape the pain," Mairi said. "I understand. I know what it's like to try to find oblivion. I know that you lost your parents when you were young and your sister too—"

He gave a harsh crack of laughter. "You know nothing."

Mairi bit her lip hard against the smart of his contempt. "So tell me," she said steadily.

Again he stared at her, but this time she was not sure he actually saw her at all. She waited, aware that she was holding her breath.

"I killed my sister," he said. "It was my fault that she died."

JACK RUBBED A hand across his face. His head ached and his eyes felt raw. He felt as though he had lost every last vestige of protection, as though there was nowhere to hide. He was never vulnerable. He hated the sensation, but he had no idea how to escape it.

He looked at the drink in his hand and from there to Mairi's face. She was so beautiful, he thought. It was not a simple matter of the arrangement of features, the color of her eyes or the autumn-red-and-gold of her hair. It was in the candor that made her gaze so clear and honest. It was in the generosity that made her reach out to him when he had been so unforgivably rude to her. There was a quality of brightness and sweetness about her then that drew him irresistibly. He ached for it. He wanted to lose himself in her. He wanted to take her and forget all else.

But the sympathy in her eyes would turn to revulsion when she knew the truth.

"I'm so very sorry," she said. "Tell me what happened."

Jack looked away from her into the heart of the fire. It might be easier to tell her if he did not have to look at her, if he was not obliged to see her disappointment and disgust.

"Our parents were desperately in love with one another," he said. "It was almost as though Averil and I did not exist, except as a proof of their love. When my father died my mother could not bear the grief. She took her own life a few months later. I found her body. She had taken an excess of laudanum one night and simply did not wake the following day."

He heard Mairi's soft gasp of shock. "Jack," she said. She put a hand on his arm, but he shook her off, rejecting the comfort because he knew he did not deserve it.

"I had tried to help her," he said painfully. "I knew she was desperately unhappy, but I had no idea what to do and I knew that whatever I could give her would never be enough. The love my parents had for each other..." He shook his head. Love was a dangerous, destructive force and he wanted nothing of it. He and Averil had been excluded from the enchanted circle of his parents' love, and there had been nothing that he could do about that.

"She left us alone," he said.

"You must have been very young," Mairi said. "Too young to carry such a weight of responsibility."

"I was sixteen when she died," Jack said. "Averil was twelve. We were sent to live with my father's sister and her husband, but they did not really want us. They sent us both away to school."

He saw Mairi flinch. Her face was very pale. "That

seems harsh," she said. "When you had both suffered so great a loss."

Jack shrugged. "We brought no money with us and were a burden on them." He raked his hand through his hair. "Well, I expect you can imagine what happened. I rebelled. After a while the school expelled me, my aunt and uncle washed their hands of me and for a time I ran wild and ungovernable." He looked at the brandy bottle. The taste of the spirit was sour on his tongue, but he wanted more. He ached for it, for oblivion. He was drunk but nowhere near as drunk as he needed to be.

"I drank too much," he said. "I fought and stole. I was no more than seventeen years old…." The misery and bitterness twisted inside him. "And throughout it all I abandoned Averil. I thought she was safe in school and that she would be well cared for. I knew she was better off there than she would have been with me. What could I do for her? I had not even been able to help our mother. I had not been able to make her happy, to stop her from deserting us. I knew I would be no good for Averil, no good at all."

He drained his glass. The bottle clinked against the rim as he topped it up again.

"And then one day I heard that she had died." He took a deep breath. "She had died in a typhoid epidemic that swept the school. It was only then that I discovered that it was a terrible place—cold, dirty, with little food and what there was poorly cooked and rotten." He stopped. "She died alone, lonely and afraid, because no one gave a damn, least of all me."

"Jack," Mairi said. "That isn't true—"

"It is!" The fury and guilt in him was like a live thing, making him want to lash out at her. "I failed my

mother and I failed Averil and that is why, my sweet—"
he spoke mockingly and saw the blood sting her cheeks
"—you should get up now and leave me and never look
back because I will be no good for you either."

He saw Mairi close her eyes. For a second a tear
dampened her lashes, but she rubbed it away angrily.
"I don't want to hear you say such things," she said. Her
gaze was stormy. "You were little more than a child,
Jack. You should not have to bear the responsibility for
this. It was not your fault."

"Are you trying to comfort me?" It was the last thing
he wanted from her. "I am afraid that there is only one
thing I want from you and that is what I took last night
in the gallery."

He heard her catch her breath and saw her eyes open
wide as the cruelty of his words struck home. She recoiled from him, stumbling backward, almost falling
over her skirts with the haste that she stood up.

"I don't understand why you have to be so brutal,"
she said. "Why are you trying to hurt me?"

He was hurting her because he hated himself. He
very nearly hated her too for refusing to walk away
from him. Jack's throat closed. There was a burning
pain in his chest. He would not answer that. He could
not. Why could the damned woman simply not leave
him? She reminded him of his grandmother coming to
the tollbooth, stepping daintily through all the filth and
squalor to save him when he deserved to be abandoned.
Mairi had the same strength and the same indomitable
spirit. She refused to leave him too. She was far, far
too good for him.

She stepped forward, but before she could speak he
turned on her, grabbing her by the shoulders.

"I warn you, Mairi," he said, "that if you stay a moment longer I will take you and use you, just to forget." He cocked his head toward the door. "Now go while you still have the chance."

MAIRI'S HEART WAS pounding. She was afraid of Jack in this mood and yet she was not; beneath the cruelty was a man who was in so much pain that she wanted to help him. If this was the only way to reach him, then so be it.

He did not move. His fierce, angry eyes scanned her face, yet he made no attempt to touch her. She put one hand on the back of his neck and drew his head down to hers, kissing him gently. She could feel the resistance in him. For a moment he did not respond at all and then he gave a despairing groan and his arms went around her. His mouth crushed hers. She opened her lips to him at once and he kissed her with desperation and frantic need. She held nothing back, offering kiss for kiss, clinging to him as the room spun about her and the floor seemed to shift beneath her feet.

He was shaking as he shed his clothes and pulled hers haphazardly from her. They sank down onto the bed, his hands roaming over her body like those of a man starved of touch, starved of love. There was nothing of gentleness in him; his lovemaking was starkly physical. He rolled her beneath him, spread her, plunging into her without tenderness. She held him, smoothing her hands down over his shoulders and back, drawing him close, sensing the tumult of emotion driving him. She whispered endearments as he took her. She knew that her body was nothing more to him in this moment than an escape from pain, but it was enough that she could give him that.

When it was over he rested his cheek against her breast, eyes closed, panting.

"I'm sorry," he said. He sounded wretched. "So very sorry."

She stroked his hair and held him close as he fell asleep. She understood now why Jack was afraid to love anyone and why he did not want the responsibility of a wife and a family. Her heart ached for him and she drew him closer into her arms. She did not know how she could convince him that he had not failed. He had been so young and had lost so much. It was hard to heal such old and deep scars. She was afraid that it might be impossible. And she was even more afraid that he would not want her to try.

JACK WOKE STIFF and aching, with a headache hammering his temples and a vile taste in his mouth. He eased himself out of Mairi's arms, stood up and slid out of the bed. Cold air washed about him; he missed the warmth of the bed but even more the comfort of Mairi's touch.

Pulling on his trousers and shirt, he walked over to the dresser and splashed water over his head and neck, welcoming the cold shock it gave him. He slicked back his wet hair, reaching for a towel. He felt deathly tired and bitterly ashamed. He had not drunk so much in years. It had not helped him escape the brutal memories. Only Mairi had tried to help with that and in return he had been cruel to her and had taken her without consideration for her feelings while she had shown him nothing but sweetness and generosity. The guilt and shame in him deepened. There was no excuse for his behavior. Nothing could justify it.

A tray stood on the dresser with a carafe of fresh

water and a vial of a thick plum-colored liquid. Shaw-cross had left it earlier on one of the many occasions when Jack, with unforgivable rudeness, had told him to bring a fresh bottle of brandy and then get the hell out of there. He drank the tonic down in one gulp. It tasted so vile that for a moment Jack thought that the valet had taken a very sweet revenge and poisoned him. Then the mixture started to work, the pain in his head lessened, the dregs of drink and tiredness started to lift and he tasted the freshness of mint rather than the sourness of alcohol on his tongue. Only the sense of shame remained and Jack suspected there was no cure on earth for that.

In the big tester bed Mairi shifted in her sleep and burrowed more closely beneath the covers, murmuring something unintelligible. Jack walked across and sat down beside her. He felt odd. He wanted to touch her and hold her close. At the same time there was a sick dread underlying his need for her. He could not understand why he had told her about his mother and his sister. He was not given to confession, least of all on the subject of his family. He had never even spoken to Robert about it, nor his grandmother. He did not want to disinter the past, talk about his failure or why he could never trust himself to love again.

Why he had spilled his secrets to Mairi was weak and inexplicable. He was skilled at protecting himself. Over the years he had built defenses he had been sure no one could breach, and yet Mairi had demolished them.

She opened her eyes and he felt a strange sense of shock deep inside and a longing so acute it shook him. He touched her cheek very gently.

"Did I hurt you?" he asked gruffly.

Mairi smiled and his heart clenched again. "No," she said.

"I'm sorry," Jack said.

She gave a tiny negative shake of the head. "There's nothing to apologize for," she said. Then: "Jack, you do know that it was not your fault?"

Jack shook his head. He could hear the words, but he could never believe them. Something was broken, wrenched apart deep inside him.

"I'm sorry," he said again, and saw the light go out of her eyes. They both knew that this time he was not apologizing for his behavior toward her but for the fact that he could not accept her words. He did not want to hear them and least of all did he want to need her the way he had the previous night.

CHAPTER FIFTEEN

MAIRI WAS SO emotionally exhausted that she slept very late, heard nothing of the housemaid when she came in to light the fire and did not even stir when Jessie brought the breakfast tray. Eventually she woke when Lucy knocked at the door and came into the room, pulling back the curtains and letting in the sunshine.

"I am sorry to disturb you," Lucy said, sitting down on the edge of the bed, "but I was worried."

"About Jack?" Mairi said. She sat up, rubbing her eyes. "He is not drunk anymore and I think he is back in his right mind."

"Well, I'm sure we will all be glad to hear that," Lucy said crisply. "But actually I meant I was worried about you." She took Mairi's hand in hers. "Did he hurt you?" she asked, her blue eyes suddenly serious.

Mairi startled herself by bursting into tears. She felt Lucy's fingers tighten on hers and then her sister was hugging her close and Mairi was surprised to discover that it felt like one of the nicest things in the world.

"I take it that he did," Lucy said. Her voice was muffled, but she still sounded ferocious. "Blackguard. I'll kill him. I don't care if he is Robert's cousin—"

"Please," Mairi said, releasing her. "There is no need for family warfare. It's fine. Really it is." She was not sure that it was, but she did not want to examine her heart too closely this morning. It felt very sore.

Lucy looked dubious. "You do know," she said seriously, "that the best sex in the whole world is not worth it if it comes accompanied by so much grief? It might seem as though it is, but it isn't."

Mairi giggled despite herself. "So now you are the expert," she said. "Yes, I do know that."

"Did Jack tell you what happened to his mother and his sister?" Lucy asked.

"Yes," Mairi said again. "He told me."

Lucy's expression had brightened. "Oh. Well, that *is* good because he has never talked about it before. Not even with Robert."

"I'm not sure that it will do much good," Mairi said honestly. "Jack was regretting it as soon as he had told me."

Lucy was watching her sister's face with her shrewd blue gaze. "A few days ago I was worrying that your engagement to Jack was a pretense," she said slowly. "Now I am worrying more that you will fall in love with him."

That was something else that Mairi was not prepared to think about this morning. "Don't worry," she said. "Even if I lose a lover I will have found a sister."

Lucy squeezed her hands again and stood up. "That's a lovely thing to say," she said, misty-eyed. She smiled, suddenly mischievous. "I am afraid that you have found a sister-in-law at Methven too, whether you wish it or not. I am relying on you to take Dulcibella on at the archery butts this morning." Pausing in the doorway, she added, "Oh, and if you could manage to hit her rather than the target, I think we would all be grateful."

JACK SAT BESIDE the bowling green watching Mairi roundly trounce her sister-in-law Dulcibella in the game. Normally he disliked being inactive, but he took a curious pleasure in watching Mairi. She rolled her bowls towards the jack with such strength, elegance and lethal accuracy. Dulcibella, in contrast, had no skill whatsoever and a weak wrist, and after losing two games to Mairi's ruthless proficiency, she was sulking.

Jack had told himself that he was dancing attendance on Mairi in order to ensure her physical safety, but he knew full well he lied. Here within Methven's walls she was as safe as anywhere and he had no need to follow her around like a lapdog. It only served to disturb him that he was doing it because he wanted to; he enjoyed watching her, he enjoyed talking to her and he adored making love to her. After the night when he had appalled himself by getting disgracefully drunk, he had tried to stay away from her in order to demonstrate if only to himself that she did not have any power over him. He had failed shamefully. In the past week he had gone to her room each night and made love to her with a wrenching need that would have disturbed him had he not resolutely refused to think about it. He had thought he would soon be sated, that boredom would set in as it had done with every woman in his life before, and yet it did not matter how many times he had her. He felt a renewed need each night—and day—and just about every moment in between.

In a vague attempt at discretion he made sure never to visit Mairi's room before the house was quiet for the night and never to be found by the maid in her bed in the morning. With his past affairs this had never presented any sort of problem. With Mairi, though, this had been becoming increasingly difficult, much to his chagrin. He actually wanted to stay with her, to sleep with her, and the fact that he could not felt frustrating. Even more exasperating was the fact that during the day they were obliged to preserve a perfect facade of a respectable betrothal. This was proving fatal for Jack's self-control as it just seemed to make the entire situation all the more seductive and made him want Mairi all the more. He realized with a sense of disbelief that he had not even looked at another woman since he had first slept with Mairi.

The arrival of tea provided a welcome distraction. The servants set it up under a huge tented pavilion to the left of the green, shaded by the tall pines. Slowly the members of the house party started to arrive; Lucy, with her sister Christina and various other members of her family came through the terrace doors from the house; Robert and Lachlan came from the stables, Lady Methven from the rose gardens. There was also a new arrival, a tall, fair, solid-looking gentleman with a serious air and a document case tucked beneath his arm. He paused on the edge of the bowling green to greet Mairi and Jack saw him kiss her hand. Mairi was smiling. Clearly they were well known to each other. Jack immediately got to his feet and went down to join them. Mairi's laugh rang out. Jack observed that the visitor was still holding her hand and they were smiling and chatting together like old friends.

"Jack." Mairi turned to him as he reached her side. Her blue eyes were bright with laughter. "May I introduce Mr. Cambridge, who manages Lord MacLeod's affairs and is an old friend of mine. Jeremy, my fiancé, Mr. Rutherford."

Jack bowed. "Cambridge." He had enough sense not to show any animosity toward the other man, although judging by Cambridge's expression the antipathy was entirely mutual.

"Rutherford." Cambridge's gray eyes were chilly. "Congratulations on your betrothal, my lady," he added to Mairi. Then, with a glance in Jack's direction, "Lord MacLeod has told me all about it."

That, Jack knew, was designed to make it explicitly clear that Cambridge was aware that the engagement was both temporary and false. He felt a flash of anger and drew closer to Mairi's side.

"Thank you," he said coolly. "I am the most fortunate of men."

Cambridge's gaze cooled still further. "Why, so I think," he said.

Mairi either had not picked up on the hostility between them or was determined to ignore it, for she drew Jeremy Cambridge toward the tea table. "Jeremy," she said, "come and sit by me and tell me all the news from Strome."

"Have you come from Strome now on business, Cambridge?" Jack asked. His implication was that if so, Cambridge should get on with whatever business that was and then leave. He knew it was discourteous of him and he did not care.

"I have," Cambridge said, without even according Jack a "sir." "I shall discuss it with Lady Mairi later."

That was pointed. Jack saw Mairi glance at Cambridge's face and frown slightly. "Mr. Rutherford will join us for that," she said, and Jack felt a flare of pleasure that startled him. He caught Mairi's hand and she gave him a little shy smile that made the sensation in his chest tighten.

The others were taking their seats around the big table. Dulcibella was already making a fuss, insisting that Lachlan set a chair for her in exactly the right place, sheltered from the breeze and where the sun would not be in her eyes. Dulcibella could have been very pretty, Jack thought, with her rich brown hair and bright brown eyes, but her mouth turned down at the corners as though she were perpetually disappointed with her life. He glanced from her face to Mairi's. Mairi too did not give the impression of warmth at first glance because her beauty was so classically perfect that it looked cold, like a statue. Remembering how she warmed under his hands, though, Jack felt both his collar and his breeches grow tight.

As though drawn by his gaze, she looked up and their eyes met. She smiled and Jack felt a tug of emotion he could not identify.

"You smell of the stables," Dulcibella was saying disagreeably, wrinkling her nose up at her husband. "Pray sit downwind from me!"

"You are looking a little flushed yourself, my love," Lachlan responded through gritted teeth. "Was the game more than usually exerting?"

"Your sister approached it as she does all things," Dulcibella snapped, "with a great deal of energy."

"I always say that if you are going to play, play to win," Jack said, his lips twitching.

Dulcibella shot him a limpid look. Jack could tell that she wanted to dislike him but her vanity was too great to allow it. She could not bear not to be admired. She patted the seat beside her.

"Do come and sit by me, Mr. Rutherford, and tell me which of Lady Mairi's many talents first drew you to her," she cooed. "Was it her proficiency with watercolors or her skill on the harp? But no..." She paused. "That cannot be it, for she has so little merit with either. Do tell."

Jack glanced at Mairi and caught the flash of amusement in her eyes. He could tell she was preparing some devastating set-down for Dulcibella—assuming he did not administer one first. Lucy was looking pink and uncomfortable at such open discourtesy over her tea table. Lady Methven was looking at Dulcibella as though she were some unpleasant form of insect she had found lurking in her cake.

"Perhaps it was Lady Mairi's charm and exquisite manners that Jack admired," Lady Methven said sharply. "Good manners are in all too short supply."

Dulcibella flushed a dull brick-red and fell silent for one long and blessed moment.

Seeing that Jeremy Cambridge was holding a seat for Mairi, Jack sat down beside Dulcibella and passed her the cup of tea that Lucy proffered. Cambridge, he thought, as he watched the man spread a variety of cakes and sandwiches before Mairi, was entirely too attentive to his fiancée. He knew very little of the man and he had no urge to learn more. He was aware of disliking Cambridge intensely while simultaneously knowing nothing about him, a lack of logic that only made him more annoyed. He watched Cambridge talking to Mairi and discerned a strangely possessive attitude in the man. It was not that he appeared to admire her, more that he seemed to think she was in some way his property. It was odd but perhaps it was because Mairi was a MacLeod by marriage and Cambridge was the Mac-Leods' man of business. Or perhaps, Jack was obliged to admit, it was simply that his judgment seemed to be shot to pieces where Mairi was concerned.

Rather than torture himself by watching Mairi smiling at Cambridge, he turned to her elder sister, who was on his other side. Lady Christina MacMorlan was the eldest of the Duke of Forres's daughters, a dull brown mouse of a woman whose life had been dedicated to keeping house for their father and helping to raise the younger children after the death of their mother. She did not resemble Lucy, who was tiny and fiery, or Mairi, who was cool and elegant, but seemed insipid, as though she deliberately chose to melt into the background.

"Do you enjoy visiting the Highlands, Lady Christina?" Jack asked.

Christina jumped as though someone had set a fire under her seat. She blushed. "Oh! I—"

"The country is so dull," Dulcibella interrupted. "Nothing but ugly mountains and bad roads. I cannot bear it."

"You will have to ask Lachlan to take you home as soon as possible, then," Lucy said. "We cannot have you suffering."

"I wouldn't dream of venturing out through the castle gates," Dulcibella shuddered. "Not with dangerous wild men on the warpath! I shall be staying here until my cousin Cardross is recaptured."

Jack saw Robert and Lucy exchange a look. Robert rolled his eyes.

"How beautiful the rose gardens are looking at the moment," Mairi said to Lady Methven. "Mr. Rutherford tells me you are a keen gardener. You would have had much to talk about with my late husband. He was a noted botanist."

A small breeze stirred the pines and set the tented pavilion flapping. Jack was aware of a feeling of extreme bad temper. The last thing he wanted was to sit here and listen to Mairi sing the praises of the sainted Archie MacLeod, damn him. He resisted the urge to kick something. Their engagement must seem as shallow as a puddle compared to the complexity of Mairi's feelings for MacLeod. And why that should bother him was anyone's guess.

He drank his tea—which he hated as a tasteless drink—and ate a piece of the Dundee cake, which was very fine. Mairi and Cambridge were now deep in conversation, his fair and her auburn head bent close together. Jack gritted his teeth.

He stood up abruptly. "Robert," he said, "do you wish to mount another patrol this afternoon? I thought I would go out riding before dinner."

This announcement was met with exclamations of shock by most of the ladies.

"Oh, Mr Rutherford," Dulcibella quavered, "do not even think of it! You might be shot, maimed, killed!"

"I'll take my chances," Jack said.

"You wouldn't catch me doing that," Lachlan muttered.

"I imagine not," Jack said.

"There is a detachment of dragoons at Kinlochewe now," Robert said. "By tomorrow I am confident that Cardross will be back behind bars."

"I hope so." Dulcibella pushed her plate away. "So very distressing to have such a renegade in the family!"

Jack caught sight of Jeremy Cambridge. He was following the conversation, eyes intently narrowed. When he caught Jack's gaze he said self-importantly, "I was telling Lady Mairi that Lord MacLeod was greatly concerned to hear of the attack on her carriage. He pledges all possible support in the capture of the Earl of Cardross."

"Thank you," Robert said.

"I'm the one that Wilfred is hunting," Dulcibella said pettishly, as though it were better to have the dubious honor of being Cardross's quarry than to be overlooked. "I am sure he only attacked Mairi's coach because he thought it was me!"

No one contradicted her. Jack suspected that everyone was wishing that Dulcibella *had* been in the coach and that Wilfred Cardross had put period to her life.

"Mairi," he said, "if you have finished your tea I should be glad of your company on the way to the stables."

Cambridge's open face fell with clear disappointment. Mairi smiled and got to her feet. "Of course, Jack." She turned to the other man. "Perhaps we could talk later when Jack has returned?"

"There's no hurry," Robert said lazily. "Why don't you stay for dinner, Cambridge? You can put up here for the night and hold your meeting in the morning." He met Jack's glare with a bland lift of his brows.

"Why do you allow Cambridge to pay you so much attention?" Jack asked as he and Mairi strolled away across the lawns. "It will only give rise to further conjecture that you are a flirt."

Mairi raised her brows. "Are we having another lovers' tiff?" she inquired sweetly. "You are being ridiculous, Jack. Why do you not like him?"

Jack raised a brow at her and saw the pink color touch her cheekbones. "I would have thought that was obvious," he drawled. "He covets what is mine."

Mairi made an exasperated tutting sound. "In the first instance, he does not. In the second, I am not a piece of property. And in the third, Jeremy is an old friend, nothing more. I value his business advice and Lord MacLeod trusts him. He is very pleasant."

"Damned with faint praise," Jack said, noting that his temper was improving. "You have never called me pleasant."

"That's because you are not," Mairi said tartly. "You are not pleasant at all."

Jack caught her and pulled her behind a huge stone-carved garden urn. "But you like me," he said. She felt wonderful in his arms, warm and soft and so tempting.

"I'm not sure that I do," Mairi said but he was intrigued to see that she was not struggling.

"Then if you don't like me," Jack continued, brushing her earlobe with his lips, "you must like how I make you feel." He kissed the tiny hollow beneath her ear and felt her shiver.

"I will come to your room tonight," he whispered.

Her lips curved deliciously. "See that you do," she whispered back.

A bevy of servants appeared from the direction of the castle with more tea and cake piled up on trays. Mairi drew discreetly away from him and Jack sighed and released her. "I wish you could come riding with me," he said abruptly.

Her gaze softened. "I would like that too," she said. "I would like to escape. I feel so penned in here."

She stood on tiptoe to press a kiss on his cheek. It

was the most chaste and sweetest salutation and yet Jack felt it through his entire body. He watched her as she walked back to the pavilion. He wanted to take her away from the oppressive atmosphere of the house party, the stuffiness of forever being under everyone's gaze. He wanted to be alone with her riding out on the high tops with nothing but the cold wind for company.

Most of all he wanted to take her on a wild ride far away from the memories of Archie MacLeod. But he could not do that. He could not replace Archie and he was not even sure what it was that he wanted from her anymore.

MAIRI MANAGED A couple of blissful hours of peace tucked away in the library reading before Jeremy Cambridge found her. She had known that he would not wait until the morning. He would not want to discuss whatever business there was with Jack. When she heard his heavy tread approaching, she was tempted to jump up and hide behind the bookcase, but she knew that would be childish. He had annoyed her over tea with his pomposity and self-importance and she would have had to be insensate not to feel the antagonism between him and Jack. They were like two territorial dogs circling each other. She wondered why men had to be so downright foolish.

Jeremy heaved himself into the chair opposite, sat forward with his hands dangling between his thighs and fixed her with a gaze that was more in sorrow than in anger. Before he had even started to speak she felt an acute sense of irritation, which she knew was hardly kind. She should try to give him a fair hearing.

"I am so very sorry, Lady Mairi," Jeremy said. He

shook his head. "If only Lord MacLeod had apprised me of his plans beforehand, this need never have happened. There was no need for you to do anything so foolish as to betroth yourself to a dangerous rake who can only damage your reputation still further."

"I assume you are referring to Mr. Rutherford," Mairi said, "since he is the only fiancé I have." She closed her book with a snap. "Was that what you came all the way from Strome to tell me, Jeremy?" she said a little tartly.

"I came to deliver this letter from Lord MacLeod," Jeremy said, unfastening the buckles of his document case, "and to see how you are after the dreadful shock of the attack by Wilfred Cardross. I promised His Lordship that I would report back on your state of health." He took the letter from the case but did not hand it to her immediately, holding it instead in his hand as though it were made of precious gold.

"That is very thoughtful of Lord MacLeod," Mairi said, resisting the urge to snatch the letter from him. "Please tell him that I am very well."

She held out her hand. Jeremy ignored the gesture, instead placing the letter neatly on the table between them. He resumed his scrutiny of her, his gaze so sorrowful it made her want to slap him.

"I told you that you should return to Edinburgh to scotch the rumors about your misconduct," he said.

Mairi bristled. "*Misconduct* is a very judgmental word," she said frostily. "And as I recall you said no such thing. You were so evasive that I had no notion of the nature of the gossip."

A shade of color touched Jeremy's cheek. "It was not my place to speak of such tawdry matters," he said.

"Fortunate for me that Mr. Rutherford was not as fastidious as you, Jeremy," Mairi said. She could feel anger bubbling up inside her again and made a monumental effort to smother it. "He was very willing to offer me his help."

"I would have offered you mine when you returned to Edinburgh and discovered the situation," Jeremy said. "I was willing to overlook your moral failings. I was even prepared to offer you *my* protection, which I flatter myself would have been a great deal more respectable than that of Jack Rutherford." By now he was bright red and spluttering and Mairi had stopped feeling annoyed and could only feel sorry that he valued himself so highly and clearly thought so little of her. She felt bereft too; she had thought that she and Jeremy had had a genuine friendship. She had always known he was a little stuffy and that like so many men he disapproved of women who were different and independent, but it was disappointing to see his opinions with such unflattering clarity.

"I am honored by your regard, Jeremy," she said, "and can only be sorry that I am promised to Mr. Rutherford when you could have offered me so much more."

"You mock me," Jeremy said sharply, "but you will regret it, Lady Mairi. The whole of Edinburgh will be talking about your betrothal—"

"They are," Mairi said, "and in tones of most flattering excitement." She reached out a hand for the letter from Lady Kenton that had arrived that morning. She had been using it as a bookmark.

"Lady Kenton says that society is quite besotted with the news," she said. She read aloud: "'When a rake such as Mr. Rutherford chooses to wed, it gives hope to all the other ladies that they may catch an equally exciting husband."' She folded the letter away again and stowed it back in the book. "So you see," she said, "I am a beacon of hope to all my sex."

Jeremy gave a disapproving snort and hauled himself out of the chair. "It isn't too late to reconsider," he said, looking down at her. "Come back to Edinburgh with me. You know you dislike being here. You hate children and you do not enjoy the company of your family."

Mairi was incensed by this misrepresentation of her feelings. "I do not *hate* children," she said with biting anger. "I am merely unaccustomed to them, as I was not fortunate enough to have any of my own. As for my family—" She felt a fierce and unexpected pang of affection. "I love them very much and I do not appreciate your criticism of them, particularly when Lucy and Robert are being generous enough to offer you their hospitality!"

She felt so out of sorts when Jeremy had gone out that she decided that nothing but some fresh air would make her feel better. Lachlan, Dulcibella and some of the other guests had gone down to the lake for a picnic; as she walked down the chestnut avenue she could hear voices and laughter. It made a change for Dulcibella to be in a good mood. Mairi did not fancy company, however. For a little while she sat in the gardens, feeling the slight breeze stirring her hair and the sun on her face.

It was odd that Jeremy's words had upset her so much. The news he had brought from MacLeod seemed slight and it felt as though he had come all this way to rebuke her for entering into an engagement with Jack. She was furious to be scolded and felt strangely protective of Jack and indignant about Jeremy's criticism. She was not sure she could be civil to him at dinner tonight.

The sun was becoming too hot and she had forgotten her parasol. She walked through the walled garden where the scent of the roses hung heavy on the still air, and through an archway into the wild garden. Here she remembered there was an ancient swing strung in the dappled shade, beside an overgrown lily pond. Lucy and Robert's children were too young to play on it yet. It must have been there when Robert and his elder brother had spent their childhood at Methven. Jack too.

The seat of the swing was a rough piece of wood, mossy but dry. Mairi sat down on it, and the rope creaked a little beneath her weight. She rocked backward and forward gently, remembering the rhythm of it from her childhood, remembering the thrill of hurtling through the air and feeling so wild and free and out of control. She wondered when she had lost that sense of lightness. Archie had left his fortune to her out of guilt and it had enabled her to do so many things, but sometimes it felt more of a burden than a gift. She remembered the wicked thrill that had coursed through her when Jack had asked her to ride with him to Methven. She loved riding and she had wanted to take a risk and go with him, but sense and self-control had won out instead. It seemed she had built walls around herself without even realizing it.

She shivered a little in the heavy air. It had been a while since she had felt that terrible loneliness and oppression of spirits that stalked her now. The sun had gone in now and the birds were quiet. A distant rumble of thunder echoed off the mountains. Through the lattice of the branches above her head she could see that the sky was gray with clouds piling one on top of the other. The storm had come sooner than she had expected.

She slowed the swing and it came to a stop with a creak that now sounded loud in the silence. Already the first fat drops of rain were pattering on the leaves over her head. She was going to have to run for the house or be soaked. The wooded shrubbery was now plunged into a gloom so deep that she tripped over a root and almost fell. The air felt sultry beneath the trees.

There was a sharp rustle of leaves away to her right and, spinning around, she thought she saw the figure of a man before he disappeared in the stygian darkness. She quickened her pace and heard again that betraying flutter of leaves and the patter of footsteps on old, dead leaves. Whoever was following her was coming closer.

She felt the first stirrings of panic. She disliked thunderstorms at the best of times, and now she could feel her fears playing on her mind and mingling with her stifling sense of isolation— even though she was a bare few hundred yards from the house. She told herself that she was being foolish and made for a gap in the trees where the wood opened out onto the lawn. The leaves beneath her feet were slippery with rain now and the thunder rumbled closer. She could feel her gown sticking to her with an unpleasant combination of sweat and rainwater and always over her shoulder she had the sense of being watched. As the trees thinned, a figure stepped out onto the path directly in front of her so suddenly that she screamed. A moment later she realized that it was Jack, on his way back from the stables. She felt enormously relieved that his was the figure she must have seen through the shrubbery. She also felt a complete fool. Jack caught her arm, steadying her, a heavy frown on his brow.

"Mairi? What in God's name are you doing here? Has something happened—"

"No," Mairi said. Her teeth were chattering. Another long tumbrel of thunder rumbled closer. "I was on the swing in the wild garden. I didn't realize the storm was so close."

As they reached the edge of the lawn, there was a fierce fork of lightning and the heavens opened. Rain poured down relentlessly, hitting the gravel of the path and bouncing back. Within seconds Mairi's shoes were soaked and the rain was running in rivulets down her neck.

"This way." Jack grabbed her arm, half pulling, half carrying her toward the little summerhouse in the corner of the walled garden. She jumped violently as the thunder crashed directly overhead and Jack had to drag her through the doorway into the room beyond.

He led her over to the cushioned bench that ran around the walls and drew her down onto the seat. The air in the little summerhouse felt warm and dry and the beating of the rain on the roof was soothing.

"We'll be perfectly safe here," he said. His gaze appraised her thoughtfully with a hint of amusement in the depths. "I'm afraid you look very bedraggled. Elegant Lady Mairi has vanished."

"It doesn't signify," Mairi said. She was shivering, although she was not cold. Another vivid flash of lightning illuminated the summerhouse interior, followed by a crack of thunder that sounded as though it were splitting the mountains in two.

"I had no idea you were so frightened at storms,"

Jack said. The amusement had gone from his eyes now and he looked concerned.

"It's a stupid thing to be afraid of," Mairi said crossly.

Jack laughed. "We all have our weaknesses," he said. "It's actually a relief to discover that you possess some. Most of the time you seem frighteningly indomitable." He put his arm about her and drew her close and Mairi allowed her head to rest against his shoulder. She felt warm and safe.

They sat there quietly while the rain beat on the roof and the thunder rolled overhead and away toward the sea. Gradually the sky lightened and the rain eased and the birds began to sing again.

Mairi got slowly to her feet. She felt unpleasantly damp with her muslin gown clinging to her and her hair in rat's tails sticking to her neck, but she also felt happy and cherished.

"Thank you," she said, smiling.

Jack did not smile in return. He looked at her for a moment and it felt as though he had steel shutters behind his eyes. She felt the chill, felt the distance open up between them.

"It's over now," he said. He walked across to the door and flung it open. "You had better get back to the house and into some dry clothes before you take a chill."

His broad back was turned to her, his manner so similar to the way he had turned her out of his room at the Kinlochewe Inn that Mairi almost flinched. Once again he was locking her out. She got to her feet and without a word slipped past him out of the door and walked away across the lawn toward the house.

CHAPTER SIXTEEN

THE STORM HAD gone by the evening, leaving the sky a faded blue. The roads were awash, though, and would probably be impassable the following day, a piece of news Jack received with bad humor since it meant that Jeremy Cambridge would in all likelihood be obliged to stay a further night at Methven. His mood improved slightly at dinner when he saw Mairi covertly rearranging the place cards so that Jeremy was seated as far away from her as possible. He wondered if they had quarreled. She had not mentioned it to him. In fact, she had spoken to him very little since that afternoon in the summerhouse.

Remembering their encounter, he found that he had lost his appetite. He put his knife and fork down slowly. The salmon was delicious and the cook would be rightly offended to see it returned almost untouched. Truth was, he knew he had behaved like a cad again that afternoon. He had not noticed the slow degrees by which he and Mairi had slipped toward a closeness that was more emotional than physical and then suddenly he had been brought up hard against it that afternoon when he had comforted her during the storm. He had recoiled from the intimacy of it. He had felt something akin to panic, and that was not an emotion he welcomed.

He glanced down the table toward Mairi. She was

seated next to Robert and they were talking animatedly. She looked the same as she ever did, poised and elegant. Yet the hairs on the back of Jack's neck prickled as though there was something wrong.

Mairi looked up and for a brief second her eyes met his and he saw beneath the gaiety something so dark and lost that he felt a pang of pure shock. It was powerful enough to have him half rise from his seat before she blinked and her gaze moved on and she was talking easily to Lady Methven about growing cabbages, of all things. Jack subsided into his seat, feeling disturbed in some way he could not quite explain, as though something had happened but he had missed its significance. The footmen cleared the covers. The meat was brought in, then the desserts. The conversation ground along; he talked about Canada with Christina MacMorlan, who proved a surprisingly astute conversationalist, and about the Edinburgh shops with Dulcibella, who did not.

It was later, much later, when the gentlemen had taken their brandy and rejoined the ladies for tea that Jack realized that Mairi was missing. Lucy, when applied to for her whereabouts, was anxious.

"I think Mairi has retired for the night," she said. "She was not feeling well."

Jack hesitated. This was one of those moments when his instincts were telling him very firmly to do anything other than get involved. Which did not explain why he found himself climbing the main staircase and knocking on the door of Mairi's bedchamber. Jessie was there laying out Mairi's nightgown, a very pretty concoction of ribbons and transparent lace, as Jack was quick to notice. "Her Ladyship went out for a breath of fresh air, sir," she said, in answer to Jack's inquiry. "I think she meant to take a walk on the battlements."

That, Jack thought, should have been quite sufficient to lay his fears to rest. There was no reason why he needed to pursue Mairi to make sure that she was safe. His very solicitude annoyed him. He went into his own room and picked up a book, but after two pages he threw it aside with a smothered curse. Reaching for his jacket again, he let himself out into the corridor and took the stone staircase in the north tower that led up to the battlements.

It was cool outside with a freshness to the air that had been missing earlier. A tiny white sickle moon was rising over the mountains. It looked ridiculously romantic. He saw Mairi at once because the pale yellow of her gown reflected the faint starlight. She was standing halfway along the battlements, her palms resting on the stone balustrade, looking out over the garden. As Jack drew closer to her he saw that her shoulders were slumped and her head bowed.

He stopped and she turned her head very slightly and he saw the sheen of tears on her cheek.

She was crying.

Hell.

Jack felt cold. His first instinct was that he could not touch her, could not offer her comfort. The last woman who had cried in his arms had been his mother and he had failed her completely. He could still hear those fractured sobs. His soul shrank from them.

Mairi had seen him. She scrubbed the tears from her cheeks in a quick, furtive gesture that had his heart lurching with recognition. He remembered that gesture from his childhood, the misery that did not want to be seen. She did not turn toward him. Instead she turned away. It was clear she did not want to speak to him.

Walk away.

And yet he lingered. He could not explain why. A moment later he realized he was walking toward her rather than away from her.

"Mairi?" he said. "Are you ill? Can I fetch your maid for you?" He wondered what the hell he was doing, getting involved. His reluctance had in all probability shown in his voice. He suspected he sounded unenthusiastic at best, churlish at worst.

Walk away, Jack. Don't get involved.

It was one of the rules he lived by.

He took her hand. She was icy cold. He felt a flicker of alarm.

"No, thank you." She scrubbed at her cheeks again. He could feel her shaking, from cold or something else. "I am perfectly fine."

"Don't be ridiculous," Jack said. "You are not fine."

She looked directly at him then, and the blank desolation in her eyes was shocking, stronger, fiercer than the flash of despair he had seen at dinner. Jack understood then. He had seen an expression like that before in the eyes of men who had lost everything, family, home, livelihood. He had seen it in his mother's eyes after his father had died. He had felt it himself when he had been at his lowest. He felt shocked as he realized he must have completely underestimated the sense of bereavement Mairi still felt. In that moment he actually wished Archie MacLeod alive again, if it spared Mairi this misery.

He had not realized that he had moved, but the next moment he had taken her in his arms. She made a little sound of surprise and protest and stiffened. He smiled then. They were such a pair, he so reluctant to give comfort, she so reluctant to take it. They could make love with all the intimacy in the world, but when it came to simple emotion they were both so wary.

After a moment, though, she drew him closer, her fingers clutching the material of his jacket. She cried silently, but harder now and Jack held her awkwardly because he had no idea how to do this and he felt terrified, although that was an emotion he was trying extremely hard to avoid acknowledging. He pressed his handkerchief into her palm and she sniffed and rubbed her eyes and after a few moments the crying stopped.

She offered him his handkerchief back again, a little dubiously. It drooped between her fingers and he smiled.

"Please keep it," he said.

"Thank you," she said. Her voice was husky. "I'm sorry."

"Come inside," Jack said. He had an arm about her now and was leading her to the tower door. On the staircase it was bright with torchlight flaring from the sconces. Mairi shrank back from the light, but he kept his arm tight about her and led her down the steps.

"I don't want anyone to see me," she said.

"They won't," Jack said. He took her along the corridor to the little sitting room that linked their two bedchambers. His valet was there, banking up the fire, tidying the room with the desultory air of a man who was waiting for orders. Jack jerked his head toward the door and the man vanished discreetly. He pulled a chair forward for Mairi, set it before the fire and pushed her into it gently. She was racked with shivers; although the night had not been cold, she had had no cloak and the thin gown gave little warmth.

There was a decanter on the sideboard with wine and two glasses. Jack poured one and took it over to her. She looked up and he felt another pang of physical shock at the blankness in her eyes. It was as though she had withdrawn herself completely.

He sat down opposite her. She turned her glass round and around in her hand and did not drink it. Nor would she look at him.

"I know you want to be alone and are wishing me in Hades," Jack said, "but I am not leaving you on your own."

For a moment it seemed she was not even going to acknowledge his words, but then she focused on him and the relief caught him like a blow in the chest. She was really seeing him this time. She had come back.

"How do you know what I am thinking?" she said.

There was a silence. The clock ticked loudly.

"Perhaps," Jack said, "I have been where you are now."

Her eyes opened wide. "When your mother and your sister died," she said slowly. "Of course."

He had been down as far—further—as she was now, in the dregs of his life, in the gutter, in jail.

"And with the drink," Jack said. "I was lost in it, sunk in misery. So yes, I do understand."

Mairi nodded. She put out her hand and caught his. Jack did not pull away. Her touch was comforting. So was the fact that she said nothing but he knew she understood.

He turned the subject back to her. "That night in Edinburgh," he said.

Her lashes fell, veiling the expression in her eyes, but a small smile touched her lips. "How you do go on about that night."

"At least I understand your reasons now," Jack said. "You wanted someone. Anyone who could help you to stave off this darkness."

Her gaze came up and met his. "But it was not anyone I found," she said softly. "It was you."

"We are not so different, you and I," Jack said. "We both sought to forget."

Their gazes held and he felt again that tightness in his chest. After a moment Mairi looked away, breaking the contact. "The doctors call it a depression of spirits," she said. "They recommended opium." She shuddered.

"Does Michael Innes know?" Jack asked.

Alarm flared in her eyes. "No! Can you imagine? He would try to have me committed to an asylum if he knew."

"Is this what you are trying to hide from him?" Jack asked.

For a moment she stared at him, and then her shoulders slumped. "Among other things. If Innes knew he would certainly exploit it to the full. He would claim that I was a hysterical woman, unfit to run the MacLeod estates. The courts would probably be sympathetic to him." She swallowed hard. "They would unite Archie's estates with the main MacLeod inheritance, and when Lord MacLeod died Innes would sell them off with no care for the people working the land. He would destroy their livelihoods for profit and he would close down all the charitable trusts that Archie established so that he could take that money too."

"You are trying to protect everyone," Jack said. He

could see now the weight of the burden she carried and it stunned him. She had been incredibly strong but it was no wonder that sometimes the sheer pressure of it was too much for her to bear on her own. "You are very brave," he said softly.

She blushed. It was endearing. "It's my duty," she said simply. She shifted. "But that is not the secret that Lord MacLeod was hiding."

Jack took a breath. Now that the moment had come, he was not sure he actually wanted to know. Some superstitious fear breathed gooseflesh along his skin. Secrets bred emotional intimacy, and emotional intimacy was something he had rejected from the age of seventeen.

Don't get involved, Jack. Don't get close.

He looked into Mairi's eyes and knew it was too late. He was already involved.

"Archie isn't dead," Mairi said. "He is still alive."

"CHRIST ALMIGHTY." MAIRI saw the rather comical look of disbelief in Jack's eyes fade, to be replaced by a welter of anger, disbelief and disgust. He stood up; backed away from her.

Well, maybe she could have broken the news to him more carefully, but it had been one hell of a night. Sometimes this secret felt just too huge to carry alone but there was no one she could trust, no one she could tell. Except that she had done now. She had trusted Jack Rutherford, of all people.

"Dear God," he said, and his tone jerked her out of her thoughts, "you are still married. All those times you were with me—"

"No!" Of course he would think that. It was the natural assumption. "Jack, please." She put out a hand to him. "The marriage was void. I told you the truth. I've never been unfaithful to my vows even when..." Her voice faltered. She had never been false to Archie even in the deepest despair of knowing that he could not love her as a man loved a woman.

Jack walked across to the chest of drawers, poured himself a glass of water and swallowed it straight down like medicine. "You'd better tell me everything." His tone was curt.

"Yes." She looked at the glass in her own hand as though she had only just realized that it was there. She did not want the taste of alcohol tonight. She felt a little sick.

"Where to start?" She frowned, her thoughts a jumble.

"Try the beginning," Jack said. He threw himself down in the chair again and fixed her with an unnerving stare. He waited in a silence that felt intimidating.

"I was seventeen when Archie and I wed," Mairi said. "Papa had wanted me to marry the Duke of Anwoth."

Jack's frown deepened. "That lecher?" He sounded incredulous. "He must have been seventy if he was a day!"

"He was sixty-five," Mairi said evenly. "The first time we met he tried to force himself on me." She swallowed convulsively. "Papa... He was not cruel, but he did not want to be gainsaid. I think that after Mama died some spark of humanity died in him also. Anyway, he was not interested in my objections to the match and so..." She made a slight gesture. "I did the only thing I could think to do. I asked Archie to wed me."

"You proposed to him?" Jack said. There was the faintest hint of a smile in his eyes as he watched her. It warmed her a little.

"I did." She raised her chin.

"You did not wait for someone else to rescue you." Jack stirred in his chair. "It is a habit of yours, isn't it, to take your fate into your own hands?"

Mairi blushed. "I couldn't afford to wait around for a hero to save me," she said dryly. "There was no time."

"So you asked your childhood sweetheart to marry you," Jack said.

"My childhood friend," Mairi corrected. "Archie and I had never been sweethearts, but we were friends. He was gentle, very kind. But he was also weak. I think I knew it, even though I was young." She hesitated. She was not sure that Jack would understand Archie's weakness. Jack was one of the strongest men she knew.

Jack was waiting but with a shade less angry impatience now. Mairi felt the tightly wound tension inside her ease a notch.

"So we wed," she said flatly. "It was a disaster right from the start." She dropped her gaze. "We tried to make love but it was painful and embarrassing and although we did consummate our marriage…" She broke off. No need to tell Jack how utterly ignominious it had been, how she had felt ugly and unwanted as well as completely baffled at how dreadful the physical act of lovemaking could be. "After a week I think we realized that if we were to preserve even a friendship we had to stop trying or there would soon be nothing between us but bitterness and shame," she said. "So we had separate bedchambers, separate lives. By this time Archie had inherited his godfather's fortune and he established endless charitable trusts and I... Well, I threw myself into good works and tried to forget that my marriage was a sham." She gave Jack a twisted smile. "I still loved Archie very much as a friend, but I was too young and too naive to realize the true reason for the failure of our marriage."

"I imagine," Jack said, "that your husband preferred men to women."

Mairi nodded. "I had no idea. He started to disappear at night. I thought he had a mistress and I never questioned where he went because it was too painful." She knotted her hands together. Those nights had been endless as she had lain awake, wondering, torturing herself. "I suppose I was to blame in a way," she said, "because I pretended there was nothing wrong—"

There was an ugly set to Jack's mouth. "You were not to blame," he said gruffly. "In any way."

Mairi stood up. She felt too agitated to keep still, hemmed in, restless. "Finally four years ago Archie disappeared one night and never reappeared. He left a letter. He said he was sorry, that our marriage had been a sham from the start and was void in the eyes of the church and the law because he had wed me only to conceal his preference for men. He had said he had wanted to help me when my father threatened to marry me off but that he had not had the courage to tell me the truth about his nature."

She heard Jack swear under his breath.

"He ran off with his lover," she said. "He said he could not bear the pretense any longer. He staged his own death to spare his family the scandal. Afterward I discovered that he had made all his fortune over to me, out of guilt, perhaps. I do not know. I never understood why he could not have told me the truth. We would have managed somehow."

"It's difficult to see how you could have done so without tearing yourselves apart," Jack said. He came over to her and took her cold hands in his. His touch was warm. It comforted her. After a moment he drew her into his arms. They felt strong, like bands of steel. He smoothed the hair away from her hot face, and although she did not want to rely on him emotionally, Mairi let herself rest for a moment in his arms.

"No wonder you feel so alone," Jack said. His tone was hard, but Mairi knew he was not angry with her. His anger was for a man he could not help despising. "He left you with too great a burden to carry on your own."

"Lord MacLeod knows," Mairi said. She shivered, feeling hot and cold at the same time as though she had the ague. "He is the only one. It was he who hushed the whole matter up, paid people off, made sure that I was legally free. Not that I had any desire to wed again." Another shudder racked her. "Archie writes to him, I believe, and Lord MacLeod sends money sometimes. He never tells me any news and I do not ask. God help me, but I cannot forgive Archie. It still feels too much of a betrayal."

Jack cupped her face in his hands and tilted it up so that he could look at her. "And throughout it all," he said, "you never once betrayed him in return."

"I was tempted," Mairi said. She felt her skin heat beneath the cool touch of his fingers. "To start with I felt crushed by Archie's lack of interest in me, but there were plenty of men who made their admiration for me plain, so I realized I was not unattractive. Why are you smiling?" she added.

"You are correct," Jack said. "You are not unattractive."

Mairi smiled too, reluctantly. "Yes, well, I could have taken a lover, but I was stubbornly loyal to my marriage vows."

"And after he left and you were free?"

Mairi bit her lip. "I was too unhappy in the beginning. I did not want to remarry and I was too inexperienced to know how to manage an affair. So I pretended." She gave a little shrug. "I flirted but it was all for show. "

Jack's gaze scanned her face and she felt vulnerable and exposed beneath that clear appraisal. "I wish I could find him," Jack said. His tone was fierce, the violence just beneath the surface, controlled but no less powerful for that. Mairi felt the force of his anger in the same way she had done when Wilfred Cardross had attacked her. "It would give me the greatest pleasure to kill him myself," Jack said, "and make the fiction a reality."

Mairi pressed her fingers to his lips. "No," she said. "Please—"

She broke off as he silenced her with a kiss. It was hard and full of turbulent emotion.

"Mairi," he said. Then: "Damn him for hurting you."

He kissed her again, so swift and fierce and yet with a tenderness in it that made her heart race. She clutched the lapels of his jacket and tried to draw him even closer. Her head spun. She wanted him very badly. The emotions of the night had stripped away all her defences.

"Don't leave me," she whispered. "Stay with me. Please."

Unbelievably she felt him hesitate. "I don't think—" he started to say, and she kissed him again, desperate.

"Don't tell me you have scruples about taking advantage of me tonight," she said, when their lips parted. "I thought you were no gentleman."

She felt him smile.

"So did I." He loosed her, scanned her face again. She could see hesitation and wariness in his, almost as though he were afraid. Then he gave a sigh, as though he were surrendering, and scooped her up in his arms and carried her through to his bedroom.

JACK LAY AWAKE watching Mairi as she slept. He knew that he should carry her back to her own room. By now it would be abundantly clear to her maid that Mairi was in his bedchamber and had been there for some considerable time. The poor girl was probably desperate to retire for the night and would not know whether to wait or simply go to bed. The discreet fiction that he and Mairi had been practicing over their affair had been blown to pieces.

The problem was that he wanted to keep her here with him. He was tired of pretense, of creeping around like a backstairs lover who was ashamed of his behavior. He had already resigned himself to the fact that his lust for Mairi was not going to burn out. What he felt for her was not so simple. He was also determined to protect her, even more so now that he knew her secrets.

He raised a gentle hand and smoothed the hair away from Mairi's cheek. She stirred in her sleep, making a soft sound and pressing closer to him, turning her face instinctively up to his. Something like a fist clenched tight in Jack's chest, sweet and poignant at the same time. He surrendered to another impulse and kissed her very softly.

Mairi stirred again and opened her eyes. When she saw him her lips curved into a smile, a smile that was sweet and warm and knowing. It sent a flare of lust through him and something else, something more potent and powerful still. Jack recognized the lust. That he understood. The rest was a mystery to him.

"Go to sleep, sweetheart," he whispered, and she closed her eyes again, snuggling closer into the curve of his arm.

Jack thought of Archie MacLeod then and felt the tenderness in him dissolve into a wave of primitive fury that was almost ungovernable in its strength. The man was weak through and through for not having the courage to tell Mairi the truth from the first. Unlike many of his contemporaries Jack had no issue with any man's sexual proclivities, but he most certainly had one with MacLeod's behavior. The fact that MacLeod had walked away, leaving Mairi and his father to deal with the aftermath of his desertion, was the act of a coward.

With a muffled curse he got up and crossed to the dresser, splashing water from the bowl onto his face, trying to think clearly. He was fairly certain now that Michael Innes could have no idea at all that Archie MacLeod was still alive. With MacLeod alive, Innes was no longer the heir to Strome or the MacLeod barony. If he raised the matter in court he would be dispossessed of his inheritance. It was not in his interests to dig up this particular scandal.

On the other hand, the penalty for sodomy was death. Jack doubted that the courts would impose such a sentence on the son of a peer, but he could understand why

Lord MacLeod would do all in his power to protect Archie from that danger. MacLeod still loved his son no matter what the man had done. He could not take the risk. And if the matter went to court at all, it would give rise to the most monstrous scandal. The entire family would be destroyed. And Mairi… Here Jack released a long breath. Mairi would suffer most of all. As the former wife of so infamous a man, she would be dragged down into the cesspit of gossip and be utterly ruined.

He wondered fleetingly where Wilfred Cardross came into the matter. Cardross's attack was no coincidence. He was sure of it. There was a pattern here, but at present he could not see it for what it was, and until he could unravel it Mairi would not be safe.

Smiling a little wryly, Jack slid back into the warmth of the bed, drawing Mairi back into his arms. He could see how thoroughly Lord MacLeod had manipulated him now. It had not merely been a matter of finding a man who would give Mairi the protection of his name until the threat of scandal had passed. The old laird had been looking for a man who would marry his daughter-in-law. He had chosen him because he was strong enough to deal with the threat Michael Innes posed, but he had also believed that once Jack knew about Archie MacLeod he would marry Mairi and keep her safe against the danger of the truth ever coming out. He had known that no man of honor would abandon Mairi to the scandal.

Jack rubbed a hand through his hair. The only question left was whether he really was the man of honor that MacLeod believed him to be.

Mairi was awake. He heard the covers rustle as she turned over to look at him. Her eyes were a hazy blue, soft with sleep and satiation. She smiled at him and yawned delicately, stretching, her throat arching, her body as sleek and satisfied as a cat in the sun.

"So," he said softly, "how do you feel?"

"It is odd," she said, "but I feel very happy." The smile deepened in her eyes. "Thank you," she whispered, and Jack knew she was not talking about the sex but about something a great deal more profound and a great deal more dangerous. She had trusted him. She had entrusted her secrets to him. There was no going back.

The thought made him feel uncomfortable and he sought steadier, less emotional ground.

"I hope," he said, "that I have managed to convince you that you are indeed an exceptionally attractive woman?"

She laughed, though he thought he saw a shade of reserve come into her eyes. She had noticed that he had refused to engage with what she had said.

"The only mystery is why you waited so long to take a lover," he said.

Her gaze slid away from his as though she was thinking back, considering. "I did not take a lover because it mattered too much, I suppose," she said. "It felt too important simply to be treated as another fashionable diversion." She smiled. "You look shocked, Jack." She reached up and touched his cheek. "You must be the only man in Scotland who would prefer his mistress to be a faithless whore."

"That would certainly be more my style," Jack said. "I've explored every vice there is and treated sex as no more than a pleasant game." He did not want commitment and he had never asked for it in return. Now, though, he considered it. If he were to take Lord Mac-Leod's commission to its logical end and marry Mairi, he would offer her, if not his love, then certainly his fidelity.

Mairi was regarding him with her clear-eyed candor. "Why have you had so many lovers?" she asked, turning his question around.

"Because it did not mean anything at all to me," Jack said. For the first time in his life he felt, if not ashamed, then regretful that matters had not been different. He sat up. "I'm sorry," he said. "I did not mean that to sound disrespectful to you."

Mairi shook her head. "You said nothing that was a surprise to me," she said. "I knew exactly where I stood when I agreed to our affair."

"What changed for you?" Jack said. "Why did you agree?"

Again she considered the question thoughtfully. "I suppose I was tired of a life lived without color or excitement," she said. "I was tired of always being in control and battening down my emotions. I wanted to know how it felt to make love with passion." She sat up and pulled back the covers, about to swing her legs over the side of the bed. "I must go. It would not do for Jessie to come looking for me. As it is she will be wondering where on earth I am."

Jack caught her hand in his. "Stay," he said. He was shocked at how much he wanted to keep her with him. He ran his hand up her bare arm, turning it over so that he could press a kiss to the hollow of her elbow. He brushed her hair aside to kiss the point of her shoulder. When she neither responded nor moved away, he laid her back against the pillows and pushed back the covers, exposing her breasts, taking her nipple in his mouth, stroking his hand down over her rib cage and stomach. He felt the tension leave him as he heard her sigh and felt her body loosen and warm beneath his hands and mouth. This was familiar, this game of seduction. Yet somehow beneath the familiarity was a difference. He felt uncertain; he was almost fearful that she would turn away from him and that if she did he would in some strange way be lost.

It was only sex, he reminded himself. Physical intimacy was very different from emotional closeness. The hot, familiar sweep of desire took him then and he surrendered himself to it. His other thoughts, doubts and questions could wait until the morning.

CHAPTER SEVENTEEN

"You failed, Cardross."

A ragged gray dawn was brewing over the mountains. Wilfred Cardross had been half-asleep, soaked, cold to the bone, huddled in the ruins of an ancient bothy halfway up the hillside. It gave him little protection against the elements, but it was a good vantage point. From here he had seen the soldiers fanning out across the glen, searching for him, city boys who hated these bleak mountains and the harsh terrain, stabbing ineffectually at the heather and the bracken as though they expected to find him hiding in a fox hole.

He had laughed then, but he was not laughing now. This predator had come up on him unseen and unheard, and by the time he was aware of him it was already too late and there was a dirk at his throat.

"You?" he said. "Here?"

He looked down at the blade. It was bright in the dawn and wickedly sharp.

The other man smiled. There was no humor in the look. "I said that if I needed you I would find you," he said. "Though actually—" The dirk pressed a little harder. "I don't need you."

"Wait!" Cardross said. Panic scrambled in his chest at what he saw reflected in the man's pale eyes. "It's not my fault I failed," he said. "They were too good for us. You said there would be no contest! You said my men would win—"

"So it's my fault now, is it?" The man was laughing at him. Cardross felt a vicious rush of hatred. "Somehow, with you, I suspect it is always some other man's fault."

The dirk gouged a little deeper. "Give me another chance." Cardross was gabbling now, playing for time. "I won't fail again. I almost took her yesterday in the gardens. I got past all the guards Methven had set. It was easy—"

"So where is she?" The other man's voice was devoid of sympathy. "You almost took her—but you didn't succeed. A broken tool is no use to me."

Cardross had meant to beg, but in the end he had no time. The conversation was over. He had expected a slash to the throat, and his hands came up in a vain attempt to deflect the blade. In the same moment he realized he had been deceived. The knife slid between his ribs. For a second he felt nothing and then the pain took hold of him and shook him like a rag doll. It was terrible. He had always been a coward, afraid of death, and now he had ample time for fear as his life leeched away. When the darkness finally took him, it was a relief.

The rattle of the bed curtains woke Mairi.

"It is high noon, milady." Jessie was placing a breakfast tray on the dresser. "Mr. Rutherford suggested I let you sleep late. He said you were quite worn out last night."

Mairi rolled over, blinking as the bright sunlight struck across her eyes. She had slept very deeply. She vaguely remembered that she had woken as the sun had been coming up. She had been in Jack's bed, wrapped tightly in his arms. She had known that she had to return to her own room, but it had been extraordinarily difficult to tear herself away. She was sure Jack had carried her back to her bed. She even thought he might have kissed her before he left her, but that might have been her imagination or perhaps wishful thinking. Then she had fallen asleep again and there had been no bad dreams.

She stretched, testing her feelings. Her mind felt lighter than she could remember it feeling in years. It felt as though a terrible weight had lifted and the darkness that had been paralyzing her life was banished because she had shared the burden at last and told Jack everything.

A sweet flood of emotion filled her. It was the same sensation she had felt when she had made love with Jack at the inn at Kinlochewe. It was the same feeling she had experienced on the afternoon of the storm when Jack had comforted her so tenderly. But it was stronger now and deeper.

She had wondered if she was the type of woman who could separate physical pleasure from emotional involvement. Obviously she was not. What she was feeling for Jack Rutherford was getting dangerous. She was falling in love with him. She had trusted him with her body. She had trusted him with all her secrets, but she could not trust him with her heart.

The thought was enough to waken her completely and she sat up, reaching for her wrap. The sunshine was flooding in and it felt warm, but she did not want its caress on her body. She felt emotionally stripped bare, and that chilled her. She needed to wrap herself up. She needed to protect herself.

Before the previous night she had thought that she would never trust a man again. Archie had betrayed her and smashed her faith. She had become accustomed to taking control and making her own decisions. Yet last night she had trusted Jack and that was because she was in love with him. She was not simply in thrall to the physical pleasure their affair gave her. She loved him and she wanted his love in return. But love was the one thing that Jack could never give her. He had made that abundantly clear right from the start.

She drew her knees up to her chest and sat hugging them, the breakfast tray forgotten beside her. An affair with Jack was not enough for her now. She loved him and she wanted more than he could give her. She wanted his love; she wanted to marry him. But the fact was that Jack, the perfect lover, would never be a perfect husband. His definition of fidelity was probably to make love to only one woman at a time. He wanted no commitment. While she had been letting down her guard he had been reinforcing his to keep her out.

She picked up her cup of chocolate absentmindedly. The rich liquid felt warm and comforting. Suddenly she had a huge craving for ice cream and marshmallow candy and just about anything else sweet that she could lay her hands on. If this was love, then it was going to make her very fat.

Jessie had come back for the breakfast tray and to help her dress.

"Mr. Rutherford sends his compliments, madam," the maid said, "and asks that you would join him and Lord Methven in the library when you are ready. There is an army gentleman here with news of Lord Cardross."

"What news?" Mairi asked quickly. "You must know,

Jessie. They say that the servants' hall is always the first to hear."

Jessie looked furtive. "They say he was found dead in a ditch, ma'am," she said. She lowered her voice. "Drowned in the storm yesterday."

"Drowned?" Mairi said. She could not believe it. "Wilfred?"

"Aye, madam. Like the sewer rat he is," Jessie said. The satisfaction faded from her voice. It turned cool. "Mr. Cambridge also presents his compliments, madam. He asked me to tell you that he had to leave early to return to Lord MacLeod at Strome. He will see you once you are back in Edinburgh next week."

"Thank you," Mairi said. She was not sorry to have missed Jeremy's departure and she would be in no hurry to seek him out.

An hour later she presented herself in the library. She had dressed in bright cherry-sprigged muslin with a matching ribbon in her hair. It gave her courage in some strange way and she felt as though her emotions needed all the protection they could get. She had to make a conscious effort not to look at Jack as she came in; she felt curiously aware of his presence, even more so than usual, as though love had made all her senses acutely sharp. She could feel his gaze on her even though she greeted Robert first and only then turned to him with a casual smile.

Jack's lips twitched at the indifference of her greeting. "I hope you slept well, Mairi," he said. "You look radiant this morning."

"Thank you," Mairi said. One compliment and he was straight through her defenses, damn him.

Jack and Robert had with them a young captain of

the dragoons; his eyes widened in blatant admiration when he saw Mairi and he blushed.

"Lady Mairi!" He sketched a bow, turning an even stronger shade of pink.

Mairi felt rather than saw Jack stir at her side. "This is Captain Donald of the Royal Scots Greys," he said. "The captain is in charge of the troops who found Wilfred Cardross."

"Congratulations, Captain Donald," Mairi said. "Thank you."

"It was my pleasure, ma'am," the captain assured her fervently. "Although I am sorry he was already dead. It would have been an even greater pleasure to drag him back to jail for you."

Mairi could see that Jack was trying not to laugh at the young man's ardor. She frowned at him; he gave her a look that said Donald might admire her but he was the one in her bed. She felt her face heat.

"I heard that Wilfred drowned," she said, turning her attention away from Jack and back to Donald. "Can that be true?"

She saw Robert and Jack exchange a glance. It was Jack who answered. "He was found facedown in a flooded ditch," he said, "but that was not how he died. He was stabbed."

"The water had washed all the blood away," Donald confirmed with rather too much relish for Mairi's taste, "but we found the wound. Whoever killed him had left him there deliberately by the side of the road. They wanted him to be discovered."

Chills chased up Mairi's spine. "Who would do such a thing?" she said.

"Probably one of the band of outlaws who took part

in the attack on your carriage, ma'am," Donald said. "My understanding is that Cardross abandoned them in the fight. They would not take kindly to being double-crossed and would be looking for revenge."

Robert leaned forward. "We are not making news of the murder public," he said. "We're putting it about that he drowned."

"Dulcibella," Mairi said, realizing. "Of course. She would have yet another fit of the vapors if she thought that another murdering outlaw was on the loose."

"We hope that Lady Dulcibella will feel able to go home now," Robert agreed smoothly. "There is no virtue in causing further alarm."

Jack turned to Mairi. "Needless to say," he said, "you will be traveling back to Edinburgh with me when we leave. I don't want you taking any risks."

"With Wilfred dead, surely there cannot be any further danger," Mairi said.

"You will not," Jack said, an edge to his voice, "put that to the test, if you please."

It felt as though the tension in the room had suddenly ratcheted up by several degrees. Mairi saw Robert watching them. There was a look of intense interest in his eyes as he surveyed his cousin's taut face.

"I think Mairi is right," he said mildly. "The danger is surely past. Cardross was killed by a criminal with a grievance. It's unlikely that such a man would attack anyone else and thereby risk being hunted down. Besides, with so many soldiers about we are surely as safe as houses here."

Jack turned on him with repressed anger latent in every line of his body. Mairi almost flinched but Robert seemed unmoved. "With respect, Robert," Jack said, "you cannot know that, and I do not wish you to encourage your sister-in-law to get any further involved in this—"

"I am involved," Mairi pointed out.

"It isn't seemly," Jack rapped out.

There was a silence. Robert looked as though he was trying not to laugh. "Now I've seen it all," he said. "Jack Rutherford preaching on propriety. I wonder at the cause of this sudden change of character."

Jack took a step toward him and Mairi was afraid he was actually going to punch his cousin.

"I am sure Captain Donald has no wish to witness our family bickering," she said quickly. "Captain, thank you again for your diligence. I wish you a good day."

Jack tore his gaze away from Robert and stepped back. After a moment he sketched a bow. "Your servant, Donald," he said abruptly and stalked out. Mairi looked at Robert, who gave her a faint lift of the brows and a rueful smile. She knew he was trying to apologize for the fact that in provoking his cousin he had disregarded her feelings and opinions. It was exasperating and she had no idea why Jack was behaving like a bear with a sore head.

"Let me show you out, Donald," Robert said, standing up to escort the captain to the door. Mairi went across to the long windows and watched the detachment of dragoons outside form up and march away. It was a glorious summer day and suddenly she ached to be out of the house and in the open air. She wanted to ride out onto the mountains and let the wind chase away the blue devils.

She went upstairs and changed into an old jacket and trews that Murdo, one of Frazer's sons, had lent to her years before, trousers being so much easier to ride astride in than a habit. She dispatched Jessie with a note for Lucy to tell her that she was going for a ride. The one thing she did not want to do was tell Jack. She had had quite enough of his overbearing ways for one day.

"You'll no' be riding on your own, milady," Murdo said as she came into the stable yard, "not with masterless men on the loose."

Mairi groaned. "You sound like Mr. Rutherford, Murdo," she said. "Did he tell you to keep an eye on me?"

A wide grin split Murdo's face. "Aye, madam."

"He's got a damned nerve," Mairi said. "I'd like to see any of you try to stop me."

"Then at least let us come with you, madam," Murdo begged as he led out one of Lucy's mares. "That way we can tell Mr. Rutherford we looked after you."

"You're afraid of him," Mairi scoffed but the groom only nodded with no trace of a smile.

"Aye, madam," he said. "If anything happened to you I'd be terrified to tell him."

He gave her a leg up and Mairi swung up into the saddle and dug her heels in. The mare was fresh and as eager for the ride as she. They galloped out of the yard, scattering the grooms like straw in the wind. Behind her Mairi heard Murdo give a shout, but it was not until she reached the knot of pines halfway up the track that edged the mountain that she slowed down to wait for him and for Hamish to catch up with her.

It was a good four hours later when they rode back down to Methven, and Mairi felt exhilarated by the ride. The sun was starting to drop behind the hills and evening was cool in the air. As soon as she entered the stable yard, though, she could feel a tension in the air. The grooms looked at her sideways from the corners of their eyes.

She jumped down from the saddle and handed the reins to Murdo with a word of thanks. And then she turned.

Jack was standing directly in front of her and it was clear he was blazingly angry.

JACK HAD NEVER felt so furious in his entire life. Only the fact that they were standing in the stable yard and were surrounded by grooms and servants who could barely conceal their anticipation of a huge row could restrain him from ringing a peal over Mairi straight-away. Lachlan and Dulcibella MacMorlan might air their grievances in public, he thought grimly, but he had too much regard for Mairi to do that even when she had gone expressly against his wishes.

Her first words to him were not conciliatory, how-ever, and he could feel his temper soar even higher.

"Good evening, Mr. Rutherford," she said, quite as though she had done nothing wrong. She looked flushed, her cheeks pink, her eyes bright and starry with the exhilaration of the ride. She looked beautiful. Somehow that annoyed Jack all the more when the im-ages in his mind had been of her lying dead in a ditch like Wilfred Cardross. The only thing he could think was that he would never let her out of his sight again.

"Lady Mairi." He bit out the words. "I wonder if we might speak privately?"

"Of course," Mairi said. She sounded cool, but Jack could see the pulse beating in the hollow of her throat. She was nervous. Well, she should be.

She turned her back on him and started to walk toward the door that led to the tack room and from there to Lucy's hothouse and conservatory. Jack nodded to Murdo and Hamish. "Thank you," he said. At least Mairi had had the sense not to ride alone, but that fact did little to alleviate his anger. She had waited until his back was turned and that was what infuriated him more than anything else.

Mairi was walking faster now. Perhaps she thought she could run away from him. Jack smiled grimly at the prospect of chasing her down Methven's long corridors. The idea did hold some appeal.

He caught up with her just as she reached the conservatory door and slammed it shut behind them. He knew it was not a particularly private place for a confrontation, but he could not wait any longer. They were immediately encased in the heavy air and gloomy light of the hothouse. It smelled of dry earth and the faint heady scent of lilies. A gardener who was working on the vines by the back wall caught sight of them and moved discreetly away. Jack heard the soft click of the door closing behind him.

He took Mairi's arm in a tight grip and spun her around to face him. "Perhaps you can explain to me how it is that I ask you not to take any risks yet I find you riding out alone the day after your cousin is murdered?" He realized that his voice was shaking with anger, within an inch of losing control. "Do you, then, have so little regard for your own safety—and for my concerns?"

"Of course not," Mairi said. She met his gaze fearlessly. Even in his anger Jack liked that about her, that she would not back down. He liked her. Respected her too. But he was still so angry with her he could shake her.

"I took two grooms with me," she said. "They were both armed and I had a pistol in my saddlebags. I fail to understand your objections."

"My objections," Jack said through his teeth, "relate to the fact that I expressly asked you not to venture out until this matter was settled. Had you even thought that your late lamented husband might be behind this? That he might be the one who set up Wilfred Cardross? That he is trying to hurt you?"

He saw by the way that she paled that she had not even considered it. She fell back a step, her eyes searching his face.

"I could not mention it in front of Robert and Donald this morning since I did not wish to break your confidence," Jack said, his tone softening as he saw her distress, "but you have to consider it, Mairi."

"No." Her hand had come up to her throat. Her words were a whisper. "Archie would never hurt me. He is too gentle."

"Can you be sure of that?" Jack said. He thought she was naive in the extreme. "You are one of only two people who know that he is alive. If he sees you as a threat in some way—"

"No!" Mairi shook her head violently. "I can't believe it. I *won't* believe it." She came up to him. In the hazy light of the conservatory he could see a tiny shadow furrow her brow. "Jack," she said slowly, "are you *jealous* of Archie?"

"I'm trying to protect you," Jack said.

"Which does not answer my question." She stood

feet planted firmly, hands on hips. "Be honest with me. Are you?"

Jack was. He realized it with a shock. It had been bad enough when he had thought the man was dead. Everyone seemed to have liked him and painted him as some sort of saint. Now, knowing MacLeod was still alive even if he and Mairi were no longer married, Jack felt a wrenching sense of jealousy.

"I feel possessive." He pulled her against him, ran his hands down her back and over her buttocks, pulling her against his body. "You're mine, Mairi. Marry me."

He felt the shock rip through her. She drew back and stared at him as though he were speaking in an entirely foreign language. To be fair he was almost as surprised as she was. He had been thinking about it since the previous night when he had finally realized the full implications of Lord MacLeod's plan, but he had not intended to propose in so abrupt a manner. It was not, he realized ruefully, something in which he had any practice at all and he had never anticipated having any.

Mairi opened her mouth. She looked suspiciously as though she was going to argue with him, so Jack kissed her to distract her and after a second she kissed him back, tangling her tongue with his, all hot and sweet and willing. He felt relief then that this must surely mean that she agreed to his proposal; relief, and a sharp desire.

"Jack—" she whispered.

Jack kissed her again, hard and insistently. She made a sweet sound of capitulation deep in her throat and again responded to his kiss with a fervency that stole his breath and made him want to carry her straight up to his chamber and seal their agreement in his bed.

He took a step toward her, trapping her against the wall. He held her gaze as his hand moved down, unfastening the buttons of her jacket one by one. She met his eyes, her chin tilted up defiantly, but beneath his hand he could feel the frantic beat of her heart.

When the jacket was undone he pulled it apart and without preamble pulled the linen shirt from the band of her breeches. She sucked in a breath but kept quite still. There was a defiant glitter in her eyes now and in the jut of that determined little chin.

Jack smiled. He slid his hands beneath the shirt. She wore nothing but a thin shift and through it he could feel the warmth of her skin. With one swift movement he pushed the jacket from her shoulders and drew the shirt over her head. She was shivering now, but not from cold.

Jack pulled the chemise apart, careless of the fastenings. He ran his hands over her breasts and felt her nipples harden against his palms. He heard her catch her breath and he kissed her again, driving his tongue into her mouth, exploring her. He released her only to bend his head to her breasts, nipping, tugging and biting softly and then a little harder against the sensitive skin. She tilted her head back. In the heat of the conservatory her hair was clinging in wisps to the damp skin of her throat and as Jack watched a drop of water ran down between her breasts. The sight was so erotic it already had him at the edge of his control.

"Marry me," he repeated. The thought of having her in his bed every night was like a dark dream of pleasure.

But then she freed herself from his grasp, slipping away from him. Her eyes were a dark blue, shadowed with passion, but there was something else there in the depths, disappointment, perhaps, or regret. She bent down and picked up her jacket, pulling it together to cover her.

"I cannot marry you," she said, and there was a wealth of regret in her voice. "I am truly honored that you should wish to marry me because I know that it is not a decision you would make lightly, but I cannot accept." Her voice changed. There was a pleading note in it now.

"Please try to understand, Jack," she said. "I was married to a man who did not love me and one day he left me for someone else he did love. I could never take that risk again."

"I would never be unfaithful to you," Jack said instantly. "I swear it." He meant it. It would not be a promise that would be difficult to keep. Yet in the same moment he could see that it was not enough for her.

"But you could not love me either, could you?" Mairi said. Then, as his silence betrayed him: "You could not love me as I love you."

Jack swallowed hard. He had known she loved him the previous night, he thought, when she had trusted him with all her secrets, turning to him when she was at her most vulnerable. But he did not know how to love her in return. Love had been crushed out of him when he had been little more than a boy.

He took her hand in his, running his thumb over the back of it, feeling her tremble.

"I don't want to hurt you," he said. His voice was rough.

She smiled but her eyes were tired. "I think it's a little late for that." She freed herself from his touch very deliberately and stepped away. "I'm not blaming you for anything, Jack. You made me no false promises. I'm not telling you I love you because I want to hear you say the words in return. I'm telling you because I want to be honest with you." She wrapped her arms about herself as though she were cold even though the air in the conservatory was so humid it felt like a deadweight. "You say that you would never be unfaithful, but without love to bind us, what is there?" She smiled, but he could see the sparkle of tears in her eyes. She would not cry, though, at least not in front of him. She had too much pride for that.

Jack felt fierce regret that he could not give her what she wanted and in the same moment an even more fierce determination that he was not going to let her go even if he could not offer her what she needed, even if he was in no way good enough for her.

"Mairi—" he said.

She shook her head. "I would spend each day wondering if you would find someone you *could* love, Jack," she said. "I would spend each day wondering if this was the day I would have to let you go. Better to do that now than to lose you when we were wed." She raised her hand and touched his cheek in the sweetest and most fleeting of caresses and then she turned on her heel and was gone. Jack heard the sound of her footsteps fade into silence and then he was alone.

CHAPTER EIGHTEEN

IT WAS FORTUNATE that Mairi met no one on her way back to her room because she was crying so hard that she could not really see where she was going. It infuriated her. She knew she had been right to refuse Jack. She just wished it had not been so damned painful.

Jessie was waiting for her. She wondered what on earth she must look like. Her lips were stung red from Jack's kisses, but her eyes were equally red from crying. Jessie was looking at her out of the corner of her eye. It was clear she was struggling hard not to say anything. Silence was not really her forte.

"Lovers' quarrel, madam?" she said after a moment.

"Something of the sort," Mairi said wearily. "Mr. Rutherford proposed to me and I refused him."

"I hope ye did not," Jessie said. "I thought the two of you were *already* engaged!" She put her hands on her hips. "Such goings-on as between you and Mr. Rutherford, ma'am! I couldnae stay in your service if ye didnae wed. I'm a respectable girl."

"I know you are," Mairi said. "I'm sorry." She sank down onto the seat in front of the mirror. She looked in what Jessie would no doubt describe as a "right state." Her hair was tousled, her face flushed and her lips looked swollen. She touched them lightly and felt a voluptuous shiver echo through her. Her body's indiscriminate response to Jack's lovemaking just made her feel more despairing. It did not care that he did not love her. It just wanted more sensual pleasure.

She half turned in the seat. "I don't feel like dinner tonight," she said. "Please would you draw me a bath? I'll maybe take supper later."

"Very well, madam," Jessie said.

When the maid had gone out Mairi quickly slipped the jacket off, throwing it to one side with the shirt and the breeches. She resumed her seat before the mirror, naked now but for her drawers, and examined her body with curiosity and more than a little awareness. The skin of her neck was stung pink in places where Jack's stubble had rubbed against her. Lower, her breasts also showed tiny pink marks where Jack had pressed those delicious tiny biting kisses over her skin. Her nipples were still swollen and aroused. She plucked at them and felt an echo of the pleasure that Jack's touch had brought her.

She sighed. She had wanted Jack very much. It was exciting to be desired with such fierce passion after so many barren years, but it was not sufficient to sweep away her scruples over a loveless marriage.

There was a knock at the door. It sounded accusatory as though Jessie thought she might have been getting up to all sort of wickedness as soon as her back was turned. Mairi grabbed her robe and slipped it on, tying it at the waist.

"Come in."

The bath was deliciously hot. Methven might be a medieval castle in origin, but Robert had spared no modern expense when it came to heat and warmth. Mairi was most appreciative. She sank back in the water and let it take the knots of tension from her neck and shoulders. She also let it wash away the niggling worry that Jack might actually be right about Archie being the one who was hunting her. She could not believe that he would set out to kidnap or murder her. It seemed an absurd idea. He had always been the most gentle of souls, with a hatred of cruelty and violence. Besides, he had loved her. Not as a husband did, never as a husband, but as a true friend. It was the friend that she had mourned when Archie had left her, that and the loss of trust.

She could feel her shoulders tightening again and consciously turned her thoughts away from Archie, letting her mind float free as she sank deeper into the scented water. She thought again of Jack and all that she had learned at his hands. He had shown her how much pleasure could be found in exploring the sensuality in her own nature. It had been a revelation.

The thought woke the arousal in her body that had scarcely been lulled by the caress of the scented water. She felt the knot tighten in her belly and a pulse beat between her thighs. Grabbing her robe, she stood up and stepped out of the bath, wrapping the material around her, feeling it cling to her skin as the water soaked through. Every touch of the cloth on her felt like a caress. Her body felt ripe and languid, heavy with desire.

She walked slowly across to the bed and lay back against her pillows, allowing her wrap to fall open, parting her legs, slipping a hand between her folds, stroking. She had been alone for so many years, forever really, since she and Archie had had no physical relationship. Sometimes this had given her release. She thought of Jack, imagining him teasing her nipples with his fingers and his tongue and his teeth, running his hands down her body, driving her to extremes of pleasure. The delicious ache started to build inside her, taking the latent arousal and spinning it into something stronger.

She opened her eyes, raised her gaze to the mirror. Her hair was tumbled over her bare breasts and her legs were splayed. She looked lewd and it was exciting. Then her gaze focused on the rest of the reflection and she almost screamed. In the mirror she could see Jack, standing in the dressing room doorway, leaning a shoulder against the frame, watching her. For a second she thought he must be a fantasy, conjured by her wicked thoughts. Then he spoke.

"I beg your pardon," he said, "but you forgot to lock the door."

He prowled forward into the room. His gaze was all over her, hot and smothering. She could barely breathe. She felt extraordinarily embarrassed and at the same time excited almost out of her skin to have been caught like this by him.

He came toward her until he was no more than a few feet away. His gaze raked her, lingering on her tousled hair, her flushed face, the open robe, the parted thighs.

"Were you thinking of me?" he asked softly.

Shame swept through her. She did not want to have to admit that even though she had walked away from him, she still wanted him.

He leaned down and braced a hand on either side of her against the bed head.

"Well?" he said. He dropped his hands to her shoulders. She was still wearing the robe and his touch was hot through it.

"Yes," Mairi whispered, and saw the flare of triumph in his eyes and heat, and hunger.

"Marry me, then," he said.

She raised her chin a notch. "No," she said.

She saw a flash of brilliant amusement in his eyes. "You need to learn to surrender control," he said.

He pulled her toward him, running a hand into her hair to hold her still as he kissed her again, long and deep, plundering her mouth. It was delicious and as carnal as she could ever have desired, his fingers teasing the sensitive tips of her breasts as a tight knot of lust pulled in her belly. She wanted to tell him to leave, but at the same time she could not bear to be cheated of her pleasure again.

When she could not stand the friction any longer, she made a sharp noise in her throat and Jack pushed her back against the bed, drawing the robe farther apart. He pressed kisses against the hot skin of her stomach and she shuddered with need. He came back to kiss her again, his mouth slanting over hers more gently this time but still with ravenous demand. He bit down softly on her bottom lip, then soothed it with his tongue. Mairi was trembling, waiting for him to shed his clothes and join her on the bed. There was such a fierce ache inside her now.

She reached for him, wanting to touch him too, but frustratingly he withdrew from her. The bed creaked as he stood. She rolled over, suddenly frantic that he was about to leave her as unsatisfied as she had been earlier.

He walked over to her discarded pile of clothes by the dresser, picking up the thin, battered leather belt she had borrowed from Frazer to anchor her riding breeches. She had had to tie a knot in it because it had been too long. Jack looked at it, head bent as he weighed it in his hands. Then his gaze came up.

Mairi's heart turned over at what she saw in his eyes. Her heart started to thump.

"Stand up."

The rough order made her tremble.

"Drop the robe."

Mairi hesitated. She saw him smile faintly. There was a mocking edge to it. "Scared?" he asked.

She was but she was impossibly excited, as well. This was a game that would take her well out of her depth, but she was too aroused to back down now. The thin silk slithered down her body like a caress as it fell to pool at her feet.

For one long moment she was aware of nothing but the heavy air of the chamber, the light and the shadows thrown by the lamp, the wood scent of the fire. She refused to meet Jack's eyes as she stood naked before him.

He moved in front of her. His hands smoothed over her shoulders and down her bare arms to hold her lightly. She quivered as he pulled her arms forward and with slow, deliberate movements wrapped the belt about her wrists.

Again he waited. There was a silence. Mairi was trembling so much she thought her legs might give way. This time he moved behind her. She could feel his breath hot and fast against her back. His tongue touched her spine, tracing the line of it all the way down to the curve of her buttocks. She shivered as the goose bumps spread over her skin.

"Very nice." His voice was a little rough. She looked down at her wrists, tested the bonds. They were not chafing, but they were firm enough to hold her. She had wondered when he had first picked up the belt if he was going to beat her. She had heard of such practices, but they did not appeal to her. She had already learned that her body responded to pleasure that was just short of pain, but she did not want more than that. Or so she thought. She had so little experience, knew so little, really, of her body's reactions, that she could not be completely sure.

But she was about to learn.

The thought made her shake all the more.

"Walk through the dressing room and into my chamber," Jack said.

Mairi cast him one swift glance, but his face was impassive now. She walked ahead of him; it was not far but she felt very vulnerable and exposed, naked while he was fully clothed.

Jack's room was a match for hers in style and design, it even had a mirror in the same position, but it looked very different, a masculine room with the faint scent of sandalwood and leather.

There was one other significant difference. Where she had a pair of pretty matching cottager chairs with embroidered cushions, Jack had one large leather armchair. He led her across to this one now.

"Lean over," he said. One hand low down on the small of her back emphasized the order. Mairi bent over the side of the chair. Her groin now rested on the padded leather arm. She was so aroused that the pressure was a torment. She put her palms flat on the leather seat, expecting Jack to release her hands from the captivity of the belt now, but then she saw that he was kneeling down, tugging on the end of the strap to draw it down and fasten it beneath the heavy wooden leg of the chair.

He pulled her gently into place; the leather bit into Mairi's wrists, obliging her to lean a little farther, arms extended across the other armrest now, legs spread wide to balance her. The tips of her breasts just touched the leather seat where a moment ago her hands had rested. Her hair fell forward, cloaking her bare shoulders.

She caught her breath, feeling hopelessly prone, shaken, acutely vulnerable. This was wicked indeed.

"Is this my punishment for refusing your proposal," she said breathlessly, "or is it some sort of inducement to persuade me to marry you?"

Jack sat back on his heels. The light was in his eyes, bright and feral.

"It can be whatever you want it to be, darling," he said softly. "It's no punishment when it will be so pleasurable."

Her heart tumbled at the endearment. She trusted him not to hurt her and she was so aroused now that she could hardly bear it.

"I won't marry you," she said stubbornly, just in case he had not taken the point.

He smiled. "But you love me," he said with so much smugness that she would have slapped his handsome face if her hands had been free.

"I wish I had not told you," she said furiously. "I am sure my feelings will be of short duration."

Jack laughed. "Unlike your pleasure," he said. "I intend to make this last as long as I can." He stood up, the slow, heated way in which he appraised her bound body making her all the hotter and all the more furious.

"Even nicer," he said softly. Then: "Are you sure you really want to surrender control? This is your last chance to change your mind."

Mairi closed her eyes. Damn her perfidious body. She would just about explode if he stopped now. "Yes," she said. "I'm sure."

Jack reached up, cupped her face in his hands and kissed with infinite sweetness, his mouth lingering on hers, parting her lips, his tongue touching hers softly. He ran his hands over her breasts, a possessive gesture that made her quiver and her body jerk in its bonds.

When he moved behind her she closed her eyes again. He adjusted her legs a little farther apart so that she was almost on tiptoe. This felt even more wicked, even more difficult to endure. Cold air touched her cleft. Her thighs trembled. Her body felt too taut to bear, already on the edge of orgasm.

Jack's hands brushed over her shoulders again, moving her hair away from the nape of her neck, tracing the path they had followed before in a soft caress down her spine, then along her sides to the flare of her waist. They paused there. She felt him move and waited in urgent, unbearable anticipation to feel him inside her.

Instead she felt something else, something silken and light, tickle the skin of her neck and the dip between her shoulder blades, following the line of her spine. She could not see what it was, a feather, perhaps. Her skin was so sensitized that the slightest flick made her tingle unbearably. The heavy scent of leather filled her nostrils, the smell so strong she felt almost drunk on it. She bowed her head between her spread arms.

She felt the silken caress again, this time against the side of her breasts where they pressed against the leather seat. It skipped over the sensitive skin, causing her to writhe; it dipped beneath her, teasing her nipples, making her groan now in frustration.

There was a flick across her cleft that had her jerking again in her bonds. This was fiercer than the caress of the feather, sharp, only a shade away from pain but so intense that it was almost but not quite enough to bring her to climax. She gritted her teeth and waited, aware of nothing but the thrum of need between her thighs and the hard beat of her heart.

A second passed, two. Still she waited, her body screaming for release. She felt a stroke across her buttocks, like tongues of fire. The sensation was extraordinary. Mairi's skin felt as though it were lifting to the touch, stinging with the most delicious mingling of pain and pleasure. She felt another stroke that was hot and sharp and in that moment she realized it was a whip, a cat-o'-nine-tails with the softest leather strands.

Shock splintered through her. She barely had time to think before she felt another light stroke and found herself pressing her groin down hard against the arm of the chair in a vain attempt to force her body to orgasm. She had to find surcease from the desperate need that spiraled inside her, and yet it seemed impossible. Each time the whip fell it took her closer to the edge and then left her hanging there helplessly.

She heard a sound, felt another blow that was gentle yet with a smart that made her body twitch and throb. She realized that she was on tiptoe, trying to spread her legs even wider in blatant appeal as she desperately sought fulfillment.

She heard Jack laugh. "You are as deliciously responsive to this as I suspected you would be."

There was another flick, this time across her cleft, a slither of sensation that made her cry out her need. The whip danced along the vulnerable skin of her inner thighs, the caress of it both sharp and sweet. Again Mairi hung on the edge of orgasm for one long unendurable minute, waiting, wanting to beg. Then the sensation of pleasure faded just a fraction, taking her a step back from climax. She could have cried with frustration.

Jack came back round in front of her, kneeling down. He put a hand under her chin, raising it so that she met his eyes. His own were dazzlingly bright with arousal.

He kissed her, slowly, deeply, ran his hands all over her body, pinching her nipples lightly so that she could not help jolting against the bonds.

"Just a little more," he said softly. "You can take a little more."

Mairi was not sure that she could but she was damned if she was going to ask him to stop. She had never dreamed of such wicked, carnal pleasures.

Jack walked away. This time Mairi turned her head to watch the reflection in the mirror, drinking it in greedily, all shame and all restraint forgotten. She shook at what she saw there, her body bound and arched over the chair, Jack with the whip in his hand.

He came to stand behind her once more. She watched him in the mirror, waiting, nerves stretched, her body so taut it trembled. She watched as the whip fell; she saw her body rock in response to the blow, felt the bite through a haze of sensual delight.

The tip of the whip touched the hot damp skin at the nape of her neck, then slithered all the way down her spine, feathering over her ribs, stroking her buttocks. It danced across the soft skin of her inner thighs again and brushed her cleft, curling for one unbearable moment against her nub.

Mairi's stomach tumbled. She let out a keening cry

and felt her body rock on the very edge of orgasm. Then, as she shuddered and burned, she saw Jack reverse the whip. A second later the cold, hard wooden handle parted her folds and pressed against her nub, rubbing back and forth against her slick core in sinful caress.

She lost all control then and tumbled over the edge of orgasm, her head filled with blinding light, the pleasure so intense she almost fainted. Her body pulled against the tug of the belt that still held her pinioned. The whip handle pressed harder against her pulsing body and she thought she would scream from the inescapable sensations, and then the head of the whip slipped deep inside her and she came again, the sensation violent and crystal-sharp, her cries muffled against the arm of the chair.

She heard the thud as the whip hit the carpet and then Jack was filling her, taking her in long, hard strokes. She was exhausted, drained with the intensity of the experience, and in this position she could do nothing to anchor herself; her body moved helplessly to the rhythm of his as he held her hips and spread her wider and thrust deeper, harder, using her unashamedly to slake his lust this time until he too came fiercely. She felt so weak with ecstasy that when he freed her from the belt she simply slumped in his arms, eyes closed, and felt him lift her, kiss her gently, and lay her down in his bed. His arms enfolded her. His lips touched her cheek.

"Are you all right?" he asked softly.

"Oh yes," Mairi said. Overwhelmed, sated, she wanted only to sleep.

"Open your eyes," Jack said, as he had once said to her before when they made love, and she could hear the amusement that laced his voice. It was inordinately difficult to force her eyelids to lift. They felt weighted by pure satiation.

"Will you marry me?" he whispered as she opened her eyes a tiny bit and forced herself to focus on his face. He was smiling, his fingers tangling gently with her hair, and there was so much tenderness in his eyes that she wanted to cry out against the unfairness of it. It undermined her. He showed her everything but love.

"No," she said. "No, thank you."

"So polite." He was looking at her with the same gentleness and suddenly Mairi could feel her heart cracking. Much more of this and she would agree to his proposal, against her better judgment, against all common sense. And that would be a disaster.

Suddenly she felt wide awake, fear chasing away her exhaustion. She sat up. "Jack," she said. "Don't do this. It's over."

There was sheer stupefaction in his eyes. "Is this because of what just happened?" he said. "I know I pushed you hard—"

Mairi silenced him with her fingers pressed against his lips. "It's nothing to do with that," she said. "I enjoyed it."

She felt him relax. "Then there is no need for us to part, " he said. "We could continue to see each other when we return to Edinburgh—"

Mairi shook her head. "No," she said again.

"If I asked you to change your mind," Jack said. "If I tried to persuade you…" He moved to take her in his arms, but she held up a hand to ward him off.

"Please," she said. "Please don't try to persuade me. I don't want to live my life hoping against hope that one day you will learn how to love again."

She sat up, looking for her clothes, realizing that she had none since she had walked into the room completely naked. She certainly did not have the bravado to walk out again in the same way. This was awkward. Sliding from the bed, she grabbed Jack's linen shirt and quickly slid it over her head. It was a mistake to borrow it; it smelled of Jack and her heart clenched with pain.

She realized that she was waiting for him to say something and as the silence unrolled she felt hope flicker within her and knew that it would always be like this. She would wait and hope and each time the disappointment would destroy her a little more.

"Goodbye, Jack," she said softly. She knew that the following day they would make a public goodbye in front of everyone, but this one was just for them. She leaned down and kissed his cheek and when he still said nothing, she left.

CHAPTER NINETEEN

THERE WAS A bitter little wind from the north as Mairi stood on the top of the steps at Methven waiting for the carriage to be brought round. She shivered; her summer spencer seemed too light for the chill. But perhaps the chill was inside her.

Lucy was looking worried. "I wish you would stay a few more days," she said anxiously. "I don't like to think of you traveling on your own."

"I'll be fine," Mairi said. She could not wait to be away, to be alone. "You know how heavily armed Frazer and the boys are. And so am I."

Lucy smiled. "But you won't have Jack with you." Her face puckered again. "Have the two of you quarreled? You seem very distant with each other."

"No," Mairi lied. She shivered again. "Not at all."

Lucy's expression conveyed her disbelief more clearly than any words.

"All right," Mairi admitted. "The engagement is over. Please don't ask me more—" She broke off, teeth chattering, aware that she was perilously close to tears.

"Oh Mairi!" Lucy hugged her close. "Send for me if you need me," she said. "And I might just kill Jack after all."

At that moment Jack came out the door. He looked sinfully handsome in a superbly cut riding coat. Mairi caught her breath. He came down the steps toward her, his expression serious. He did not speak but took both her gloved hands in his and raised them to his lips. Mairi's eyes jerked to his face, and her heart did a curious little twist. His eyes were deep and dark, their expression so different from the usual mocking amusement with which he faced the world. She knew he was telling her without words that he cared about her, respected her, and that what had happened between them mattered to him. He was telling her everything except that he loved her. She had no idea how to deal with this, what to say, how to behave. It had never happened to her before.

Her fingers trembled in his. She felt his clasp tighten for a moment and then he half smiled, the corner of his mouth tilting up in the way that always made her stomach tumble with longing.

"I will send word when I am back in Edinburgh," he said, "and I will come to see you when I have spoken to Mr. Innes."

"Thank you," Mairi said.

He nodded, hesitated, then bent and brushed his lips against her cheek. It was a cold caress. He handed her up into the carriage, hesitated again over releasing her hand, then let her go.

Three days later, back at Ardglen, she felt even worse. She should have gone to Edinburgh, really, where there would at least be some company and some entertainment, but she could not bear to be there while Jack was in the city. She was too afraid of seeing him with another woman. She did not fool herself that he would be without female companionship for long. Everything seemed to hurt. It hurt dreadfully. The blow of losing Jack never seemed to ease. The pain seemed to sharpen rather than decrease, and it exhausted her to put on a brave face and deal with all the paperwork from the estates. She even considered going to Jack and telling him she had changed her mind about his proposal because anything would feel better than this dragging pain. Pride and principle made for cold bedfellows, she discovered, particularly because she was in love. She got as far as calling the carriage. But in the end she sent it away because she knew that nothing had changed. Jack did not love her and that was all there was to it.

EDINBURGH WAS DRY, dusty and largely empty of company since most of the aristocracy had left the city to spend their summer on the grouse moors. Jack found it curiously quiet and lonely. It was not that he craved the excitement of balls and soirees; what he wanted, what he needed, was Mairi.

He had thought that once they were apart he would be able to move on. After three days, though, he had been obliged to acknowledge, if only to himself, that this had been naive. Privately he was terrified of the power Mairi still had over him. He had been away from her for only ten days and yet he missed her desperately. Her wanted to see her, talk to her, hear her voice. He had to resist the urge to ride out the seven or eight miles to Ardglen simply to see her. He was shocked how difficult it was to withstand that impulse. It felt not only inexplicable but outrageously sentimental as well. He wanted to be with her all the time, to touch her—of course he did—but to hold her as well as make love to her. It felt as though a part of him was missing. Whenever the door opened, his hopes would surge that she had come to find him and then they would drop like a stone.

The only thing he could hope for was that action would drive out this peculiar obsession, and so he exerted himself to find and deal with Michael Innes in the quickest and most ruthless way possible. The other advantage of that was that as soon as he had news he could take it back to Mairi. Yet it would make no difference. She would still refuse to marry him and he could see no way past that impasse.

Business was a welcome distraction. It was Jack's firm belief that every man had his weakness and it proved easy enough to use his contacts to discover Michael Innes's Achilles' heel.

Innes's one vice was a gambling habit that kept him particularly short of money. What he earned, his wife spent. He was gambling with debt. Jack suspected it was that which made Mairi's fortune so unbearably tempting to him and made the perceived unfairness of her inheritance stick in Innes's craw.

It was past eleven on his third night back in Edinburgh when Jack presented himself at a discreet establishment just off the Royal Mile. His host, a tall, dark man with jet-black hair and eyes almost equally as dark, drew him into a small reception room off the side of the entrance hall. Lucas Black was said to be the illegitimate offspring of foreign royalty but no one knew for sure. The only thing Jack had discovered about the man was that he was ruthless and determined to succeed. That made them two of a kind and from that they had forged a friendship.

"Your quarry is here, Jack," Lucas said. If he genuinely had foreign antecedents no one would have guessed it from his speech. He sounded like the product of the best English public school. "You owe me a favor. Mr. Innes is so overawed he has already lost several thousand pounds." He smiled. "But then I doubt he would ever normally receive an invitation to play in a house like this or in such exalted company."

Jack grinned. "I'm grateful to you, Lucas, especially that you were able to find sufficient players when Town is so sparse of company. I'll cover Mr. Innes's losses against the house."

Lucas inclined his head. "That is thoughtful of you."

"My pleasure," Jack said. "I have already bought up most of his other debts."

Lucas gave a soundless whistle. He sat down on the edge of the desk, foot swinging. "Poor fellow. What can he have done to displease you?"

Jack hesitated. "It is Lady Mairi MacLeod he has displeased," he said. "I am here on her behalf."

There was a gleam of laughter in Lucas's dark eyes now. "He has upset Lady Mairi? Then it is surprising that he still has his balls. I hear she is a crack shot."

"The best," Jack agreed. "But on this occasion she prefers to work through me—and with subtlety rather than with outright violence."

"I heard the news of your betrothal," Lucas said. "My congratulations."

"Thank you," Jack said. It was odd; the words hurt. They made him realize that soon, once he had spoken to Innes, he would be sending a retraction to the newspapers and his connection to Mairi would be formally severed.

Lucas was looking at him speculatively. "I never thought to see you of all people in love, Jack," he said. There was a hint of amusement in his voice. "But actually it rather encourages my faith in human nature."

"I'm not—" Jack started to say automatically, then stopped.

"Spare me the conventional denials," Lucas said. "A man does not go to the amount of trouble that you have done for Lady Mairi MacLeod without some fairly strong reason. Your cousin wrote to me," he added, "to put me in the picture once he knew your plans for Innes."

"Devil take Robert," Jack said, but he said it without any heat. Lucas was right on both counts; he was in love with Mairi and there was no point in denying it. It had taken him a hell of a long time to realize it—too long—because he had not wanted it to be true.

He realized that he was shaking. He felt strange. The one thing he had not wanted to do—to love and risk losing again—and there was not a damned thing he could do about it. Lucas was smiling as he led him through a large salon where a smattering of Edinburgh society was at play. It was an exclusively male gathering. Cigar smoke wreathed the air. A number of gentlemen nodded to Jack as he passed. Lucas ushered him into a smaller salon through a door at the back. Here there were only a half dozen players. Introductions were brief, as Jack already knew several of the people around the table. Michael Innes met his gaze without a flicker of recognition, which pleased him. Evidently the business that had taken the lawyer out of the city until recently had meant that he had not heard the gossip of Mairi's engagement.

The game was deep basset and the atmosphere in the small room was already tense. Jack held his own for the first hour, winning a little, then losing a little, watching with interest as Innes became completely engrossed in the game. He had the air of the hardened gambler, his attention rapt on the turn of a card.

Jack exerted himself a little and was soon winning steadily. As Innes lost he drank more and it was apparent he could not hold that drink, for he soon became flushed and erratic. He had a run of luck; Jack saw how it gave him confidence and the confidence made him careless, so that his concentration waned and he lost all that he had gained. By the time the game broke up Jack had a number of Innes's IOUs in his pocket.

As the others filtered out of the room, Innes plucked at Jack's sleeve. His fair face had a high color now and his eyes were a little glazed. He swayed on his feet like a sapling in a gale.

"Sir…"

"Mr. Innes?" Jack said smoothly.

"Apologies," Innes said. "There will be a slight delay in settling my debts."

Jack raised his brows and said nothing. Innes looked uncomfortable. "I have expectations," he muttered.

"So I understand," Jack said coldly, "but I hope you do not expect me to wait for Lord MacLeod to die before you pay me. I don't care to wait on a man's death."

The dull color settled deeper into Innes's cheeks. His pale eyes slid away from Jack's hard gaze.

"No," he said. "You don't understand, sir. Sooner than that… My cousin Lady Mairi is vastly rich and soon that money will be mine."

Jack glanced up. Lucas Black was standing in the doorway. At Jack's nod he came into the room, closed the door behind him and leaned back against it. Innes shot him a glance, then turned so swiftly back toward Jack that he lost his balance and almost stumbled. Jack pushed him not ungently back down into the chair he had so recently been occupying, where he scrambled back against the cushions as though he were trying to make himself as small as possible.

"Sir—" he protested, and his voice was a bat's squeak of fear.

"You interest me very much, Innes," Jack said. "Tell me more about these expectations of yours."

MAIRI WAS STILL at breakfast when word came from Jack that he had talked to Michael Innes the previous night and would call on her later that morning to discuss the matter with her. The note was very formal. Even so she felt a wild flare of hope and then an equally abrupt tumble of spirits. She was doing it again, she thought, refusing to relinquish her dreams. Whoever had said that hope was the very last thing to die had been in the right. It seemed she never learned.

She had no taste for breakfast anymore, so she decided to take a walk instead. She needed to be outside, to think, to plan what she would say to Jack, how she would deal with seeing him again. But she did not want to do it here in the gardens that reminded her so vividly of Archie. Suddenly at last she could see that she needed to escape the hold Archie had had on her life. She had to start afresh. Telling Jack about the past had freed her and even if her future could not be with him, she knew she could move forward now.

She let herself out of the little gate in the walled garden and took the path by the stream that led uphill behind the house. The earth was tinder-dry, crumbling beneath her feet. The sun beat down hotly and she was glad to have remembered her parasol. The air was thick with warmth, so unusual for a Scottish summer. It made walking hot and tiring, but she was still happier to be out in the fresh air.

By the waterfall halfway up the hillside she stopped and sat down to rest, soothed by the sound of the water and the buzz of the bees in the heather. From here the house at Ardglen looked a tiny neat oasis in the midst of the surrounding wild countryside. This had been one of Archie's favorite places; it was odd that she had felt drawn here when she had not walked this way for years. It was as though she still could not quite escape Archie's spirit, as though there was something unfinished in their business.

She stood up and carried on with her walk. The path passed behind the waterfall across a narrow rocky ledge made slippery with spray. Here the ferns and bracken grew thickly. As she came out onto a little open grassy expanse on the other side, she thought she could smell smoke carried on the faint breeze, but it seemed so unlikely on such a glorious day that she shook her head and forgot about it. She followed the path around the jut of a rough stone buttress. A little farther and she would turn back because she was starting to feel tired. There was a tumble of rock here, too fresh a fall to be covered in the mosses and lichens that grew in profusion in this little valley.

She sat down on one of the rocks to catch her breath, resting her parasol against the stone beside her, closing her eyes and turning up her face to the sun. It should have felt peaceful and yet she was aware of a sense of disquiet, as though someone was watching her.

With a little sigh she bent to pick up the parasol but it had slipped between a cleft in the rocks and she had to scrabble to retrieve it. One of the stones shifted a little; she saw a splash of color among the rock, vivid blue against the grays and greens....

She jumped to her feet. All the hairs on the back of her neck stood up on end and a cold, sickening sliver of dread slid down her spine. She recognized that blue. When she had bought the jacket for Archie on Prince's Street five years before, the tailor had assured her that there was not another like it in the whole of Edinburgh.

"A very special dye, madam," he had told her. "There are not two made the same." He had beamed. "It is exclusive to you, madam."

Mairi backed a step away. She felt cold although the sun was still as bright and hot overhead. The rocks were piled up in a cairn. At a distance it had looked random, but now she could see that it was not the work of nature but of human hands. And she could see too that beneath the jumbled heap of stone, wrapped in the shreds of blue, was something paler and more brittle, something that looked like human bone.

She turned away and was violently sick. For a moment she thought she might faint, as well. She felt sweatily hot, then clammily cold. Ears buzzing and her head feeling too light, she groped her way to a rock some distance from the body and sat down. She was shaking uncontrollably.

Archie. Archie was buried here beneath that tumble of stone. He had never made it as far as the Indies or China or all the other places she had imagined he might have run off to with his lover. All the time she had thought he was alive he had been lying here. He must have died the very night he had left. Someone had buried him here by the waterfall, his lover, perhaps, if this was where the two of them had arranged to meet. She wondered if there had been an accident, or a quarrel. And then she remembered that someone had been writing to Lord MacLeod in Archie's name, sending news, asking for money. Someone had been pretending that Archie was still alive.

She rubbed her arms fiercely to try to drive some heat into her chilled body. She had to get back down to Ardglen and send Frazer for help. She tried to stand. Her legs felt as though they were made of ribbons, but they held. She took a few shaky steps toward the path and resisted a look back over her shoulder at the cairn with its telltale splash of blue.

A shadow passed across her from the bank high above the path and she looked up. There was no one there, but she could smell smoke again. She was sure of it. The breeze had picked up a little now and there were puffy white clouds sailing across the sky and the sun seemed a shade less hot. Again she felt the hairs on her neck stand on end. She felt as though she was being watched.

The shadow passed over her again and this time when she squinted upward it was to see the silhouette of a man descending the bank toward her. For a long moment the sun was in her eyes, and though she shaded them with her hand she could see nothing of his face but a dark blur. There was something about the way that he moved, though, that was familiar. Then the sun shifted and she blinked and it was Jeremy Cambridge who was standing on the path in front of her, dusting the soil from his immaculate town clothes and looking ludicrously out of place. It struck her then, irrelevantly, that Jeremy was a creature of drawing rooms and city pavements and she had never seen him out in the countryside.

"Jeremy!" she said. "What on earth are you doing here?"

"They told me at the house that you had gone for a walk," Jeremy said. "I saw you on the path and followed you up here." His voice sounded odd, detached. The coldness in it sent a shiver of ice down her spine. Then she saw that he had a pistol in his hand and the cold intensified.

"What a pity," Jeremy said. He was looking over toward the cairn of rock and then his gaze came back and fastened on her so hard and fast that she flinched to see the expression in his eyes.

"What a pity you found him because now I am going to have to kill you."

CHAPTER TWENTY

JACK HAD BEEN almost ready to leave for Ardglen when Lucas Black was shown into his rooms. The meeting with Michael Innes the previous night, satisfactory in some senses, had also proved frustrating in others. It was clear to both men that Innes had not been in league with Wilfred Cardross. He did not have the stomach for violence, and his threats against Mairi were largely hot air, based on scandal and malice. He knew nothing of Archie MacLeod's secrets, and his bullying bravado had disappeared like mist in the sun when Jack had told him that Mairi was under his protection. All of which should have been reassuring to Jack and yet left him with the same air of disquiet, the same feeling that he was missing something that he had felt at Methven. The only other candidate for the role of attacker was Archie himself, and yet Mairi had been convinced that her former husband was too gentle a soul and had too deep a regard for her to hurt her. Jack tried to see past his jealousy to believe her, but he was not convinced. In the end he had decided to trust Lucas with the details of the case and had shared his thoughts with him and the two of them had talked deep into the night but had come to no useful conclusion.

"I apologize for holding you up," Lucas said, his gaze going to Jack's riding clothes, "but there is something here I think you should see." He held out a document. "I had a thought after you left last night. If MacLeod had been intending to flee the country with his lover, then there would in all likelihood be a record of their departure on a sailing from Greenock."

"But MacLeod had faked his own death," Jack said. "The booking would be in a false name."

Lucas nodded. "Yes, but there would be two names if he was fleeing with a lover. As a long shot I thought I would check the records for around the time that Mac-Leod was supposed to have died and see if anyone on the manifest sounded familiar." He unrolled the document and pointed. "This is what I found."

Jack looked. The ship was the *Jura*, bound for Madras in India, the date the day after Archie MacLeod's apparent death had been reported in the Edinburgh papers. He scanned the list of passengers impatiently. MacRae, parents with two children, Mr and Mrs D MacReavy, Mr S Oakes, and then, scored out, Mr A Oxford and Mr J Oxford, brothers, and the word *cancelled....*

"Oxford," Lucas said eagerly. "Cambridge. You see the connection?"

It took Jack a minute. His mind felt frustratingly slow. He remembered Mairi telling him that no one other than herself and Lord MacLeod had known about Archie's secret lover. McLeod's man of business had most certainly not been in on the secret. Or had he? Jack thought of Jeremy Cambridge coming to Methven and of Wilfred Cardross dead in a ditch the following morning. He remembered Mairi saying that Cambridge had promised to visit her when she returned to Edinburgh. Suddenly he felt paralysed with fear.

"Oh God," he said. He thrust the paper back into Lucas's hands. "I have to go."

It was only seven miles from Edinburgh to Ardglen and he could only pray that he was not too late.

"YOU WERE ARCHIE'S LOVER," Mairi said. "I had no idea." The sun still poured down, the water still ran in the stream, but it was as though she could not see it nor hear it. She felt as though she were encased in a separate world, a world encompassed by Jeremy and the pistol and the ghastly truth that he had killed her husband.

She trawled back through her memories, sifting, searching. Had she ever seen any indication that Archie and Jeremy were more than simple acquaintances? She thought not. But then there had been no reason to notice. It would have been the last thing she would have expected. She had imagined Archie's lover to be a woman, not a man.

"You've been deceiving Lord MacLeod, making him think that Archie is still alive," she said. "Why would you do such a cruel thing?"

Jeremy blinked. There was no emotion in his gray eyes, only a blank emptiness that was more chilling than any anger. "I wanted money," he said. "I kept Archie alive so that I could make Lord MacLeod pay."

Mairi glanced toward the cairn and saw him smile. "I meant in spirit," he said. "He died the night we left."

"Was it an accident?" Mairi asked, and shrank before the contempt in his eyes.

"Of course not," Jeremy said. "We quarreled. He was supposed to bring the money with him, but the sentimental fool had made it all over to you! He said he owed it to you, as though he could ever make up in money for what he had done! He said you would use it to do good." His lip curled. "Poor Archie, he was so weak, so weak and so broken with guilt."

"He was a better man than you will ever be," Mairi said with a flash of anger, but it slid off Jeremy as though it could not touch him.

"I'm not interested in being good," he said. "I'm interested in being rich. For seven and twenty years I've been Lord MacLeod's lackey and my father before me. We were meant for better than that."

The faint scent of smoke drifted down the valley and Mairi turned her head sharply. Immediately Jeremy raised the pistol and gestured to her to keep still.

"You can't shoot me," Mari said. "The servants know you are here. They will know it was no accident."

"I've no intention of shooting you unless I absolutely have to," Jeremy said. "No, I will be the one to find your body. I'll try to save you like the hero I am." He saw her frown and smiled with broad satisfaction. "The hillside is alight, my dear. The heather and bracken is tinder-dry. A flame dropped here and there..." He shrugged. "Soon we will be surrounded. You'll never get out alive."

Mairi could hear the fire now. She made an involuntary movement and once again Jeremy jerked the pistol at her.

"I want to tell you the rest," he said.

"Why?" Mairi snapped. "To gloat?"

He shrugged. "If you like. I killed Wilfred Cardross after he failed to kidnap you and bring you to me. I would have killed Michael Innes if Rutherford had not shut him up first. As it is..." He shrugged again. "I'm still thinking about it. Maybe in a little while..."

"Another accident?" Mairi said. "They will be becoming a little too frequent, Jeremy. People will start to suspect."

"It's all your fault," Jeremy said, suddenly fretful. "I had been intending to marry you, to get hold of the money that way. Then you accepted Jack Rutherford instead. Lord MacLeod told me it was all a pretense, but I knew you were Rutherford's mistress and I could not take the risk."

"So you sent Wilfred to kill me," Mairi said.

"To kidnap you," Jeremy corrected. "You were no use to me dead. But now—" he sighed as though her behavior had been particularly annoying "—now I have no choice because you know about Archie. It's damned irritating."

He smiled suddenly, shrugging off his ill temper with the whim of a child. "Anyway, I must be off. Fortunately I can run a good deal faster than you." He looked at her pretty kid boots with amusement. "Those dainty little things won't help you in a fire."

He raised the pistol in a mocking salute and then he was gone, scrambling up the bank and disappearing over the top. Mairi fought viciously against the relief and nausea that threatened to turn her dizzy. This was no time for weakness. She set her teeth and started to climb up after him.

By the time she had reached the top of the bank her leather half boots were in shreds just as Jeremy had predicted, and her skirts ripped to pieces on the heather and rock. Her legs were already aching. She crested the rise—and fell back with a cry at what she saw. The little valley had been a temporary oasis that gave no clue about the inferno that was blazing across the hillside. It surrounded her, wave upon wave of wildfire that ate through the tinder-dry heather and bracken and roared down toward Ardglen. Smoke had turned the blue of the sky to a hazy threatening gray. She could hear the hiss and crack of the flames and smell and taste the acrid scent of burning on the breeze.

Mairi had never seen a wildfire before. The speed and the sound of it terrified her. Jeremy had got through just in time. She could see him fleeing down the path, racing ahead of the fire, running at a pace she knew she could never match.

A sudden gust of wind drove the sheet of flame so close she could feel the heat. She fell back, scrambling back down the side of the valley the way she had come, her heart thumping and the roughness of the rock scoring her palms. When she saw the fire top the bank and follow her down she screamed.

The water. She had to get into the water.

Despite the heat of the summer the stream was brutally cold and she caught her breath on a gasp of shock. She plunged downhill, following its course, heedless of the mossy stones slipping beneath her ruined shoes and the brambles that tore at her clothes. Twice she fell, scraping her raw hands and bruising her knees. There was only one thought in her mind and that was that she was not going to die here to oblige Jeremy Cambridge so that he could keep the secret of Archie's murder. In some way it felt as though she would be failing Jack. It felt as though he was calling her on. Yet even as she scrambled along the stream, soaking now and cold, the flames kept pace with her, dancing along the bank, reaching out to her, so close it was terrifying.

About fifty yards from the bottom of the hill she knew she was not going to make it. Here the stream disappeared underground through caves hollowed in the sandstone thousands of years before. A dry old oak, deadwood, overhung the water and as she watched it caught fire and split apart. The sound was indescribable, a fierce blistering crack like a gunshot. The tree fell across the stream, burning fiercely, and the flames jumped the water to catch on the other side and turn her only escape route to a wall of flame.

JACK HEARD THE sound of the tree falling as he came up the slope of the hill. The entire landscape seemed to be alight. By the time he had arrived at Ardglen, Frazer was evacuating the house. Servants were running around frantically, the grooms leading out the horses. Of Hamish and Murdo and Ross, there was no sign. Frazer, pale and his face drawn into tight lines of strain, told him that Lady Mairi had gone for a walk earlier and had not returned. The boys were out searching for her. He said that Jeremy Cambridge had called and had set off up the hill after her. It was then Jack felt the dread encase his heart like ice.

At first he thought it was a shot he had heard; then he saw the tree fall across the stream. Beyond that he saw a flash of white against the dazzling brightness of the sun on the water. Of all incongruous things, it was a parasol.

Mairi.

Even as he started to move, Murdo came up at a run and caught his arm. The man's face was already filthy with sweat and soot and soil. The heat was fierce here and the fire only yards away. There was desperation and grief in Murdo's eyes.

"You can't go up there, sir—" he started to say.

"I can," Jack said, "and I will. The fire is not going to take her. I won't let it." Even as he spoke he felt the despair, the fear that he was already too late. He crushed it down.

Murdo and Hamish and Ross surrounded him.

"Let me pass," he said on a burst of fury, "or I'll knock you all down." They fell back, respect in their eyes even though they knew and he knew it was a death trap.

Jack ran toward the fire, meeting it just at the point where the stream vanished into the rock. He leaped for the water, blinded, deafened by the roar of the fire, feeling the flames reach out to catch at him. Then he was down on the streambed and the cold of the water surrounded him. He stumbled, momentarily shocked by the chill. He reached out and touched flesh and caught Mairi's hand. She was cold, soaking wet and trembling, but she felt like the most wonderful thing in his arms and he dragged her to him and pulled her beneath a sandstone overhang as the fire raced overhead and turned the water red.

Her face was pressed into the curve of his neck and he had a hand on the back of her head and his arm about her waist holding her still against his chest. He was shaking, he realized, and his breath came in great shuddering pulses that threatened to wrench him apart.

"Mairi," he said, and could not recognize his own voice. He felt her move then, burrowing closer still into his arms. They were both chilled and drenched to the skin, but where their bodies were clasped together they heated each other and the blood beat warm. Jack pressed his lips to her hair and breathed deeply, smelling the smoke that clung to her. She was singed and filthy and she was the most beautiful thing he had ever seen and he felt as though his heart were cracking open.

He was not quite sure what happened next. He had thought only to find them both some cover, pitifully small as it was, from the fire that roared overhead. But then the ground beneath them seemed to give way and they fell, tumbling over and over, until they came to rest on the floor of the cave below.

MAIRI CAME BACK to consciousness to find herself clasped close to Jack's body. Her head was against his chest, and his body was curved over hers to protect her from the falling stone. Her lungs were choked with dust and dirt. She felt frozen, filthy and shaken to the core, but she was alive. She shifted slightly, angling her head up toward him. The bank above them had collapsed, but there was just enough light coming in to see his face.

"Jack?" she said.

He shifted. His hands on her were urgent. "Mairi? Are you all right?"

"Yes," Mairi said. She started to shake with cold and reaction, shivering uncontrollably. "You?"

"I'm still alive." Astonishingly she could hear the smile in his voice. "Mairi, darling—" His tone changed, turned so fierce it made her tremble. "God Almighty. I thought I had lost you forever and I could not bear it."

Mairi stopped feeling afraid then. There, with the sound of the fire roaring overhead and the slither of the rock still falling about them, she was aware of nothing more than an infinite peace. Jack held her tightly. His eyes were closed, but she could feel the thud of his heart, hard and strong beneath her ear, and she knew suddenly that if forever lasted only a few minutes more, that would be enough.

Jack's fingers were against her face, turning it up to his as he kissed her with infinite gentleness. "You taste of salt," he said a little later. "And ash." He kissed her again. "I love you," he said. His voice fractured. "I thought I was never going to have the chance to tell you."

She had known, in the moment that he had held her, known he loved her and known that to be with him was the most important thing in the world. Now she felt a ripple of laughter bubble through her. "Jack," she said. "You have the most terrible sense of timing."

"You've never complained about it before," Jack said. He kissed her again. "I love you," he repeated. His voice sounded stronger this time, more certain, as though he was trying out the words and finding them slightly more comfortable.

"Marry me," he said. Then, with fierce humility, "I know I'm not good enough for you—"

"Hush," Mairi said. She kissed him. "You are all I want, everything I want."

She heard him give a shaken laugh. "I love you hopelessly. I'll love you forever."

"You are doing frightfully well," Mairi said demurely, "for a man who until today thought himself unable to love at all."

"Minx."

She could feel his smile as he kissed her again, with tenderness and infinite sweetness. His body had relaxed into acceptance now, acceptance of his own emotions and of the love she had for him in return. He held her protectively and with a sort of blazing, defiant pride that made her feel humble and astonishingly happy all at the same time.

"Sir!" There was a shout from the top of the shaft where the faint light gleamed. "Madam? Lady Mairi?"

"Damn," Mairi said. "They've found us." She scrambled up. "Murdo! Over here!"

It was a half hour later that she and Jack finally emerged into the daylight, filthy, cold, blinking in the sudden brightness. The wind had taken the fire away down the valley to the west, leaving nothing but charred and smoldering heather and scorched ground in its wake. A dark pall of smoke hung over the hill. Ardglen still stood looking peaceful and immaculate beside the sparkling sea.

"We found Mr. Cambridge's body by the stream," Murdo said. "Had he come looking for you, ma'am? Looks like the fire caught up with him. It moved so fast. I'm very sorry, ma'am."

Mairi held Jack's gaze. She thought of Lord MacLeod and of Archie and of the scandal and she knew Jack was thinking of them too. She took a deep breath.

"I'm sorry too," she said. "I don't know what Mr. Cambridge wanted. I didn't even know he was here."

She saw Jack smile ruefully, but he said nothing and in that moment she loved him even more. In a little, she thought, she would tell him about Archie and they would arrange for a decent burial and his parents could mourn him properly. But for now she was going back for a bath and clean clothes and salve for her cuts, bruises and burns.

She looked at Jack. "Please will you take me to Glen Calder soon?" she asked. "I would like to be married there."

Jack smiled at her brilliantly and the love she saw in his eyes made her heart turn over. "With the greatest pleasure," he said. He swept her up in his arms. "I'll take you home."

* * * * *

An indecent proposal

Lady Lucy MacMorlan may have forsworn men and
marriage, but that doesn't mean she won't agree
to profit from writing love letters for her brother's
friends. That is, until she inadvertently ruins the
betrothal of a notorious laird…

Robert, the dashing Marquis of Methven, is on to
Lucy's secret. And he certainly doesn't intend to let
the lovely Lady Lucy have the last word, especially
when her letters suggest she is considerably more
experienced than he realised…

www.mirabooks.co.uk

Henry Atticus Richard Ward is no ordinary gentleman…

As maid to some of the most wanton ladies of the *ton*, Margery Mallon lives within the boundaries of any sensible servant. Entanglements with gentlemen are taboo. Wild adventures are only in the Gothic novels she secretly reads. Then an intriguing stranger named Mr Ward offers her a taste of passion and suddenly the wicked possibilities are too tempting to resist…

Covent Garden,
London, October 1816

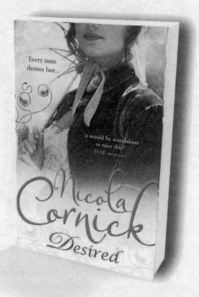

Tess Darent's world is unravelling. Danger threatens
her stepchildren and she is about to be unmasked as a
radical political cartoonist and thrown into gaol.
The only thing that can save her is a
respectable marriage.

Owen Purchase, Viscount Rothbury cannot resist
Tess when she asks for the protection of his name.
Will the handsome sea captain be able to persuade the
notorious widow to give her heart as well as
her reputation into his safekeeping?

www.mirabooks.co.uk

M285_D

An innocent pawn
A kingdom for the taking
A new dynasty will reign…

1415. The jewel in the French crown,
Katherine de Valois, is locked up by her mother
and kept pure for the English king, Henry V.

For Katherine, a pawn in a ruthless political game,
England is a lion's den of greed, avarice and mistrust.
And, when the magnificent king leaves her widowed
at twenty-one, she is a prize ripe for the taking.

This is the story of the forbidden queen who
launched the most famous dynasty of all time…

'Extremely compelling historical fiction'
—*Cosmopolitan*

www.mirabooks.co.uk

M310_TFQ

One marriage. Three people.
Proud king. Loving wife.
Infamous mistress.

1362. Philippa of Hainault selects a young orphan from a convent. Alice Perrers, a girl born with nothing but ambition.

The young virgin is secretly delivered to King Edward III—to perform the wifely duties of which ailing Philippa is no longer capable.

Mistress to the King. Confidante of the Queen. Whore to the court. Power has a price and Alice Perrers will pay it.

'An absolutely gripping tale.'
—*The Sun*

PARIS, 1919. THE WORLD'S LEADERS HAVE GATHERED TO REBUILD FROM THE ASHES OF THE GREAT WAR.

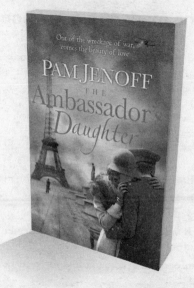

For one woman, the City of Light harbours dark secrets and dangerous liaisons, for which many could pay dearly.

Against the backdrop of one of the most significant events of the century, a delicate web of lies obscures the line between the casualties of war and of the heart, making trust a luxury that no one can afford.

www.mirabooks.co.uk

M304_TAD

HMIRA_WEB2